THE BOYFRIEND LESSONS

Jenna Fiore

Copyright © 2023 Jenna Fiore

All rights reserved

The characters and events portrayed in this book are fictitious. Any similarity to real persons, living or dead, is coincidental and not intended by the author.

No part of this book may be reproduced, or stored in a retrieval system, or transmitted in any form or by any means, electronic, mechanical, photocopying, recording, or otherwise, without express written permission of the publisher.

ISBN-13: 9798374830767

CONTENTS

Title Page
Copyright
One — 1
Two — 9
Three — 18
Four — 29
Five — 38
Six — 47
Seven — 56
Eight — 64
Nine — 71
Ten — 80
Eleven — 91
Twelve — 99
Thirteen — 109
Fourteen — 120
Fifteen — 131

Sixteen	140
Seventeen	149
Eighteen	159
Nineteen	176
Twenty	186
Twenty-One	195
Twenty-Two	205
Twenty-Three	215
Twenty-Four	227
Twenty-Five	237
Twenty-Six	249
Twenty-Seven	258
Twenty-Eight	270
Twenty-Nine	285
Thirty	293
Thirty-One	307
Thirty-Two	317
Thirty-Three	324
Thirty-Four	332
Epilogue	347
About the Author	357
More Books by Jenna Fiore	359

ONE

Olivia

Panting, I jogged around the corner, my glasses slipping down my nose from the sweat. Only a few feet to the entrance of my building and I'd be done with this run.

Counting the seconds, I glanced up, nearly plowing right into my neighbor from across the hall, Luke, who was staring into his phone, repeatedly rubbing his finger on his forehead.

"What are you doing?" I asked.

"Huh? What?" Startled, he looked at me then returned his attention to his phone. "Damn it! This isn't working, is it?"

"Uh, what's not working?"

He frowned at me, pointing to his forehead. "*This*."

Okay. I was really starting to be concerned for his sanity.

His eyes darted around like he was looking for

something. "You know what I need?"

"No. I have no clue what you need."

"I need water. I need this dirt to be just a little bit wet so it'll stick." He searched harder. "Shit. I don't see anything I could use. And I don't have time to go inside."

Yeah, he was going insane. For sure.

All the sudden, his eyes cleared and he stuck his finger into his mouth as I slowly backed away. Stunned into silence, I watched as he placed his wet pointer finger into the planter next to us, straight into the soil. Then focusing on his phone, he brought his dirty finger to his forehead making a smudgy dirt cross.

With a triumphant grin, he met my eyes. "It worked! Oh, my God, it worked."

"Why? Can I just ask why?"

"My boss told me Monday if I'm late one more day I'll be fired. And of course I overslept this morning. But in the elevator just now, I saw a woman with a cross on her forehead and realized it was Ash Wednesday. Well, guess what? You can't fire me if I was at church. Right?"

"But you weren't at church."

"Ever hear of lying?" He grabbed his bag from the ground and headed off. "I gotta go."

"You're going to hell, you know that?" I shouted.

"I'm already there," he called over his shoulder.

Shaking my head, I went inside to wash off the sweat and get ready for work. Wednesdays were my absolute favorite day of the week because of *him*. But they were also my craziest day because of story time, both toddler and preschool back to back.

Who ever thought that was a good idea? My lovely boss, that's who.

Regardless of the insanity ahead of me, I put extra care into how I looked, a gut feeling deep down that today would be the day. It had to be.

There was something in the air as I walked the short distance to the downtown library. And it wasn't the usual salty sea smell that pervaded San Diego's shores. It was something else. *Something* was going to happen today. I could feel it, practically taste it. I just didn't know what.

Greeting all of my co-workers, I sailed through the morning, prepping for my story times, that magical hour of nine o'clock coming upon us as I hung out at the front desk, discreetly running my hands through my hair to make sure it was as perfect as could be. My eyes flashed between the computer and the front door, watching and waiting while trying not to be too obvious.

"One more minute," my co-worker-turned-bestie Nadia said.

Yeah, everyone knew about my teensy crush. "Hmm? I don't know what you're referring to."

But in he walked, right at that exact moment, causing Nadia to snicker to herself. I was fooling exactly no one.

A smile on his face, his envious long hair flowing, he came straight to the counter, straight to me, not Nadia. *Take that*, I thought to myself smugly.

"Hi," I said in a squeaky voice. Pathetic. I cleared my throat and tried again. "Hi."

"Good morning, Olivia."

O-liv-ia. The way he said my name, stretching out the syllables, letting them flow off his tongue like a piece of fine chocolate to be savored... "How are you today?" I managed to ask.

"Great. Just stopping by to pick up my holds."

Oh, huh. That was rather abrupt. Usually, we chatted for a bit. "Sure. Sure."

"Sorry. Running a bit late and I have a big day today."

"No problem." Jumping up, I went to the shelves where we currently kept the holds, having to move them yet again back behind the counter because of people messing things up. *People*. I quickly grabbed the books there under his name.

Did we have self check-out? We sure did. But with certain customers, I was all about that personal touch, and I could easily check them out at the reference desk. And not just hotties like Jared. I was into helping the elderly or anyone else for that matter.

Smiling, he handed me his card as I went through each book and scanned it. Poetry. Poetry. The latest Booker Prize winner. The newest literary fiction sensation that had hundreds of holds. More literary stuff and even more.

"So yes," he said amongst the beeping noises of my computer, "I actually scored a gig tonight."

"You did? Wow, congratulations."

"And if it goes well, it might become a regular thing."

"Even better." I smiled into his dreamy blue eyes, trying not to get too lost in them. "That's amazing."

"I'll let you know how it goes next week."

I handed him his books. "Can't wait."

He turned to go as my heart sunk. A week was a very long time.

"Hey, Jared?" I called after him without thinking.

"Yes?"

"Break a leg tonight."

His grin brightened the entire library. "Thanks."

Once he left, Nadia suddenly appeared at my side. "You totally should have asked where he was playing."

"What? Why?"

"So you could go see him. Duh."

My eyes went to the ceiling. "So I'd just show up and be a groupie?"

"One of you has to make the first move. This is absolutely agonizing to watch."

Instead of being insulted, I grasped at the subtle straw she had thrown me. "So you really think he likes me?"

"Of course he does. What's not to like?"

And that's why Nadia had become my best friend these last four years of working together. She'd stuck by me through *the break-up* and always cheered me on.

"Ooh, you better get ready." Nadia glanced at the front door as a large family came in. "I've got the desk. And you might want to think about standing up to Nikki about this monstrous double story time."

While I made my way over to the children's area, my arms loaded with books, I thought about what Nadia had said. Yes, it made for an exhausting day. But I knew why my boss did it and pushed for so many programs at the library. More programs equaled more patrons which equaled more books being checked out which meant better circulation. So it was a win overall. Even if it was tiring.

And the rest of the day turned out to be just as exhausting. By the time I made it home, I could barely put one sore foot in front of the other. Being on your feet all day took a lot out of a person. So did singing "Old MacDonald Had a Farm" at the top of your lungs while putting on a puppet show.

All I wanted to do was curl up on my couch, read my book, and not talk to a soul until tomorrow when I went in to work again. My new book was practically burning a hole in my purse, a why choose romance that Nadia had said I had to read as she'd quickly stuffed it into my bag at the end of the day after making sure no one was watching of course.

Everybody else who worked at the library couldn't stand romance books. I read other genres, of course, because I had to keep up with the current hot books and trends. But if I could, I would only read my spicy books.

You'd think someone who'd had their heart broken recently like I had would hate romance. But I still believed in love, and I knew someday I'd find it. With any luck, maybe Jared would end up being *the one*.

Trudging down the hall, take-out in my hands, my ears perked up when I heard raised voices... well, more like a raised feminine high voice mixed in with an occasional low rumble. Where was it coming from?

"You never initiate things! I have to do *everything*."

Ohh, this sounded interesting. Slowing my pace, I tilted my head trying to make out that deep voice that was indistinguishable. Damn it. I couldn't hear his side.

"I don't even think you *like* me let alone *love* me."

Rumble, rumble.

"It's all so one-sided! And I'm sick of it!"

Now nearing my door, I realized exactly where the voices were coming from. Luke's apartment!

Apparently, his day wasn't getting any better. Resisting the urge to stall even more, I slowly keyed into my place, directly across from his.

"I'm done. *Done!* You hear me?"

Oh, we all heard you, honey. I couldn't resist giggling as I shut the door behind me, tossing my keys into the bowl. Poor Luke. I almost felt sorry for him. Almost.

I'd seen this girl around for the last month or so, the latest in a string of women that never seemed to last. Yep, Luke was a player. Loved them then left them. Another reason I couldn't stand him.

Flashy car. Flashy job. Fuckboy. I could only imagine the inside of his place. Dude central. But I'd never know because I didn't plan on spending any time with the guy. Ever.

TWO

Luke

I popped open a beer—the good kind that my friend Aiden had brought me, telling me I had to try it. Flipping on the TV, I took a sip. He was right. It was pretty decent.

With a sigh, I clicked around until I found the Padres playing the Dodgers, losing one to zero. Ninth inning. Great. Looked like an exciting game.

Fuck. Fuck my life. Another one gone. What the hell was wrong with me? Same complaint as always. I wasn't putting in the time or effort. It didn't seem like I even cared. Everything was always one-sided. Yep, yep, heard it all before.

I was sick of this shit. I'd been with plenty of hot girls, sweet girls, cute girls, trying them all out, trying to find one that made me feel something, one that took away the numbness, one that made me care. But it was always the same. Nothing.

What the fuck was I even doing with my life? I hated my job. Hated my family. Hated the small talk. Hated getting up early. Hated *everything*.

Smashing my beer down on the side table, I stood up, determined to find something stronger. I needed Jack for this night. And I knew I didn't have any. So the corner liquor store it was.

That was the only thing I liked about my life... where I lived. The Gaslamp, downtown, where the ocean met the city. It made me actually feel alive. Most of the time.

Not tonight though. I didn't care about the historic lights I passed, the people, the cool vibe, and trendy restaurants. I just needed to get plastered. Inside the store, the annoying music and bright fluorescent lights didn't help my mood. In a hurry, I grabbed my bottle and waited for the girl ahead of me to pay.

She was buying ice cream. Two pints. One of them my favorite—mint chocolate chip. Maybe I should get some of that too, be typical, eat ice cream when you get dumped. But there was already a line behind me, and I didn't want to lose my place.

When she finished, she whirled around, and I was surprised to see *her*. My neighbor. The hot librarian who despised me. Fantastic.

"Oh, hey," she said, her eyes wide behind the dark frames she wore.

"Hey," I mumbled as I made my way up to the counter, quickly paying with some cash.

When I turned to go, I realized Olivia hadn't left. She was still standing there, right by the door, a strange expression on her face while she spun her bag in circles.

"Did you forget something?" I asked.

"Huh?" Those big brown eyes looked up at me. "No. Uh, I was just wondering if we could walk back together."

If she had asked me to marry her, I wouldn't have been more shocked. Olivia actually wanted to be in my presence? When she'd first moved in a year ago, we'd been fine, making small talk in the elevator. But for some reason, in the months since, she seemed to avoid me for the most part, and I had no idea why.

"Some creepy guy followed me here," she suddenly said.

Ah, that explained it. In her mind, compared to some creepy guy, I must be all right. But also, fuck men like that. "Where is he?"

She glanced around, shrugging. "He didn't come in here. I mean, I can handle it. Just, you know, worried about *you*."

"Me?" I barked out a laugh. "You're worried about *me*?"

"Yeah. The bigger they come, the harder they fall. And all that." She waved her free hand and headed out.

A surprised chuckle escaped me while I

followed. That was twice she'd made me laugh on a night I didn't think I was capable of it. And wait just a damn second, was there a dirty joke in there somewhere? Did my neighbor have a naughty streak?

"So anyway," she said as we fell into step beside each other for the short walk, "I also know you've had a rough day."

"What?" I said without thinking. She couldn't know about my breakup, could she? She had to be talking about this morning. "Oh, you mean with the whole being-late-to-work thing?"

"Yeah." She tilted her head at me. "That and..."

She knew. She fucking *knew*. "You heard my, um, ex?"

"So you did dump her then?"

"Nope. I was the one who got dumped," I admitted, not seeing any point in hiding it from her.

"Oh," she said in a small voice. "I see."

What did that mean exactly?

An awkward silence ensued as I punched in the code and we entered our building, both of us nodding a quick hello to the security guard.

That weird quiet stretched on in the elevator until she broke it by clearing her throat. "Well, I'm sorry about that."

"Yeah, thanks."

I felt her eyes on me as the elevator opened, so I gestured for her to go first. See? I was a total and complete gentleman. What had Chloe been talking about anyway? Calling me uncaring and self-absorbed. That wasn't true at all. I cared about others. Of course I cared.

Lost in my head, I realized we'd arrived at our doors.

"So," Olivia said, her eyes darting around, looking anywhere but at me.

"So," I answered, wondering why she hadn't already disappeared inside like usual, wanting to be away from me as soon as possible.

"Um, do you want to come over?"

Literally, my mouth fell open. "What?"

She swung her bag around. "I have ice cream. And you kind of need that when you get dumped. Unless of course, you already have some. And then, well, you don't really need to come over, you know, if you have it at home because then, well, you—"

"I don't have any," I interrupted. What was going on here? Did Olivia feel sorry for me or something? I didn't need her pity. But what the hell? I did need some ice cream. "And yeah, sure. I could use some mint chocolate chip."

She smiled, and for a second I forgot where I was. Wow. I hadn't really seen her smile before. Or if I had, it'd been a long time ago.

In a flash, it was gone, and she was flinging her door wide open. Okay, this might be interesting. Not might. It would definitely be interesting.

Like a dumb-ass, I stood in the center of her living room, the exact replica of mine, but worlds away it seemed. Where I was a minimalist, Olivia's place looked lived in. She disappeared into the kitchen, and I could hear the sounds of dishes and drawers being opened.

"Need some help?" I asked.

"I got it. Just have a seat, and I'll bring out your ice cream before it melts in this heat."

Yeah, her place was kind of warm, and I noticed her windows were open rather than using the AC. Oh, well, to each their own.

Spotting her couch covered in a million cushions and blankets, I pushed some aside, took a seat and looked around. Books. Books. And more books. A whole wall lined with bookshelves, every single spot filled, paperbacks and hardbacks all crammed in there.

And as if that wasn't enough, there was a huge pile stacked on the side table next to me, threatening to topple over if just one more book was placed on top.

"Sorry for the mess," she said as she came around the corner, a wooden tray in her hands.

She set it down on the plush ottoman, and I eyed the two large bowls, a container of chocolate syrup, and glasses of ice water.

"Did I forget anything?" she asked.

"No. This is perfect."

And there was that smile again. Huh. I kind of liked that look from her.

She sat down next to me on the couch. "Well, help yourself."

I did just that, squirting out a generous portion of chocolate onto my ice cream. I never thought to buy the stuff. She did the same, and for a few minutes, we both worked on our bowls, silence again.

Shit. I needed to remember how to make small talk with her. My brain tried to reach back to when we used to chat in the elevator. What exactly had we talked about again?

All I could remember was where she worked. At the library. Something about kids.

For a brief moment, I'd debated asking her out. But there was something intimidating about her, something that told me she was off limits, like she was way out of my league. And I hadn't bothered, knowing that she'd turn me down anyway. So why not spare myself the humiliation.

The clanking of our spoons sounded loud as my mind whirled. I wasn't usually this bad at conversation. But today had been a day.

"So," I said, turning to face her, "this is really good. Thank you."

"No problem." Her tongue darted out to lick some chocolate from her lower lip. "I've been there. And it sucks."

"I don't believe it."

"Don't believe what?"

"That you've been dumped. Who would dump *you*?"

A ghost of a smile formed on her face. "A real

asshat. That's who."

I couldn't help laughing. "I guess so."

After taking my last bite, I set my empty bowl back on the tray, wondering if I should go.

"Feel better?" she asked.

"Yeah, actually. I do."

And that was without the alcohol that currently sat by the door in its brown paper bag. But Olivia had been right. The ice cream did dull the pain somehow, even making me hopeful about my future once more if I could just figure out why I was in this predicament. Again.

Clearly, I had some kind of problem within myself that I needed to fix—a fundamental flaw. It was plain and simple really. I was a shitty boyfriend. There was nothing wrong with Chloe. On paper, she'd been perfect. Most of them had been. It was me, something in me that was wrong then.

"I guess I have some work to do on myself," I blurted out, immediately regretting it and wishing I could take it back.

But of course, she wasn't going to let that one go. She turned her whole body toward me, tucking her feet under her. "What do you mean?"

With a heavy sigh, I rubbed my forehead, now desperate for that Jack and Coke. "It's not the first time I've been called a terrible boyfriend," I admitted.

For a long minute, she didn't say anything, and I watched the expressions play out on her face. Surprise, confusion, and finally an unfamiliar emotion to me, her lips compressed in a line.

"Well," she said, "with some work, you can always change that. You can change anything about yourself really... if it's something you truly want."

"In theory, I suppose." Honestly, I wasn't so sure. In my years of experience, people didn't really change all that much. Except maybe to get worse.

Her eyes narrowed at me, she opened her mouth to speak then shut it again.

"What?" I asked. She obviously had something to say.

Pursing her lips to the side, she shook her head. "Hey, it's your turn to share."

"Share?"

She nodded her head toward the door. "Yeah. Your Jack Daniels."

Ah, was that how she was going to play it? Was this her plan all along? "Sure. Sure. You got some Coke?"

"Yep. Stay right there. I'll be back in a minute."

As I listened to the sounds of ice clanking in glasses, I couldn't help thinking this night had taken a turn. A weird turn. And by adding alcohol to the mix, things were definitely about to get weirder.

THREE

Olivia

I might have made the drinks a little strong. Not a little. Way strong. Whoopsie. But tonight was strange. And getting stranger by the minute.

Some demon must have possessed me to invite Luke inside. Or maybe it'd been the lost look in his eyes when I'd first spotted him at the liquor store. Or maybe the way he'd paid for his whiskey with his head down and shoulders slumped.

And then when he'd revealed that he'd been the dumpee and not the dumper, well, that had cemented that spark of empathy in my chest. It had shocked me, frankly. I would have thought he'd have been the one to do the deed, his player reputation and all. So to find out the opposite was surprising.

I brought the drinks out to find him still

sitting in the same spot on my couch. Boy, did he look odd there amongst my mess of cute throw pillows and cushions. The window was open behind us, and a slight breeze came in, carrying not just the ocean scent but a whiff of cloves too.

"Here ya go," I said, offering him a glass.

"Thanks."

His eyes didn't leave my face as I sat down, turning toward him again, holding out my drink. "Well, cheers?" I said, unsure if that was the right thing to say under the circumstances.

That brought a soft laugh as he clinked his glass with mine. "Cheers."

I was beyond curious to return to our previous conversation, to see this new side of my neighbor that I never dreamed existed, the cocky attitude turning to self-doubt. Wiping the condensation on my glass, I debated how exactly to bring it up.

"So," we both said at the same time. Then laughed together. Weird.

"You first," he said with a nod.

Before speaking, I took a long drink, chickening out at the last second. "So, uh, how's work? Did they buy the whole improbable Ash Wednesday scenario?"

"Hey, it's not that improbable. I've been to Ash Wednesday services before."

"You have?"

"It's been a while, but yeah. And yeah, they bought it. Saved my job and get to work another day. Woohoo." He spun his finger around in the air, the sarcasm dripping from his voice.

"Wait, you don't like your job?"

He wiped his hand on his knee. "I *hate* my job."

What? He had to be kidding. He hated his job as some kind of finance VP where he had to be pulling in six figures? But as the expression on his face mirrored his disgust, I realized he wasn't joking. "You're serious."

After taking a long drink, he met my eyes. "Definitely serious."

"But why?"

"It's boring. It's dull. It's health insurance."

Oh, I had forgotten that part, that he worked for a major health insurance company. "Then why do you keep working there?"

He shrugged one shoulder, like he couldn't be bothered to lift both. "What else am I going to do?"

And that's when I felt it, that tiny niggling feeling inside that I wanted to help. My little fix-it gene, or whatever you wanted to call it, came out. Sitting right in front of me was a classic case of someone needing a life makeover. Bad job. Bad boyfriend. Where to even start?

"Well, what calls to you?" I asked.

His brows lifted, a smirky smile taking over his face. "What *calls* to me?"

My excitement level grew. "Yes. You know, what's your dream job? What would make you happy to go do every day?"

He swirled his drink in small circles, the

remains of the ice cubes knocking around. "What would make me happy?" he said quietly, almost to himself, like he was hypnotized watching his glass.

While he was apparently deep in thought, I took a moment to study him, really look at him, something I hadn't done much since he was so obviously not my type. His deep brown hair was a touch longer than it should have been for a business type, not to mention the fact that it appeared he couldn't bother to shave every day. Or maybe he didn't have the time to with his lateness habit.

I already knew he was tall and broad with arms that strained at his sleeves. What I didn't know was that he had a small scar that cut through a part of his left eyebrow. Or that he had one tiny freckle near his ear. He suddenly seemed more human to me.

"I have no fucking clue," he finally said then drained the last of his drink.

Well, that was unexpected. How could he not know? "How did you get into this field anyway?"

"First job I got after my MBA. I mean, not my current position obviously. I worked my way up. Moved around to several different companies. All health insurance. This latest one the worst with a real asshole of a boss who's obsessed with being punctual. Which is crazy because I work late all the time, or bring home work. But that doesn't count unless I'm there every single day at exactly seven-thirty."

"Sounds like you need to be your own boss."

Leaning back, he exhaled. "That would be the dream. Yeah."

Spotting his empty glass resting against his knee, I said, "Would you like a refill?"

"Sure. Yeah. That'd be great."

While I made more Jack and Cokes for us, again on the strong side, I heard a whirring noise from the other room, a familiar sound that made me laugh as I came back in.

His head against the back of my couch, Luke had found my foot massager, his shoes placed next to it. Eyes closed, peaceful expression, he looked like he was in heaven.

When he heard me, he practically jumped, removing his feet instantly. "Oh, shit. Sorry. I couldn't resist."

A giggle escaped me. "No worries."

"I kept my socks on?"

I laughed some more. "Really. It's fine. It was sitting right there. How could anyone resist?"

After I handed him his drink, I went to turn on my fairy light curtain, the sun disappearing early behind the tall buildings downtown and making it too dark.

"That thing's cool," Luke said in his characteristic deep, low voice.

"Oh, thanks. I guess I like my ambiance in here."

His eyes glanced around, and I couldn't help

wondering what he thought of my place. It was odd sharing myself like this with him. "I can tell. You've nailed the whole cozy, bookstore thing."

Ha, yes. Exactly what I was going for. "Good."

I plopped back down next to him, admiring my handiwork, the air now a bit cooler, another breeze ruffling the gauzy light curtain. Something about it all felt weirdly intimate, having this guy sitting on my couch, my big splurge when I'd moved in.

A warm feeling hit my toes as I took a sip of my drink, the alcohol buzzing through my body, making me feel a little lighter, a little looser. I could sense my cheeks turning pink like they always did whenever I imbibed.

"You, uh, make a stiff drink there, Miss Librarian," Luke suddenly said, chuckling.

The way he said librarian made me laugh, and of course, my mind went there. "Please don't start with the librarian jokes."

"Librarian jokes?" he asked innocently.

Was that just an act, or was he serious? "You know. All the dirty, sexy librarian stuff."

"What? I would *never*."

Glaring at him, I spotted a wicked gleam in his dark eyes that betrayed his words. "Anyway, what were we talking about?"

"I have no clue. But can I use the foot massager again?"

I burst out laughing. "Of course."

And then he was off, exploring all the different

speeds and modes, admiring the gift my parents had given me last year after I complained about my aching feet from standing most of the day at work.

"This thing..." Luke groaned. "...is amazing."

"Right?"

My drink was halfway gone by the time he was done, turning it off and slowly leaning back. "Mint chocolate chip. Strong Jack and Cokes. Foot massager. I might never leave."

There was that familiar lightness in his expression, his usual cocky demeanor coming back, probably fueled by the alcohol. I had no idea what to say to that.

"So what about you?" he asked, his eyes suddenly serious again. "Why don't you have a boyfriend?"

Oh, what a thing to ask. "How do you know I don't?"

He frowned like the question had taken him aback. "You do?"

"Not currently." My mind turned to Jared and his sweet smile. "But I'm working on it."

"Oh, yeah? What's that mean?"

Crap. Why had I said that exactly? Damn whiskey.

"Come on. Who's the guy?" Luke prodded.

What the heck? Why not tell him? "His name is Jared. And he's... well, he's a frequent customer at the library, and he's really nice, and he's a musician, and he's smart, and he's funny. And nice. Oh, I think I already said that."

Luke whistled. "Somebody's got it bad."

"Yeah, I kind of do," I said with a sigh. Jared was the polar opposite of my ex, and that was exactly what I was looking for in a man.

"So what's the hold-up?"

"The hold-up?"

"Yeah. The hold-up. If he's so amazing, why aren't you together already?"

"Duh," I said, shaking my head. "Because he hasn't asked me out yet."

Luke shot me a wry smile. "You do know what year it is, right?"

"Of course."

"So you know you can ask *him* out?"

The exact thing Nadia always said and in that same annoying tone too. "It's highly inappropriate for me to ask a customer out."

"So maybe he thinks the same thing, that it's *highly inappropriate* to ask you out at your place of employment."

His words gave me pause. "That's actually a good point," I admitted. "Why on earth didn't I think of that?"

Luke shrugged. "I have no idea. It seems pretty obvious to me."

The whiskey made my head spin a bit, but I could still recognize an insult when I saw one. "Hey. Rude much?"

He threw his head back and laughed. "I'm joking. A joke. J-o-k-e."

"I know how to spell joke. And I hate it when people do that."

His brows came together. "Do what?"

"Say something mean then pretend it's a joke. Then when you're still annoyed or upset, they call you sensitive. And 'Sheesh, can't take a joke?'" I'd heard that too many times with my ex, and I was over it.

Luke stared at me, assessing, his eyes shrewd. "Got it. Got it. That *is* an asshole move. Sorry."

Sorry? Had he really said that word? His intense gaze stayed on me, making me squirm under the scrutiny.

"So what else you got?" he asked abruptly.

"What else? What do you mean?"

"Other pointers. That was a good one."

Was my buzz making this conversation difficult to follow? Or was it just a weird conversation period? "Other pointers about what?" I asked, grasping for clarification.

"Life, love, relationships, all of that. Clearly, I suck at it."

"You don't suck at it," I said quickly, reeling from his admission yet also wanting to reassure him for some reason. "You're, um, doing great."

He arched a single brow at me. "I know we've had a bit to drink, but you must remember I just got dumped for like the millionth time for being an awful boyfriend."

"I remember."

He glanced down, his index finger spinning a

loose thread on one of my pillows. "I'm thinking that if the same problem keeps happening over and over again, then it's maybe not the other person's fault. Maybe *I'm* the actual problem. You know?"

Never in my life would I have dreamed of having this discussion with Luke. "Wow, that's actually quite insightful."

He chuckled softly. "I'm not all brawn."

I snorted, I really did, which made him laugh. Loudly. And then I shoved his shoulder. "You're a hoot."

"A hoot?" he asked in a teasing tone, his smile infectious.

"A total hoot. I had no idea you were so entertaining."

He made an attempt at a sitting bow. "Well, I'm glad me and my pathetic love life can entertain you."

Funny and self-deprecating. Who knew?

"Hey, we're both empty," he said. "Can I make us another round?"

"Yeah, I'll take another drink. Thanks."

As he took off for the kitchen, I thought about everything he'd confessed, thinking he was terrible at love and relationships, and a little seed of an idea formed in my hazy brain. The tiny part of me that was still somewhat sober wondered if I'd regret it, but drunkenness overruled all else.

Giddiness swelled inside me, and I could hardly wait to ask Luke. I was ninety-nine percent sure he'd be resistant, but that was okay. I liked a good challenge. After all, what better way to add some excitement into my "boring" life?

FOUR

Luke

As I walked away, I couldn't stop smiling. Olivia was turning out to be a lot more fun than I would have imagined.

I rounded the corner into her kitchen which was neat, clean, and a tiny bit cluttered. Apparently, blue was her favorite color. It was everywhere—the hand towels, the rugs, the canisters on her counters. There was just something about her place, something I couldn't even name. But I liked it. And I was kind of liking her.

Finding the ice cubes, I filled our glasses, thinking about our conversation. One thing about Olivia that was more than obvious, even to me, was that she had her shit together. She was poised, self-confident, and sure of herself. Clearly, she was smart, not just book smart but emotionally as well.

Pouring the coke, I watched the bubbles fizz, thinking about how different Olivia was compared to anyone else in my life—my friends, my parents, even my numerous exes.

Grabbing the drinks and returning to the living room, I was well aware of her eyes on me, watching me, studying me for some reason. I settled down next to her, handing her a glass, hoping I hadn't mixed them up. But really, who cared?

I met her intent gaze, noting how her face was practically glowing, her cheeks flushed, her eyes bright, giving me a strange feeling in my gut. Something was definitely up, and given the fact that I really didn't know Olivia at all, I had no clue what it could be.

"So?" she asked, the "s" sound kind of slurry.

After I gulped down nearly half my drink, I placed my glass on the tray, turning to face her fully. "Yes?"

She set her glass down forcefully on the side table. "So I have an idea."

"Uh, okay."

Blinking her big eyes at me, she gnawed on her lower lip like she was nervous or something.

"What is it?" I asked, my curiosity growing inside me.

"So I was wondering if, you know, if you'd be interested in some kind of, um, boyfriend lessons." Glancing down, she muttered the last part quickly.

"Boyfriend lessons?" I repeated in a shocked voice. "What's that exactly?"

"Honestly? I-I'm not really sure yet." Her eyes darted back up to mine. "But you just asked me for pointers, and it got me thinking."

Stunned speechless, my head spun around in confused circles. Huh. Boyfriend lessons. In a million years, I would never have guessed at those words coming out of her mouth.

She stared out the window at the darkening sky. "So maybe I could do some research, come up with some sort of curriculum."

"Curriculum?" Wow, she was absolutely serious about this, I realized as I watched her, that mind of hers obviously in full gear, already coming up with this so-called curriculum. But as I looked at her, I took in her lit-up expression, and something dawned on me.

I really did need some help, and who else could I ask? My friends? Besides being as clueless as I was, they'd totally laugh at me. My parents? Yeah, right. Maybe some kind of therapy? I'd already tried that, and it'd helped but apparently not enough.

It hit me like a ton of bricks that Olivia was actually the perfect person to help me. Or at least I thought so. It was certainly worth a try, and getting "lessons" from Olivia could potentially be a blast. Tonight, I'd discovered that I liked being around her.

And then, because I was a total dog, my mind

took a turn. "This isn't just your way of getting me into bed, is it?" I asked.

Her head whirled to face me, her mouth gaping open. "What? God, no."

At that, I had to laugh, and she must have realized I'd been joking. With a surprisingly strong hand, she shoved me again in the shoulder, both of us cracking up.

When we quieted down, she wiped away the tears that had formed at the corners of her eyes and looked at me. "So no sex, mister. This would strictly be all about emotional stuff... communication, caring, thoughtfulness, that sort of thing. Affection."

"Got it. No sex. Unless you initiate it," I added.

She rolled her eyes at me. "Not gonna happen."

"Ah, right." I nodded knowingly. "I forgot about your man, Jim."

"Jared. His name is Jared."

"Of course. Jim."

"Oh, God." She leaned forward, dropping her head into her hands. "You know what? I take it all back. You're beyond my capabilities. Forget it all."

"Oh, no, no, no. I want these boyfriend lessons. I'm *dying* for these lessons. No taking it back. It's out there now, and I fully accept your offer. One-thousand percent."

Now that the thought had settled in my mind, I really was dying for these lessons. Having Olivia tell me all about how I could be a better boyfriend had the potential to be the time of my life, and I could hardly wait to begin.

"So when do we start?" I asked, trying my best to lock her in.

Squirming a bit, her eyes wandered around the room. "Ummm. I don't know. When are you free?"

That was easy. "Well, as of this evening, I suddenly have a lot of free time on my hands."

She stared at me like she didn't comprehend for a minute. "Oh, oh, I see. Because of the break-up?"

"Bingo."

"Well, let me find my phone, and I'll check my calendar." She shoved herself up from the couch, a little wobbly on her feet once she finally made it up. I reached out my hand to steady her, but she was already off. "And I need to pee," she added with a giggle. "I mean, use the ladies' room."

Man, she was cracking me up. And how drunk were we? How hungover would I be tomorrow? You know what? I didn't even care. So what if I was late? They could fire me for all I cared. Get dumped and fired within twenty-four hours. That sounded great to me actually.

I tapped my hand on the arm of the couch, and it caused an avalanche of books to literally fall into my lap. Oops.

Olivia the Librarian wasn't very organized with her books at home. I chuckled to myself as I began to stack them up neatly on the table. One by one, I studied the titles that swam a little in front of my eyes. But I could still read them at least.

It seemed like a wide variety that she had there—everything from non-fiction and self-help to mystery and thrillers. I placed one that said something about inner peace on top of the rest, reaching for the next. And this one... holy shit. Was that a... was that a nipple I saw?

Bringing it closer, I tried to make my eyes focus. There was definitely a ton of skin. Bare skin touching bare skin. Oh, that was the dude's nipple. Okay then. But what was the girl wearing? Next to nothing it seemed. And where exactly was his hand? And wait a damn second. Was that another guy on the cover too?

I looked around for a lamp or something. How did Olivia read in here anyway with just her fairy light curtain thing?

Hearing a noise down the hall, I put the book back on the table with the rest, doing my best to make the stack neat and even this time.

"Okay," she said, holding onto the wall, "I found my phone, and I'm free tomorrow night and Friday night but not Saturday or Sunday."

"How about tomorrow?" I asked.

Her narrowed eyes caught mine. "Tomorrow? You sure you can handle me?"

Was she being flirty? Or was I completely misreading her? Or maybe it was due to the alcohol. "Definitely. I can handle whatever you throw at me."

"We'll see about that. I'm not going to go easy on you."

"Bring it on," I challenged.

She stumbled toward the couch and collapsed in a heap, her legs knocking into me. It was probably time for me to go, but I couldn't bring myself to leave just yet. My place across the hall might as well have been in another country, a country that was dull and lifeless, devoid of all color.

And suddenly, I dreaded it, dreaded my lonely existence. Fuck. Here came the depressant stage of drinking that I hated.

Olivia's bare legs suddenly crossed over me, catching my attention. Eyes half-closed, she sprawled out on the couch, her head on one armrest, her feet stretching beyond me to rest on the other. The weight of her calves suddenly pressed into my lap.

Whoa. That was unexpected. I swallowed hard at the wave of lust—damn it—that swept through me. And now I was that horny drunk guy.

But I was also shocked that she'd trust me like this. She didn't really know me either, yet here she was nearly passed out next to me.

"I'm gonna head out," I said.

There was no response except for a heavy sigh. Studying her face in the growing darkness, I realized she was out cold. Carefully, I put my hands under her legs and raised them, trying my hardest not to notice how good she felt, how soft and warm her skin was under my fingers. Nope, I definitely didn't notice.

Once I'd maneuvered myself off the couch, I gently placed her feet back where they'd been, debating for a minute if I should leave her there or try to move her to her bed.

In an instant, I decided that was too much. Her couch was certainly comfortable enough, and I was sure she'd be fine. Feeling a slight breeze come in from the window above her, I reached for a blanket, spreading it out over her, beginning with her legs all the way up to her arms.

God, she looked so damn peaceful, and I felt a twinge of envy, wishing I could steal some of that for myself. She was light, and I was pure darkness. For sure, she'd regret this night in the morning and call off the so-called boyfriend lessons. There was no way a girl like her would want to spend time with a guy like me.

With a sigh, I realized she might wake up thirsty, so I went to her kitchen and filled up a glass full of water, leaving it on the tray. Her phone sat on the ottoman, and I wondered if she had some sort of alarm set on there like I did.

Lifting it up, the lock screen lit up automatically, and I spotted the tiny alarm clock in the corner. So good. She was probably okay then and wouldn't be late for work tomorrow.

The photo she had on there caught my eye, and

I studied it for a minute, a knot forming in my stomach at the image. There was Olivia, along with another girl who looked just like her, arms around each other with big smiles on their faces. Behind them stood an attractive couple, most likely her parents, clearly laughing at something. All of them dressed up in front of the ocean. Probably La Jolla by the looks of it.

They were a beautiful family. The perfect family really. The perfect girl. Everything the complete opposite of me.

FIVE

Olivia

The hangover was rough, and I couldn't help wondering how Luke fared. Had I passed out last night? I didn't remember saying goodbye. But that didn't mean it didn't happen? I hoped anyway.

Ugh, how embarrassing. The girl who couldn't hold her liquor.

Returning to the desk, my arms loaded down with books, I groaned, making Nadia glance up.

"What's all that?" she asked.

"Oh, it's just, um, for a customer."

She looked at me, eyes full of suspicion. "What's going on? You've been acting weird all day."

Since Nadia was the definition of tenacious, there was no use trying to keep up the lie. So I told her, confiding in her about last night and the upcoming boyfriend lesson that I believed we'd set up for tonight?

"You have got to be kidding me," she said, her startling blue eyes piercing me. "You know you can never fix a guy, right?"

"I do know that," I huffed. "But here's the thing. Don't you think that only applies if it's *your* guy? Like a guy you're married to or in a relationship with?"

She scrunched her nose up as she thought. "I don't know," she finally admitted. "Maybe."

"Not maybe. Definitely. I'm not in a relationship with him, and I never intend to be. So it's okay. It's all good. I'm just helping him for the next girl that comes along."

"Oh, dear Lord. This seems like a bad idea."

Ignoring her, I began to check out my pile of books, all about relationships and understanding each other, the perfect place to begin hopefully.

Nadia peeked over my shoulder, reading the titles. "What is with you and wanting to rescue everyone and everything? Is this like that time you went running around Nimitz Boulevard stopping traffic to save that dog? You know Luke isn't a stray dog, right?"

"Of course, I know that. And I guess I can't help myself. I just feel like with a little research and effort, anything can be fixed."

"Well, good luck with that. I'll be breathlessly waiting to hear how it all goes tomorrow."

This was all easy for her to say, with

her wonderful, amazing marriage to the hottest firefighter alive. I knew it hadn't been *exactly* perfect for her, what with leaving her family in the Czech Republic behind for love, so I resisted saying anything.

"God, I'm sorry," she said. "I don't mean to be so cynical. I just feel like this has the potential for you to get hurt. Again. And I'm gonna go psycho on this Luke guy's ass if that happens."

Underneath Nadia's tough exterior was a heart of gold. But at the same time, she was dead wrong about me getting hurt. "You think I'm going to fall in love with Luke or something?"

Her eyes went heavenward. "What do you think? Before you know it, your boyfriend lessons will extend into practice dates, and you'll go on an apple-picking weekend in Julian and get trapped in a brutal snowstorm and have to use your bare, naked bodies to keep each other warm."

A wheezy laugh came out of my poor lungs, and I whirled around to grab my books, trying to catch my breath even more because, at that exact moment, in walked the true love of my life... Jared.

Even the way he walked was delicious, all confident and panther-like as he headed straight for me. Luke's words from last night flashed into my mind about how Jared probably didn't want to ask me out while I was at work. I mean, if he wanted to ask me out at all.

Butterflies took off in my belly at the thought of maybe asking *him* out. Oh, gosh. I couldn't do it because that wasn't right at all and totally, completely unprofessional of me.

"Hey, Olivia," he said, walking up with a book in his hand. "Finished this and wanted to bring it back for the next person in line."

"Oh, that's thoughtful of you," I gushed. It really was. The book he was returning had a months-long wait list. "How was your gig last night?"

His beautiful eyes brightened. "Great. Just great. So great in fact that it's going to be a regular Wednesday *and* Saturday night thing."

"Wow. That's amazing. How exciting." I just knew he was a brilliant musician.

"I'm beyond thrilled."

"So where are you playing?" Nadia asked, sneaking up behind me, my not-so-sly best friend.

"Not far from here, actually." He pointed toward the back of the library. "At Paradiso, two blocks over."

"Ooh," Nadia cooed, "they have the absolute best food there, don't they, Olivia?" Her sharp elbow hitting my side almost made me jump.

"They do," I agreed, seeing immediately where this was going.

"You've been there before?" he asked.

"Many, many times," Nadia lied.

We'd both been there exactly once.

"We'll actually be there this Saturday," she added.

"We will?" I asked her.

"Yes. Don't you remember? That's where Javi wants to go for his birthday dinner. *Remember*?" She shot me a pointed look before turning her attention back to Jared. "Javi's my husband."

"Wow, that's fantastic. I'll definitely keep an eye out for you all." He patted his hand on the counter. "Well, I've got to go. Can't quit my day job just yet. See you Saturday?"

His eyes lasered in on me, and I muttered out a "Yes, yes. Hopefully."

Once he disappeared out the door, Nadia turned to me, a triumphant expression splashed across her face like she'd just conquered world peace. "Well, would you look at that? You've got a date for Saturday."

"You're not in the least bit subtle," I said, smiling as I swept past her.

"Well, the early bird never catches the worm."

Laughing, I carried my books to the back. Nadia was known for butchering idioms—and for her lack of subtlety—and I absolutely adored her for it.

***

Hours later, I sat on my couch, sifting through the material, trying to come up with what to do tonight... if tonight was indeed happening. My mind struck a blank when I tried to remember our conversation, the specifics, the actual time.

And I didn't have Luke's number to double check.

For all I knew, he'd completely forgotten about it, and next time I saw him, we'd act like nothing had happened. Of course, I could take the mature route, be the grown-up thirty-year-old that I supposedly was, and knock on his door. But nope. You couldn't pay me enough to do that.

This whole thing had been my idea. I at least remembered that part. And maybe he'd just played along, humored the drunk girl, and had a good laugh about it later, joking around with his friends about me and my ridiculous boyfriend lessons.

Ignoring my growling stomach, I was deep into discovering my love language, realizing I could learn a thing or two as well, when there was a knock on the door. Could it possibly be Luke?

My heart in my throat, I went to check the peephole, and sure enough, it was him. He'd remembered! Or he was calling it off. Or he'd just forgotten something over here.

With a deep inhale, I opened the door and maybe stared for a minute longer than I should have... because there was a rare smile on his face that I hadn't seen very often, and it kind of stunned me.

"Hey," he said, holding up a bag in his hand, "I don't think we set a time, but I'm hungry, so I brought some food."

"You remembered?"

His brows lowered. "Of course. I've been waiting all day for this."

My face filled with heat at his obvious joke, and I gestured for him to come in, noting his super casual attire topped off with a Padres baseball cap. I tried not to notice his legs as he walked in, heading toward the kitchen, but I did notice them because they were the perfect combination of tan, strong, and muscular.

"Do you like Greek?" he called.

Shaking my head, I followed him, determined not to ogle him anymore. And I mostly succeeded as we organized the delicious smelling food, both of us filling up our plates and soon sitting at my cluttered little table, shoving aside papers and books to make room.

"Sorry about the mess," I said, scooping up some hummus with my pita bread.

He began digging into his salad. "No worries."

"And thanks for this food. I'm starving."

"Drinking will do that to you."

I laughed because he was absolutely right. "So do you remember much about last night?"

His forkful of sliced cucumbers and tomatoes paused halfway to his mouth. "Of course. I remember it all."

"Oh, oh, that's good. I do too."

Those deep, dark eyes of his narrowed at me like he didn't quite believe me. "Okay then. So we're all set with these boyfriend lessons, right?"

I gulped down my bite of food. "Yep. All set."

We were really doing this thing.

"Good. I can't wait to see what all you have in store for me."

Did I detect a teasing twinkle in his eye, or had that been my imagination? "We could start right now if you'd like."

"That'd be great."

In no corner of my mind would I have predicted his unlikely enthusiasm. I took a minute to think about the notes I'd taken earlier until I decided on a perfect place to start. "So why don't we begin by taking a trip down memory lane, you know, a little Ghost of Christmas Past."

His brows shot up. "So basically, you want to know all about my past relationships. Is that it?"

"Exactly." Smart man. "I need to know what was said. Why exactly did, um, what's her name break up with you? What did she say?"

"Chloe. That's her name." He sighed, putting down his fork for a moment. "And she said I didn't put in any effort. She was the one who always had to make plans. She always had to reach out to me to see each other. Basically, she thought everything was always on her and that I didn't care."

Taking a few bites of falafel, I let that whirl around in my head a bit, not too surprising because of what I'd heard in the hallway. But still. "And is all that true?" I asked.

He chewed some food thoughtfully before shrugging. "I guess so."

"So in other words, you never called her or texted her. She always had to do it, the reaching out to you."

"Uh, yes? Maybe?"

"And did you care?"

"Of course, I did."

"Did you love her?"

"No," he scoffed. "Definitely not. I don't think I'm capable of it, to be honest."

Was he kidding me? "You're not capable of love?" I repeated slowly, trying not to sound too judgy. After all, I was here to help, not judge.

His shoulders lifted in a half-hearted shrug. "I'm beginning to think that. Yeah."

"And why is that, do you think?"

He looked down at his plate, every feature on his face tight, rigid, like he was dredging up something powerful within. "I don't know," he said in a low voice that I had to strain to hear.

Oops, I'd touched a nerve. *Way to go, Olivia*. I needed to backpedal and quickly. "Well, let's not worry about that just yet. I'm sure we'll get to the bottom of it eventually. Until then, why don't we move along to some other fun stuff."

"Other fun stuff?" he questioned, our gazes catching, that spark back in his eyes I was happy to see.

"Oh, yes." I grinned at him. "A quiz."

He laughed loudly. "Oh, crap. I'm scared."

"Yep, you totally should be. But first, let's enjoy our meal. And then, I'm going to drill you."

SIX

Luke

I stared at her while she ate a forkful of her salad. She was going to drill me? Wow, she couldn't have meant that the way it sounded, right? No, definitely not. Olivia had specifically said no sex, and I knew she meant it.

God, I was a horny shit.

We finished our food, making small talk about our lives, how both of us had grown up in San Diego, although she'd spent most of her time in North County, pretty far from where I'd lived as a kid in Clairemont. It was strange that we'd both ended up in a downtown high rise as neighbors.

And while her parents had moved to the East Coast a few years back for her mom's job as a professor, mine still lived here. Same house. Same everything. I didn't tell her too much about my family because who wanted to hear that really? And it was pretty boring anyway with me being an only child, unlike Olivia who had a little sister currently renting a place in PB, living that party lifestyle.

It was strange getting to know Olivia this way after a year of being neighbors. I had no idea that her laugh was so cute, or that she crinkled up her nose when she thought something was especially funny. But I liked it.

And I liked it even more when she grabbed a pencil, wrapped her hair around it, and jabbed it into some kind of bun thing at the top of her head. Strands escaped her makeshift hairstyle, and I had to fight the urge to tuck them behind her ear while admiring her long, slender neck.

Fuck, I needed to chill for sure, especially because Olivia was all business suddenly, standing to grab our empty plates and clean up.

"Quiz time," she said.

I helped her pile up the dishes in the sink, wondering what on earth this quiz could be about. Was I nervous? Maybe a little. It was weird to open up to her like this, thinking back to when we'd talked earlier about my capacity for love, something I didn't really want to talk about.

But what the hell had I expected? Of course she'd want and even need to discuss that. I really did want to be a better boyfriend, so I had to at least be open to whatever she had prepared for me.

With that on my mind, I followed her back to her now-familiar couch where she turned on her little curtain thing again, making the room glow.

"Should I be concerned that you have a clipboard in your hand?" I asked, half-kidding but half-serious too.

She giggled as she settled into the same side of the couch she'd occupied last night. "No. This is more of a fun one to start with. We'll get into deeper stuff with more time. If you make it that long," she added in a teasing tone.

"Oh, I can last a long time... a very long time. And I'm more than ready to go deep."

Biting her lip, she studied my face a beat, and I couldn't help cracking up. Shaking her head, she let out some kind of sigh as her attention returned to her clipboard. "Clearly, I have my work cut out for me," she mumbled, a small smile forming on her face.

I made myself comfortable in the same spot, taking in the stack of books next to me that had grown even higher since last night.

"Okay. Let's start," she said, drawing my attention back to her. "So first off, have you ever lived with a girl before?"

"Briefly." My mind stretched back a few years to the two or so months that I'd lived with, um—fuck, what was her name? Corrine. That was it.

"Good. Good." She nodded. "That helps. So during that time, if you needed to throw something away and noticed the trash was super full, what did you do? Shove it all down and add to it or actually take it out?"

I had to think about that, and Olivia watched me carefully, tapping a pen against her cheek as she waited.

"Take it out. Of course," I said.

Her eyes turned squinty.

"Okay, most of the time," I admitted, holding my hands up in surrender. "It just depended on if I had time right at that exact moment. So yeah, on the rare occasion, I did smash it down and walk away quickly."

"Mm-hmm." She scribbled something on her clipboard. "And how about this? When you lived with your girlfriend and you took the second-to-last tissue from the box, you know how the last tissue usually pops up too?"

"Yeah?"

"So what did you do? Put that last one back in there and leave it, or get a new box?" Leaning forward, she studied me.

"Um," I hedged, "do I have to answer that one?"

"You. Just. Did."

Damn it. This was obviously not going well.

Olivia cleared her throat, back to busily writing things down. "Okay, moving on. So your girlfriend's birthday is coming up. How do you approach it?"

"How do I approach it?" I asked, not quite understanding what she wanted to hear.

"Yeah, like, the gift, the plans for the day, for the night, etcetera."

"Oh, well, let's see." My mind scrambled as I

tried to think back through the girlfriends. How many birthdays had I celebrated? Somehow not that many it seemed.

"You do *remember* their birthday, right?" Olivia shot me the stink eye.

"Of course. Of course. And I do get them a gift. A very thoughtful gift. And whatever they want to do that day or night." All a damn lie. I couldn't really remember any birthday celebrations if I was being honest. Shit. What did that mean?

"Hmm, okay." She did that tapping pen thing again. "And when your girlfriend texts you something like, 'I'll be over at eight,' how do you respond exactly?"

Feeling some heat, I took off my hat and flipped it backward, Olivia's eyes watching me closely. "Uh," I began, "I usually just write 'K.'"

Her eyes widened, and her nostrils flared, her lips compressed together like she was struggling to keep her mouth shut.

"Is there a problem with a K?" I asked slowly.

"Is there a problem with a K," she repeated, her voice low and ominous.

Crap. Somehow I'd really stepped in it.

"Okay. So I should probably wait until the end of the quiz," she huffed, "but I'm gonna pause right here because you never, ever, *ever* respond with a K. Never."

Grimacing, I sat back, trying to put some space between me and her obvious wrath. "Okay. I get it."

Closing her eyes, drawing in a big breath through her nose, she regained control, her features relaxing once more. "Sorry," she exhaled. "But that one really gets to me for some reason. It's so dismissive, that K. Like you can't be bothered to type the whole damn word."

"So it'd be better if I wrote 'Okay' then?"

"It'd be better, but it's still not ideal." She paused a moment, eyes lasered in on me. "Can you think of anything even better?"

My brain swam around in platitudes while I tried to think of the perfect response. For some reason, I wanted to impress Olivia. And then it slammed into the forefront of my brilliant mind. "Yes. 'Will you wear that hot pink bra I like?'"

She clapped her hand over her mouth, stifling a laugh, but I could still totally see it in her eyes. "Uh, not exactly what I was going for. How about an 'I can't wait' or a 'Sounds great.' Or even better... 'Are you hungry? Can I feed you?'"

I nodded. "Got it. Got it."

She scratched something out before continuing. "So it's getting down to the end of the toilet paper roll... do you leave just one square on there or replace it?"

"Oh, always replace it," I lied.

"Mm-hmm, okay. And tell me this, what's the recipe for ice cubes?"

I busted out laughing. "You're kidding."

"I most certainly am not. When you take the last ice cube, do you fill the tray back up? Or do you put the empty tray back in the freezer?"

"Always fill it. Of course." Lies. Again.

"Right. Okay." Her eyes were penetrating, probably seeing right through me. "So let's just use Chloe as an example. What's her best friend's name?"

Fuck. Think of a name. Any name. "Elizabeth."

"And does Chloe like her boss or not?"

"Hates her." That one I knew for sure. Chloe had talked endlessly about her job. See? I wasn't a complete asshole.

"And when Chloe told you the latest drama with one of her friends, did you listen, or did you nod and go along while you were thinking about something else?"

Kind of a leading question there. All of these were really. "I totally listened."

"Mmm," she hummed before continuing. "So your girlfriend comes home, and she's upset because she had a bad day at work. What do you do?"

"Uh, listen? Order some food?" Olivia waited like I needed to add something else here. What else? What else? "Massage?"

With her smile, I knew I'd hit the jackpot with massage. "Okay. That's about all I've got. For now."

My stomach did a quick flip, taking me back to college when I was about to receive an exam score. "So how'd I do?"

Obviously enjoying herself, she made a big

show out of circling and crossing things out, dragging out my unease. At least her pen wasn't red.

At last, she looked at me. "So I know you lied your way through most of this..."

The girl had made me speechless.

"But my point wasn't to get the right or wrong answers," she said. "It was to get you thinking, you know, something to contemplate, maybe how some things could improve, how we can always be more considerate and thoughtful with our actions."

I liked how she tried to take the edge off by using the word we, even though it still reeked of condescension. "Right. Okay. Well, it definitely gives me stuff to think about. And can I ask *you* a question?"

"Sure."

Leaning closer, I captured her gaze. "What's your obsession with ice cubes and toilet paper? Who did you wrong?"

Even in the faint light, I could see the flush grow on her cheeks. "This isn't about me. I'm all good."

"So you're perfect in relationships then," I challenged.

"No. That'd be impossible. There's always room for improvement."

Her prim and proper tone told me I'd hit a nerve, and I decided to let it go. "And can I ask you another question?"

"I guess."

Ignoring her hesitation, I plowed onward. "So these boyfriend lessons you're giving me... what's in it for you?" I asked.

She examined her nails for a beat before glancing up again. "It's just my contribution to womankind. And I like to help people."

"That's it, huh?"

Gnawing at her plump lower lip, her gorgeous eyes appeared wide and thoughtful behind her dark rims. "And—and I wanted to help *you*."

With that shy little admission, Olivia had no idea, but she'd just locked in her fate.

SEVEN

Olivia

"Wow, Livs, you look amazing! Doesn't she, Javi?" Nadia elbowed her husband in the side.

"Yes, yes. Absolutely," Javi agreed, making me laugh at his uncomfortable expression while straddling such a fine line.

I gave them both a quick hug, careful not to mess up my hair or makeup. "Happy birthday, Javi," I said.

"Thank you."

"You even wore your contacts?" Nadia said in awe. "You mean business."

"You know I do."

I was ready to act on this crush and take it to the next level, even if my contacts annoyed the heck out of me. Last time I'd worn them had been to a wedding a year ago, but it was best not to think about the eye irritation too much. So with a deep breath, I put my focus back on my friends as we stood there, soon greeting the rest of our big group.

That was the thing with firefighters. They had lots of friends. And even though the restaurant switch had been last minute, Nadia had somehow managed to finagle a reservation for a large number of people. She could definitely be persuasive and impossible to say no to. I almost felt sorry for whoever had dealt with her.

Once we were inside, my head swiveled around, trying to figure out where exactly Jared was. But it didn't take long, the sounds of piano music drifting into the front lobby. Wait, was that Gershwin I heard?

My heart fluttering away in my chest, I followed our rowdy group to the table, peering around a few big guys to get a look. And there he was! At the far end of the room, playing his heart out. How absolutely, utterly romantic. He looked positively dreamy sitting there while entertaining the entire cavernous room.

Thank goodness Nadia took charge in the seating arrangements, making sure I was facing Jared and the piano so I could stare all I wanted. He hadn't noticed me yet... not really a surprise considering the ginormous firefighters filling up our table. I sat sandwiched between Nadia and one of Javi's friends, Lars, whose seat could hardly contain him, our thighs rubbing together constantly. At least he was a cool guy that I'd seen many times before.

Now if I could just get up the nerve to go say hi to Jared, that would be the goal. But how did that work exactly? I didn't want to interrupt him mid-song. That would be awkward, wouldn't it?

"I'm sure Jared will take a break sometime. Or he'll just spot you in the crowd at some point," Nadia murmured next to me, apparently reading my mind.

She was right. For now, I'd cool my jets and sit here, enjoying the music he made. He really was incredible. I knew he had his own original songs, but I supposed at a place like this, they wanted him to play classics and old standards.

Soon after we ordered, which took a long time, I let my eyes drift around the restaurant. Jared still hadn't noticed me, and I wasn't inclined to get up and wave from across the room. So I studied all the other people, Lars and Javi leaning across us to carry on a heated conversation about some work stuff.

The place was pretty crowded. No wonder Jared hadn't found me in this sea of people.

A group of three guys following the host to a table caught my eye, and my breath hitched in my throat. Luke was here? Of all the people and all the nights! How absolutely surreal.

How was this even possible? I racked my brain, thinking back to the last time I'd seen him. Had I mentioned that I was coming here? I didn't think so actually. He'd left soon after our "quiz"

Thursday night when I'd stifled a few yawns, exhausted from drinking the night before.

Nadia noticed my shifting posture, followed my stare, and whistled quietly when she spotted the three ridiculously handsome guys.

"See the guy in the blue shirt?" I lowered my voice to a whisper. "That's Luke."

"*That's* Luke from across the hall?" she gasped.

My eyes veered to her stunned expression. "Yeah? Why are you saying it like that?"

"He's insanely hot! Why didn't you tell me?"

"I don't know. Does it really matter?"

"Yes, it matters. It always matters." She leaned back, trying to put more distance between us and the Javi versus Lars conversation. "Wow, I didn't mean to sound so shallow. Of course, it's what's inside that matters the most," she whispered. "But, well, you know."

I did kind of know. Because Luke was incredibly good-looking, and he was becoming even more so as we got to know each other better.

The food arrived, and our table quieted down so much I could actually hear the piano now. My attention darted back and forth between Jared and Luke, the strange dynamic of them both being here throwing me off. And the weird thing was that neither of them had noticed me.

Whoops. A split second after that thought flashed through my brain, Luke turned his head my way, his eyes instantly catching my stare. At first, his eyebrows shot up in surprise only to be replaced by a quick smile.

He said something to his friends then stood up, heading straight for me, something about the predatory look on his face making my heart gallop. What was that about? He was just coming over to say hello. Obviously.

I sensed Nadia tense beside me. "Holy shit," she muttered around a bite of food.

"Hey," Luke said, bending down to give me a kiss on the cheek, shocking the daylights out of me at the feel of his lips on my skin. "What a coincidence running into my teacher."

Between that and the kiss, I had no words, just a weird giggle-snort escaping from my mouth, causing Lars to give me the side-eye as he shoveled a meatball into his mouth.

"So you're Luke?" Nadia said.

"I am." For a beat, he looked between the two of us before zeroing in on my friend. "Olivia's been talking about me, huh?"

Now it was Nadia's turn to snort. "Just the basics."

And then somehow Javi got involved, and the whole table needed introductions while I had an intense silent conversation with Nadia, my eyes pleading with her to be cool, girl.

Once everyone resumed eating, Luke lowered himself to my level. "So I noticed you checking out the piano dude. Is that your man Jim?"

"Jared. Jared is his name," I corrected before I realized he was doing it on purpose, goading me for some reason.

"Right. Right." Luke studied Jared for a long moment. "Well, I guess he's all right if you're into that artsy wannabe rocker vibe."

The angle was awkward, but I managed to get in a good shove to his shoulder, and of course he didn't budge, just wore a shit-eating grin.

"Do you like to annoy me or something?" I huffed in his general direction.

"Always." He leaned in closer to me, and I tried to ignore the warm feeling it brought deep in my stomach. "You look so fucking beautiful tonight. But for the record, I like you better in your glasses."

My mouth fell open as his words resonated through my shocked mind. But before I could even come up with a response, he was gone, already strolling back to his table, shoulders broad and relaxed like he owned the place.

And this was how he'd managed to get a whole slew of girlfriends, that easy confidence combined with his holy hotness. Plus—plus the words he'd just said to me. Wow, what a... I didn't even know what to call him.

Nadia shoved me in the side as I watched Luke sit back down.

"What?" I grumbled, shaking my brainless head while I picked up my fork to eat again.

"You know what you have?"

Her smug tone set me on edge. "Um, no?"

"You've got yourself a love triangle."

I groaned. "No, I do not."

"Yes, you do. And it's even more ironic because I know that's your least favorite trope. And here you are smack dab in the middle of one."

"It's not a love triangle," I insisted. "It's a line. A straight line to Jared. Point A to point B. There's no point C."

"You sure about that?" I followed her gaze to Luke's table, where our eyes caught briefly before I looked away. "So why won't he stop staring at you?" she asked.

"He's not staring at me."

"Oh, yes, he is. The man likes you. It's totally obvious to everyone but you. You're *that* girl." Her knee bumped mine beneath the table.

"I am not *that* girl," I said adamantly.

"Are too."

"Am not."

"Are too."

Biting my tongue, I realized I needed to put an end to this silly argument. I already had one annoying little sister, and I certainly didn't need another. But sometimes, it was exactly what Nadia was to me.

As I bit into my pasta, I couldn't stop thinking about what she'd said, though. Did Luke like me as more than friends? I highly doubted it. We had nothing in common besides living in the same building. That was it. And that was nothing really. And I was absolutely positive it would stay nothing.

"Pick the piano dude," Lars said, startling me. "The other guy will break your heart."

EIGHT

Luke

Jesus. Did she have to be surrounded by fucking firefighters? And the guy she'd been obsessing about was a brilliant piano player with the most gorgeous head of hair I'd ever seen? What the hell?

"Dude, why do you look like you're plotting someone's death?" Aiden asked, biting off a hunk of bread. "And who was that girl?"

"That's Olivia, the girl from across the hall that I told you about."

His eyes lit up, his head swiveling around to get a closer look.

"Don't stare, man."

"Sorry. Just trying to see who's brave enough to give you boyfriend lessons."

"She's obviously into masochism and torture," Trevor said, giving me his always amazing insight.

"Fucking hilarious."

Grabbing my menu, I studied the options. Pretty much traditional Italian food, a few items with a little bit of a twist.

"So what's good here?" I asked Aiden who was friends with the head chef.

"I'm going to try the steak gorgonzola. Rafe says it's the best thing on the menu."

I thought about getting the same thing but also wanted to try something different. While I read through everything, I noticed a change in the room, the voices growing louder. Glancing up, I realized the piano had stopped, and there was Jared, a big dumb smile on his face as he crossed the room, heading right for Olivia.

Shit. I didn't like this one bit. And I definitely didn't like the look in her eyes as they began to talk.

"Who's this asshole?" Trevor said.

"That's the guy she likes."

Aiden whistled. "Looks like you have your work cut out for you."

"No shit."

"He looks like a total douche. She'll realize it eventually," Trevor said, ever the optimist.

I exhaled a tight breath. "I hope so."

Using my menu as a shield of sorts, I really tried not to stare. But damn if I couldn't help it. I hated the way they talked so effortlessly together. And when Jared touched her arm? My blood pressure took off in a dangerous slow boil as I genuinely did start to plan Jared's death, especially when he leaned in to hug her.

Fuck me.

"Dude, relax," Trevor said next to me. "You're the one spending so much time with her, right?"

He had a point.

"You just need to up your game," he continued. "Actually *try* for once. That's my boyfriend lesson for you. You never really try."

With a sigh, I turned my head away from Olivia, thinking about Trevor's words. The man certainly knew what he was talking about. Out of everyone in my life, I should listen to him the most. He'd been with the same girl since high school, Krystal, and they'd be getting married in a few short months.

The server came around with our drinks, and we put in our orders at the same time. Once he left, I sensed someone nearby and glanced over to see Olivia quietly walking past.

"Hey," I called. "You leaving?"

She tucked some hair behind her ear, shyly meeting my eyes. "Oh, um, no, just looking for the ladies' room."

Trevor stood up, holding out his hand. "Hey, so you're Olivia?"

A soft smile lit up her face. "I am."

"I'm Trevor, and this is Aiden." He pointed to Aiden who swiveled his chair around to say hi.

It was incredibly odd to see these two parts of myself merge like this—my oldest friends meeting my neighbor who'd become something more all the sudden.

"Great to meet you all." There was an awkward pause, but Olivia filled it, thank goodness. "So how do you all know each other? Do you work together?"

"Nah, I've known these clowns since middle school, Aiden even longer, actually," I admitted.

Her brows shot up. "Wow. That's cool that you've kept in touch for *so* many years."

Was Olivia throwing us shade? Calling us old? Her sly smile told me she was, and then her little laugh completely gave it away.

Trevor and Aiden stared at her for a second before the laughter hit them as they took in her not-so-subtle humor.

"Just joking. Totally joking." She giggled, making me wonder how much alcohol she'd consumed tonight. "But that is pretty cool. Let me guess, you were all part of the debate team or math club?"

Again with the teasing. Who knew Olivia was like this?

Trevor was the one who answered her. "Not exactly. We met each other on the football field."

"Ahh, that makes sense," she said, her eyes penetrating mine.

What did that mean? Was Olivia being judgy about my football player past?

"Yeah, and also basketball," Aiden added.

"Ooh, I can just picture it," Olivia said, eyes

widening with this additional information. "If I had more time, I'd ask to hear all the embarrassing stories about Luke. If there are any."

Both Trevor and Aiden laughed loudly. "There's a few for sure," that traitor Aiden said. "And I'd be glad to share sometime."

"Same," that bastard Trevor agreed.

Standing up quickly, I cut them off. "Hey, I need the restroom too. Be right back. Oh, and don't you dare touch my food if it comes."

Aiden saluted while Trevor said a polite nice to meet you to Olivia. With my hand barely touching the small of her back, I indicated for her to go ahead, and we made our way to the lobby area.

But just before she went in the direction of the ladies' room, I stopped her. "Wait just a sec?" I asked.

"Sure, yeah." She whirled around to face me. "What is it?"

"I saw you talking to Jared..." A whole lot of words stumbled around in my brain trying to make their way out, but I realized I had to be careful. Something told me Olivia wouldn't care for the jealous caveman type. "So how'd it go? Did one of you finally make a move?"

The smile that lit up her face knifed me like a sharp, hot dagger to the gut. Was she beaming because of *him*? As she leaned in closer, her eyes glancing around the room, the sweet scent of her hit my nose.

"He actually asked for my number." She poked her finger into my bicep. "Can you believe that?"

I swallowed hard. "No. That—that's great. I'm really happy for you," I lied. Again.

"Thank you." Her elegant shoulders went up in a shrug. "I'm not getting my hopes up or anything. He might never get in touch with me."

Exactly what I was wishing for. "You never know," I said instead. "He'd be crazy not to."

Now her smile was all for me, loosening up that knife in my abs. "That's sweet of you to say."

"Well, I mean it."

A heavy silence stretched out as we watched each other, but Olivia broke it when she gestured down the short hallway. "My bladder's about to burst so..."

We laughed together and went our separate ways. I'd never used the bathroom so quickly in my life, in a rush to beat Olivia and "accidentally" bump into her again on the way back to our tables. And that's exactly what happened.

"Feel better?" I asked her as we headed into the dining area.

"Like a new person. And all ready for dessert. I think Nadia's going to embarrass her husband with the whole singing thing."

"Gotta love that." We'd reached my table, and she started to walk away until I touched her elbow. "Hey, real quick. When should we meet next?" I asked.

"How about Tuesday?"

"Great. I'll see you then," I added right as Jared walked by. I hadn't exactly planned that, but apparently, the universe was on my side at the moment.

"Well played, man." Trevor clapped me on the back after I sat down. "Well played."

NINE

Olivia

Sitting on the seawall, I polished off my slice of pizza, washing it down with my drink. The sun played on the water's ripples as I looked to my left at the Coronado bridge.

"Do you like driving over that thing?" I asked Luke who was sitting beside me.

"I guess." He shrugged. "Why? You don't?"

Despite the warmth, I shuddered. "No. That one just seems extra high, and every time I'm on it, I think about earthquakes, which is even worse if I'm stuck in traffic."

"Which is pretty much every damn time," he said wryly.

We both laughed as a loud group of tourists walked past behind us. Then Luke gathered up our trash and disappeared for a minute before we started our latest boyfriend lesson. I'd decided we needed to get out of my apartment just to change it up a bit.

Once he sat back down, I brought out my phone, excited to get started. "Okay. You ready?"

"Uh, I guess so?"

Giggling, I nudged his knee with mine. "Don't worry. I'll take it easy on you. So we're going to learn about our love languages tonight."

"Love languages? What on earth is that?"

"It's based on a bestselling book," I explained. "First, let me say that I'm not implying this is the solution to every relationship issue, but it's definitely interesting to think about. So basically, there are five different ways we each feel love the most, and you know I have another quiz for you."

His grunt made me laugh.

"I'll send you the quiz and we'll each take it, then compare results," I said when I realized he had nothing to add to the conversation. "Okay?"

"Okay."

I elbowed him in the side. "Don't sound so excited there, mister."

"Oh, I can hardly wait," he grumbled.

But I caught the half smile on his face, making me realize that Luke was sometimes all bluster. After sending him the link, we both got busy answering the dozen or so questions, Luke very quiet and serious about it, taking the time to read every word thoroughly.

I patiently waited for him to finish, thinking about my results while I watched some pelicans dive into the water in the distance. Acts of service. I supposed that made sense. And maybe that was why things hadn't worked out so well with my ex. Or part of the reason anyway.

I had to wonder what his love language had been. I really didn't know. You'd think after four years, I would have known him so well that I could have figured it out. But I could only guess.

"It's a tie," Luke said, busting me out of my pointless thoughts. "Quality time and touch."

"Hmm, that's interesting." And very different from my results.

"What's yours?"

"Acts of service. So apparently, I feel loved when my partner does stuff for me."

Luke's chuckle vibrated through me as he bumped me in the shoulder. "Like take out the trash and fill up ice cube trays?"

I bumped him back. "Yes! Exactly that."

"All right. Well, that's good to know. And mine is pretty self-explanatory."

"I think so."

We were both lost in thought for a moment as we watched a fishing boat go past, sending the wake rippling toward us.

"So what's the point really?" Luke eventually asked. "Just make sure you find out your partner's love language and show them you care by doing the things they like and vice versa?"

"Exactly. Look at you. I don't think you even need these lessons, to be honest."

"Oh, I definitely do," he argued.

Not sure if he was serious or not, I studied his face, the lowering sun glowing on his tan skin. It suddenly dawned on me that if Luke didn't need these lessons, that could only mean one thing. "I think the real issue is you haven't met the right person."

He glanced away from me suddenly, his eyes trained on Coronado across from us. "That could be."

A strange silence permeated the air around us as I thought about what to say. This lesson had proved to be incredibly short.

"So what about you?" Luke asked.

"What about me?"

"You haven't met the right person either I'm guessing. Or was there one that got away?"

Closing my eyes, images of Henry flashed through my brain. On paper, we had been perfect together. And at first, it really seemed like that was the case. But somehow, over the years, things had soured. "I wouldn't say he got away. It's more like we drifted apart."

"How long were you together?"

"Four years."

Luke whistled. "That's a long time."

I studied my nails, resisting the urge to pick at them under Luke's scrutiny. "Yeah, we were engaged actually... for the last year of it. Living together too."

"Oh, wow."

"I thought he was the one. But he definitely

wasn't."

I could feel Luke's eyes burning into the side of my face, but I didn't turn my head. "So what happened?" he asked. "Did he cheat?"

"No, no. Not that I know of anyway." Henry's parting words whirled around in my brain, but there was no way I was going to say them. Ever. I hated even thinking about it and wished I could scrub that moment from my mind permanently. An entire year later, it still hurt. And the real estate I'd given him in my head was annoying and ridiculous. "In the end, I guess we just grew apart. Or we were never really right for each other in the first place."

Luke nodded. "So a learning experience."

"Exactly. A learning experience." His insightful comment was surprisingly comforting. "I guess all of our relationship failures are just that, right?"

"Right. That's one way to look at it."

"Thank you," I blurted without thinking.

"For what?"

"I guess for not shoving it back in my face." I exhaled forcefully. "Like really, who am I to give you relationship advice? I know nothing. *Nothing*."

"That's not true," he said with a scowl. "You actually know a lot more than you think. And if you don't know something, you're pretty damn good at research."

His vehement tone made me smile. "I hope I'm

good at research. That's a decent portion of my job."

"Well, you're obviously a fantastic librarian. I'm sure everyone you work with appreciates you."

I tilted my head to the side, daring to glance at him. "Mm, so-so."

"What? You're fucking kidding me," he said, practically growling. "Who doesn't appreciate you? I need names so I can kick their asses."

Goodness, he made me laugh. "Just one person. And it's my boss. She's actually okay most of the time, but she puts a crapload of pressure on me about programs. It's like she's obsessed. And I see the importance. I really do. But it's exhausting, and I'm trying my best to come up with new ones while at the same time carrying through on all the current ones."

"That's terrible. Why does she put so much pressure on you?"

Shrugging, I thought about the why. "Because I'm number two I guess. Second in command."

Luke's eyes widened. "You are? I didn't know that, but that's pretty impressive."

"Thanks," I said, not so sure how impressive it was when your boss was always so critical.

"Really. It is," he insisted. "I mean, how old are you and you're already in that kind of position?"

"I'm thirty, not exactly a spring chicken."

He scoffed loudly. "Younger than me and my ripe old age."

"Well, you're not doing so badly yourself." Hoping to change the subject and take the focus off myself, I asked, "Hey, how's your job going? Have you been late at all this week?"

"My boss is on vacation, so yeah, I've been late every single day."

I couldn't help giggling. "Have you thought about a new job maybe?"

"Nah. You know that line in that Who song? About how the new boss is exactly like the old one?"

"Oh, my God. That is so true. Always. I think all bosses just suck."

"They do. It's in their contract. And if you happen to have a good one, they always move up or get transferred after like a month."

"Yes! Exactly." Not only did Luke make me laugh, but our conversations were so effortless which wasn't always the case with me and the people of the world. Sure, I was decent at customer service. But out there in the wild, I pretty much kept to myself, only clicking with a select few on this planet.

"Hey, should we head back?" Luke said. "I don't want to keep you out too late."

"Sure."

The sun at our backs, we meandered through the winding shops and eateries of Seaport Village, filled with tourists on a warm summer evening.

Luke turned his face my way, his brows raised.

"So have you heard from Jim yet?"

My snort was the only response I gave him for a good minute. But I finally relented because I was curious to know his reaction. Was Jared just not interested or a slow-mover? "I did hear from *Jared*. But..."

"But what?"

"He didn't ask me out or anything. It was more like small talk, the same exact thing that happens when he comes in to the library. And I was convinced that he'd, well, that he'd take it up a notch."

Luke didn't say anything right away, making me extra curious to know his thoughts.

"So," I prodded, "what do you think?"

"I think he's definitely interested, judging by the way he was looking at you at the restaurant. But he'd better hurry the fuck up before someone else snatches you up."

"Snatches me up?" I glared at him. "That makes me sound like some helpless little kitten on the streets who needs rescuing."

Luke held out his hands in surrender. "You hardly need rescuing. I just meant someone else might swoop in and sweep you off your feet."

I had to laugh at that. "Ah, yes, the long line of suitors at my door. There's just *so* much competition."

"You never know."

We walked the final block in a companionable silence, strolling through the people reading outside menus, trying to decide the best place to eat. I called this section restaurant row, all with outdoor seating areas, making it easy for me to check out everyone's food. And I noticed Luke doing the same.

The closer and closer we drew to our building, the more I found myself not wanting this night to end. Hanging out with Luke was surprisingly fun. He was turning out to be a good friend, something shocking that I would never have predicted. I had been one-hundred percent wrong about him.

The more we talked, the more I realized he probably hadn't been such a bad boyfriend really. He simply hadn't been all that interested. And once he met the right person, he'd probably be a great partner. He just had to meet her.

TEN

Luke

Damn it. I hated being caught in this weird limbo. I wasn't used to being patient and hanging on the sidelines waiting for a girl I wanted. And I'd never even come close to wanting a girl like I wanted Olivia. Every time we were together, that feeling grew exponentially. And now, it was turning into agony.

So many times sitting on that seawall, overlooking the harbor, I'd wanted to reach for her, put my arm around her beautiful shoulders, squeeze her into my side, or even hold her hand.

But I couldn't make that move, not when she was obsessing over Jared. Yeah, I knew the fucker's name. I just liked to tease her, liked to see the way her lips curved in a disapproving smile, the way her eyes glinted with part annoyance and part amusement.

When I'd said someone else might swoop in, I had been dead serious. But for the first time in my life, I didn't know how to make a move. Olivia didn't seem interested in me in the slightest, and I had no idea what the hell to do with that. The only thing I could think of was to bide my time and see how the Jared thing worked out.

She'd either get tired of waiting for him, or they'd get together and she'd see how lame he was. Yeah, I was being a dick when it came to him. But something about him rubbed me the wrong way. And a gut feeling told me they wouldn't work.

Walking into the building, I held the door open for Olivia, and we stopped to grab our mail before heading up in the elevator, both of us rifling through a few envelopes.

"Anything exciting?" she asked when she was done.

"Nope. Never."

"Same."

Once we exited and started down the hallway, I sensed Olivia wanted to say something the way she was shooting me sideways glances.

"What's up?" I asked, stopping outside our doors.

Licking her lips, which I didn't notice of course, she looked behind me, not quite meeting my eyes. "You wanna hang out a little more?"

There it was. Take that, motherfucker! "Sure. Yeah. Your place or mine." Yep, I'd played that cool, right?

"Uh..." she hesitated.

Something inside me wanted to be at her place. I didn't know what it was, but I liked being in there. It was like an inner part of her revealed itself to me. Everything shouted Olivia, and I couldn't get enough of that sweet vibe.

"How about your place?" I asked. "I'm kind of getting addicted to your foot massager."

She nearly doubled over in laughter before turning to unlock her door. "Help yourself. Have a seat and I'll get us some wine."

And that's exactly what I did while Olivia walked around, first turning on the lights, then heading to the kitchen. With a content sigh, I sat down on my side of the couch, shoving off my shoes and kicking them out of our way. This was nice... the cool evening breeze coming in the window behind me, the sounds of Olivia pouring drinks, the fairy light thing glowing.

Maybe I liked this a little too much.

Before I could overthink, Olivia brought in the wine, and we clinked our glasses together. "To becoming a better man," I said.

She grinned. "To becoming a better woman."

"I don't think that's necessary. You're perfect just the way you are."

The way her gaze softened did something to me. "Stahp."

Not taking my eyes off her, I moved my arm to place my wine on the side table, a sudden cascade of books falling into my lap. "Ah, what do we have here?"

Olivia reached to help me, her closeness making it hard to breathe. "Oh, gosh, I'm sorry," she said.

"No, no. That's cool. It was my clumsy move."

One by one, I started to stack them again, reading the titles out loud, Olivia telling me most of them were for work, for a program called Books and Breakfast.

"That actually sounds like fun," I admitted, sincerely meaning it.

"It's good. It really is."

"But...?"

She didn't answer, so I continued stacking until I came to the last one, holding it up close, that same book from before with two dudes and a girl on the cover. Olivia grabbed it out of my hands, shoving it behind her.

"Wait a second," I protested. "I want to see that one."

She laughed in my face. "Why?"

Thinking hard, I took a long sip of my wine, this time taking care when placing it on the table. "Uh, curiosity?"

"What exactly are you curious about?" she asked with narrowed eyes.

What did she think I was curious about? The thought of Olivia reading that book blew my mind. "That cover implied something, and I want to see what's inside."

She paused to gulp down about half of her drink. "You're a smart guy."

"I hope so." As much as I appreciated the compliment, it wasn't that difficult to figure out really. I held out my hand to her. "So? Can I read it?"

The seconds ticked past as she thought, nibbling on her lower lip the whole time. I couldn't figure out the big deal. Surely, whatever was inside that book couldn't be that graphic. During the weird silence, we both drank down more of our wine, and Olivia shot up to retrieve the bottle from the kitchen, taking the book with her.

"Okay," she said once she returned and began refilling our glasses, "here's the deal."

The mischievous smile playing about her lips made my pulse take off. What was going on here? "Yeah?" I asked.

"I'll give you the book, but you have to read it." She sat back down, that smile turning into a triumphant grin. "Out loud."

"What? Are you serious?"

Her head bobbed up and down in a slow nod. "Yep. Absolutely."

It only took a few beats for me to agree. I mean, how bad could it be? "Okay. Deal."

With my agreement, that snorty laugh that I liked came out of her, and she quickly paged through the book. "And you have to read to the end of the scene. No quitting. Or I'll never let you live it down."

"I'm a lot of things. But I'm not a quitter."

She cracked the spine, apparently finding what she wanted, and handed the book to me, her eyes lit up brighter than I'd ever seen them. Careful not to lose her place, I grabbed the book and held it up.

"Do you have any more light in here?" I asked.

"Hmm? No. Sorry."

"No worries. But you really need more light in here if you read all the time."

"Okay, Daddy."

Shaking my head and laughing, I brought the book back up, getting ready to read. "Where do I start?"

"Top of the page."

I cleared my throat and began. "Christine could hardly believe that her husband had agreed to this. But after years of marriage, the need within her had escalated to unbelievable heights, and maybe he was feeling the same. They still loved each other deeply, but the physical spark was long gone. And they desperately needed it back." Pausing, I looked at Olivia. "That's really a bummer."

She nodded, a strange sparkle in her eyes that matched her curtain. "Keep going."

First, I took a drink then returned to reading. "Emerging from the restroom, Christine clutched the edges of her flimsy robe around her naked body, rounding the corner of the hallway into her bedroom where the two men waited for her."

Whoa. Okay. Was this going where I thought it was going? No, it couldn't be. No way.

"The way they looked at her like she was a tasty morsel they wanted to devour made her so hot, the need gripping her low in her belly. 'Christine,' her husband said, coming toward her. 'You look beautiful.' Christine's throat tightened so much, she couldn't respond to Liam... a first."

Olivia giggled and I gave her a glance, her quickly disappearing wine tinging her cheeks pink already. How was she so fucking pretty? And why had I spent the last year screwing around when I could have been relentlessly pursuing her?

"Please go on," she urged. "You're about to get to the good stuff."

Exactly how good was this going to get? I had to wonder. Once more, I knocked back some wine, then breathed deeply. "Liam's best friend, Wesley, looked at her with wonder, also walking forward, his eyes lingering on her chest. She met them halfway, eager to get started, beyond excited to be with two men at the same time."

Oh, shit.

"Slowly, she let the silky edges of her robe fall away, revealing her heavy breasts to both men, a gasp from Wesley as he saw them. Of course, Liam had seen her naked many times, but his eyes still held heat and appreciation for his stunning wife."

Why was Olivia's place so warm all the sudden? What had happened to that breeze?

"Wesley held out his hand to her, leading her to the bed, where he gently pushed down on her shoulders. 'You both have too many clothes on,' she said as she sat down, her knees not letting her stand anymore. The two friends laughed as they shed their clothes quickly, Christine not sure which man to look at, both of them muscular beyond belief, with hot, cut Vs leading to their stiffening cocks."

Jesus.

"Where Liam was thick and veiny, Wesley was long, and she couldn't wait to feel him inside her, at one end or the other. She wasn't sure of the plan, but secretly, she really wanted Wesley to fuck her, and she already knew that was okay with her husband."

Wow, this Liam dude was one hell of a confident guy.

"Kicking aside their clothes, Liam and Wesley crawled up on the bed on either side of her, her heart thudding in her chest. First, Liam kissed her, slowly, sensually, while someone began to palm her tits, her already hard nipples throbbing and achy."

Fuck, this was hot. Squirming a bit, I dared to glance at Olivia, who was attempting to hide her smile. "Don't stop now. You've got a ways to go, sir."

"Oh, dear God." Was Olivia getting as turned on as me? Shit. I couldn't think about that. "Christine could hardly contain herself as Liam's tongue massaged her own, while at the exact same time a hot mouth enveloped one of her nipples, sucking hard before biting her and flicking her with a tongue. The fact that it was Wesley, a man she'd been admiring for years, made her burn brighter than the sun."

All the blood in my body was swiftly running south, but I was determined to prove to Olivia that I could get through this.

"Then they switched places, Wesley's kisses moving upwards along her chest till he reached her mouth. It was odd to kiss someone else after so long, and it took a bit to find their rhythm, but once they did, holy hell. And it didn't hurt that Liam was moving his mouth down every inch of her body, someone's hands kneading her ass cheeks and more hands on her breasts. Had she ever in her life been more turned on?"

I'm asking myself the same damn question, Christine. Especially with the world's hottest librarian sitting beside me hanging on every word.

"Everything was multiplied. Four hands on her. Two tongues. And two hard cocks pressing into the sides of her body. Once upon a time, she'd been a calculus genius. But even with no math skills, she knew it all added up to infinite pleasure."

I couldn't help chuckling at the cheesy line, and Olivia joined in. "You're doing better than I thought you would," she said through her laughter.

"Thanks. I, um, didn't know I had it in me." Another sip of wine and I plunged onward, wondering if this was going to fade to black at any point. "Her body writhing in ecstasy, she didn't know how much more she could take of this teasing foreplay. She was more than ready for the both of them, and clearly, they were ready for her too."

Flipping the page, I fought the urge to look ahead and see where we were headed.

"Wesley tore himself away from their kisses, once more returning to her breasts while at the same time, her husband wrenched her legs apart, his mouth coming down on her dripping wet..."

"Dripping wet... what?" Olivia asked, her voice strangled.

Oh, fuck. I wasn't the least bit shy in bed, and I had no problem with the dirty talk. But crossing this barrier with Olivia? Holy shit.

"Pussy," I mumbled to Olivia's giggles. "All right? Pussy."

After her signature snort, I rallied myself, placing a pillow in my lap to hide my growing erection.

"Just the way she liked it, he sucked on her... clit." *Fuck me.* "At that exact moment, Wesley bit down on her nipple, and that was all it took to send her over the edge, her body nearly convulsing off the bed as both men didn't let up."

I looked over at Olivia, to find her face pinker than usual while drinking. "You're doing great."

Something about those words made me think she wanted me to continue? But weren't we at the end of the scene? "You want me to go on? Isn't that it?"

"Oh, no, honey. That's not it."

Honey? She'd called me honey? The way her full lips went into a pout, I thought I might bust a nut right there on her couch. Jesus Christ.

"Please go on," she slurred.

Ah, that explained a few things. Drunk Olivia seemed to have much lower inhibitions, and there was no way my buzzed ass could resist her.

ELEVEN

Luke

Draining my glass, the words took a second to focus in front of me. "'Your turn, gentlemen,' Christine said once her heart rate had returned to normal."

Well, that makes one of us.

"Christine climbed up onto all fours, her shaky limbs somehow supporting her. She stuck her ass in the air, wondering which one was going to plunge his hard cock into her still throbbing... pussy."

Olivia made a noise beside me.

"When her husband moved in front of her and kneeled, she could barely control her quivering body, realizing that Wesley was about to fuck her. She hadn't been with another man in years, and the love in her heart grew infinitely that her husband was okay with this."

That was actually pretty sweet.

"Just like she'd done many times, she slowly sucked Liam's fat dick into her mouth, reaching up with one hand to fondle his balls. It was hard to support herself with just the one arm, and she wished to heaven that Wesley would grab onto her. But when he finally did, she thought she might die. For a split second, she wondered if she could actually do this, if she was strong enough to take two men at once."

You got this. Oh, shit. Had I said that out loud? Olivia laughed hysterically while I tried to bury my red face back in the book.

"But all doubt fled from her mind when the head of his long cock nudged her soaking entrance. She pushed backward, shoving herself onto him, as a loud groan sounded in the room. The feel of him inside caused her walls to pulse, and more sexy noises filled the air. My word, he was huge. And he was patient, still, waiting for her to make the first move."

He did sound pretty cool. I had to admit.

"'Does that feel good, baby?' Wesley asked her. Her mouth was full of cock, so she just moaned her answer, her fingers letting go of Liam's balls to fall back onto the bed. As hot hands gripped the flesh of her hips, she knew she was about to get fucked hard. And damn if she didn't want it as hard as he could give."

Fuck me, but I needed some water. And some air. And to relieve the pressure building in my own balls.

"You gonna stop?" Olivia teased.

"Water," I croaked out. "Need water."

Laughing, she rushed off to the kitchen, walking a little funny I noticed. Oh, God. Was Olivia feeling this heat? The thought that her underwear might be wet made me feel faint. Just when I didn't think I could get any harder, that thought alone made me throb. I was desperate to finish this scene and get the hell out of here so I could rub one out.

She returned, a big glass of ice water in her hands, her eyes gleaming and her face flushed as she stared at me. "You're actually really good at this. Your voice... is, um, perfect."

Olivia liked my voice?

"It's deep and sexy and hot."

Fuck if my dick didn't pulse at those words spilling from her mouth. I swallowed down a ton of the cold water, wishing it could cool the temperature of my blood. But it didn't. Not even a little.

"I might ask you to narrate all of my books," she said, sitting down and tucking her feet under that sweet ass. "I could listen to you all day. And night."

What the hell?

"But you're not done yet, good sir. Please do go on," she added with a flourish of her hand.

Okay then. The girl could be persuasive, and I was powerless under her spell. "Where were we? Ahh, Christine's about to get fucked hard. Right."

Olivia's laugh swept through me. Talk about being able to listen to something all day.

"It took them a minute to find the right rhythm, all of them new to this. And Christine especially had to get it right, taking two cocks at once. Her mind drifted to how else they could do this. One in her pussy and one up the ass? Yet another dream to add to the list."

Whoa, um, okay. Christine sure liked her cocks.

"But once they found the right rhythm, it was pure heaven. And anybody who happened to walk by the open window would have known it for all the moaning, groaning, and gasping coming from the room. Her sweet husband had always been loud, bless his heart. And she knew how to suck his dick in the exact way he loved, rubbing his tip against the roof of her mouth."

Nice. Generous women were awesome, and I had a feeling my little librarian over here was just as generous. *Fuck*.

"But what was really sending her to heaven was how Wesley was hitting all her sweet spots with that long cock. He plunged into her over and over, balls slapping against her, stroking that g-spot before actually slamming into her cervix. She'd never been with anyone so big, and she wondered if she'd actually be able to have that mythical thing she'd read about a few times—a cervical orgasm."

Cervical orgasm? My jaw hanging open, I

turned to Olivia to see her hand clamped over her mouth, her eyes dancing above her fingers. I had to read more.

"'You like it deep, baby?' Wesley asked her. The way he checked in with her made her heart flutter. She nodded as best she could while still sucking off her husband. Somehow, Wesley penetrated her even more, his fingers digging into her skin harder and harder. Christine was about to pass out from the sheer pleasure coursing through her veins."

I feel ya, woman. Was that a fucking moan I heard from Olivia? I couldn't look at her or I'd explode.

"The pressure built and built inside her, every part of her aroused and swollen—her clit, her g-spot, and now her cervix. It was going to happen. She just knew it. Relaxing into it, she shifted her ass up higher, holding onto the sheets for dear life. She was on the verge of the biggest orgasm she'd ever had, and she didn't know if she'd survive it."

"You can do it, Christine," Olivia murmured, shifting her gorgeous body.

Sweet Jesus.

"By the sounds of it, Liam was about to explode in her mouth, and she was about to shatter, her walls beginning to clench and unclench around Wesley's big cock. And then it happened. A shudder racked her frame as Wesley reached around to flick her clit in time with his thrusts. It started deep, deep inside her, spreading out in an all-encompassing wave that pulsed through her, a whole body sensation that reached all the way from her toes to the ends of her hair."

Holy shit. I could hear Olivia's fast breathing, but I didn't dare glance her way. I needed to get the hell home. And soon.

"At that exact moment, Liam's cum filled her mouth as he grabbed onto her hair while she took everything he had to give. And then she felt Wesley let go too, hot pulses filling her still quivering channel, her pussy wrecked in the best of ways. Dripping with cum from both ends, Christine soon collapsed on the bed, a happy smile on her face, like the cat who'd gotten the cream."

I'll say.

Olivia snickered, and I finally glanced at her. But fuck if that wasn't a mistake. Everything about her called to me—her bedroom eyes, her pink cheeks, her slightly messed up hair that made her look like she'd just been fucked.

"Um, I gotta go," I mumbled.

"So soon?" Her eyes looked wounded.

With a gulp, I nodded. How could I explain to Olivia that there was a massive tent in my shorts without coming off like a perv?

"I need the coldest shower ever," I eventually said, my brain not thinking clearly with the lust pounding through me.

A huge grin covered her face. "Ohh. I see."

Standing up, I dropped the cushion covering my lap, grateful for once of the awfully dim lighting in here. Walking toward the door, I tried to ignore the giggles coming from the couch. "We can never speak of this again," I joked, swiftly opening it and rushing across the hall.

I heard more laughter behind me as well as the sound of her lock clicking. Good. Olivia was safe inside, and I could finally take care of myself. Maybe she would do the same? Oh, God. Not wasting a second, I hurried toward my shower, images of Olivia crowding my mind.

After cranking up the water, I shed my clothes and stepped in, not even waiting for it to warm up. Ice water would do nothing for this hard-on, the fact that I'd just read something filthy to my hot neighbor absolutely blowing my mind.

One hand against the wall, I fisted my cock, stroking up and down, knowing it wouldn't take me long with how turned on I was. Olivia's face flashed through my mind, imagining her taking off her clothes and heading to her bedroom right now. What would she use? Her fingers? A vibrator? Or maybe a shower head?

That. I thought of her in the shower, water dripping from her wet, hard nipples. Oh, shit. I was close. Imagined her grabbing the showerhead and aiming it at her pretty pussy, lifting one leg up on the side of the tub to get a better angle. What if she also touched herself?

Rubbing her clit to help things along. Then moving to her breast, tweaking a nipple.

My dick had never been so hard. And for some reason I wanted to prolong it. Jerking off to thoughts of Olivia did something *more* to me, and I never wanted it to be over.

But it wasn't meant to be. Especially because that little moan I'd heard from her flashed through my mind, a sound I'd never forget. A sound I wanted to hear again and again. Because of *me* next time.

And then I imagined her riding me, her face, the way her eyes would close, the way her sweet pussy would feel gripping my cock. That was it. I exploded, my cum shooting out against the shower wall in hot streams, the orgasm rocking my whole body.

I'd never come so hard in my life. And it was all Olivia. What would it feel like if I ever had the real-life experience of fucking her? I had to find out. I wanted it with all my body and soul.

TWELVE

Luke

Standing in line at the concession stand, my eyes kept going back to Olivia who was sitting between her parents at a table they'd managed to snag. They were in town for the weekend, a quick visit before they all went off to Italy in a few months, and somehow I'd ended up spending this day with them at the Safari Park. And somehow I'd ended up in charge of getting the food with Olivia's little sister Emily.

Olivia said it was all part of her boyfriend lessons curriculum, although I couldn't quite connect those dots myself. It's not like we were pretending to be together or anything. Maybe she just wanted to see how I was around parents and family, in general, that I'd never met before.

Emily edged forward in the line. "So I know you're neighbors with Olivia, but she's never talked about you until now."

"Right. Well, we were more acquaintances before. It's only lately that we've become friends."

She raised a brow at me, a familiar gesture, which wasn't surprising considering the physical similarities between the two sisters. Now that I'd seen the parents in person, it wasn't hard to figure out where Olivia got her good looks. The entire family was incredibly attractive.

"So do you have a girlfriend or boyfriend?" Emily asked.

Wow, straight to the point, this girl. "Not currently. How about you?" If she could ask, so could I.

"Nope. No desire for one. I don't want to be tied down. And I don't want some dick to break my heart."

Okay then. I had no response to that except for an awkward chuckle. Man, I wished this line would move a bit faster. But that's what life was like at a major SD touristy spot during the summer.

So I sucked it up, taking a second to wipe the sweat from my forehead. God, it was hot here. And it didn't help to be under scrutiny like this.

"Especially not after what happened with Livs," Emily said.

Wait. What? People called Olivia Livs? And she'd had her heart broken? What the hell? "What do you mean?"

"Oh, she hasn't told you?"

"No."

For a few seconds, Emily appeared torn, her eyes darting between me and Olivia in the distance. With a huff of air that blew some hair off her face, she stepped closer, now staring at Olivia. "It's not like she can hear me, but she's weirdly good at lip reading."

So did that mean she was going to tell me? I wasn't sure how to feel. Would Olivia be mad that we'd discussed her personal life?

Emily angled her body so her back was to Olivia, and then started to talk under her breath. "Did you know she was engaged?"

"Yes, she told me."

"Okay. Did she tell you how it ended?"

I thought back to our conversation a few days ago. "She just said they drifted apart, that they weren't right for each other."

Emily made a funny noise in her throat, like a sound of disbelief. "You can say that again. Henry, this guy we all loved, this guy we thought was absolutely perfect for Olivia, turned out to be a total and complete asshole."

For some reason, I found my blood pressure rising along with her tone.

"They were together four years," Emily went on, "living together too, and they were happily planning the wedding and all, when out of the blue, totally shocking Livs, he dumps her. One day they were tasting cakes, and literally the next he said the meanest things to her."

"Like what?" I spit out.

Emily blinked at me before taking a quick glance back at her sister. "The last thing I want is for her to hear me."

"Of course."

Whirling around, she moved up half a pace with the line. "So anyway, yeah. He said some awful things about how she never wanted to do anything, how she was such a homebody, how she was obsessed with her job and books. Said things like being with her was so incredibly monotonous he felt like he was already dead. Or if he wasn't, he wanted to die just from sheer boredom."

"What the hell?"

"Right? And this is the part that really chaps my hide. He called her *boring*. And that word almost killed her because she was already sensitive that maybe she was boring. So for him to say it?" She shook her head, her lips in a tight line.

A muscle ticked in my jaw, and I had to consciously make an effort to unclench my fists. "If she was so boring, why'd he stay in a relationship with her for four years and then ask her to marry him?"

"Exactly. Between you and me..." Emily leaned in closer. "...I think Livs must be super hot in the sack."

And now my anger blended with jealousy

until I couldn't tell the two apart.

"What can I get for you today?" a cheery voice said.

It took a second to orient myself, the anger simmering in my veins. At least Emily was on it, stepping up to order from the list on her phone. By the time it was my turn, I could communicate again.

Once we were standing to the side, waiting for our number to be called, Emily picked up right where she left off.

"It destroyed her. The wedding was only two months away, and Livs had her entire life planned out. They were already looking at houses, the whole shebang. And it's taken her all this time to even come close to resembling her old self."

"So about a year to get over this jerk?"

"Yep. And I know she talks about some guy that comes into the library, but I think it's just an act."

I fucking wish. "I'm not so sure about that."

Emily tilted her head at me. "She's told you about him? Some musician guy?"

I couldn't hide the roll of my eyes. "Unfortunately, yeah."

At my dry tone, her eyes widened. "You don't like him? You've met him?"

"Not officially. But I saw him. And Olivia talks about him quite a bit."

She waved a hand at me in a dismissive

gesture. "I don't buy it. I think she just wants to move on, and he was the first decent guy that came along. He's like her safety."

Interesting.

They called our number, and the two of us balanced trays and drinks, carrying them over to the table where we divvied up the burgers, fries, and salads. Once we were all situated, I mentally prepared myself for some sort of grilling.

Sure, we'd been here for a few hours already, but aside from the usual pleasantries, I hadn't really talked to Olivia's parents since we'd been too busy. But I knew this was the perfect relaxed setting now for a conversation.

In the past, I'd avoided meeting families like it was the plague. I hated meeting the parents... because it meant something bigger, always, something bigger that I definitely didn't want to commit to.

Biting into my burger, I noticed Olivia's mom's eyes were pinned on me. She smiled softly, and I knew I was in for it. "So, Luke," she said, "what do you do with your time? What kind of things do you enjoy?"

Whoa, what kind of question was that? I had expected the typical "What do you do" question, people's not-so-sly way of classifying and ranking others. So to get this instead totally threw me off.

"Um, I work a lot." Brilliant. "I'm a finance director at a health insurance company."

Looking back and forth at her parents, I expected to see the usual—assessing me, wondering how much money I made. I'd actually had one girlfriend whose dad asked me my salary. Yeah, that was the last time I'd met anyone's family.

"Well, that sounds like... fun," Mrs. Lindquist said, a teasing twinkle in her eye.

So she hadn't been impressed by my job. Did I need to throw in the MBA? Maybe toss in the fact that I made well over six figures?

"Do you like it?" Mr. Lindquist asked.

What a strange line of questioning we were heading into. Besides Olivia, no one had ever asked me before if I liked my job. Wait a second.

My eyes fell on Olivia who was very preoccupied with her salad and pushing it away from the fries on her plate. Had she been talking about me with her parents?

Realizing they were waiting for an answer, I shook my head. "Not really. No. But it keeps a roof over my head. So..."

"Look out," Emily said. "Mom's a psychology professor, and Dad's a school counselor."

To my amazement, the whole table dissolved into laughter.

"Guilty," they both said at the same time, only making everyone laugh harder.

Glancing around the table, taking in their faces, amazement hit me. This family really loved each other. They were tight. Anyone with half a brain could see that.

Emily poked me in the arm. "So really. What do you do for fun?"

Fun. What *did* I actually do? My partying days were long gone. Sure, I went out on occasion. But looking around at bars, I felt old and out of place.

Taking a long drink of my icy cold water, I thought for a second. "You know what I like to do? I like to eat. I like to check out all the cool restaurants where we live. And then, of course, I have to work out a lot to make up for it."

My God, you would have thought I was the funniest comedian alive at the way they all lost it. I shoved in some salad, beginning to fully appreciate this conversation that had taken such an unexpected turn from the norm.

"So that's it," Mr. Lindquist said. "If you're so into food and restaurants, you could be a reviewer, you know, a food critic. Or..."

"Or a supplier?" Emily nudged me in the shoulder. "Like go start an organic farm and do the farm-to-table thing."

Mrs. Lindquist cleared her throat. "Or you could be a consultant."

"Or open your *own* restaurant," Olivia chimed in.

"Yeah, that's totally it!" Emily squealed beside me.

And then they were off, trying to figure out what kind of food I would serve.

"American with a twist."

"Or seafood. It's San Diego. You have to have seafood."

"Or Pacific fusion."

I couldn't even keep track of who was saying what with how fast they were taking off with the idea.

"Maybe a sports theme," Olivia's dad added. "High end though. It is the Gaslamp after all."

And then they started talking about specific menu items I should serve at my amazing new hypothetical restaurant.

"You have to have burgers."

"And pasta. Always."

"And a kids' menu. And crayons in an empty tomato sauce can."

"Oh, oh, you could give them playdough."

"You could have the tables covered in paper so everyone can color."

"What about a whiskey tasting room?"

"I know. I know," Emily said, drawing everyone's attention. "Do away with tipping, and pay the servers higher wages."

"Ooh, that's a good one."

Seriously, my head began to spin... not just from the ideas, but because of the positivity and optimism circling around the table. I'd never seen anything like it.

Was it any wonder Olivia had become such an incredible person with these two parents. What had her childhood been like? What would it be like to grow up in a household like this?

"Or you could get a boat," Mr. Lindquist said, "and do some harbor cruises."

"Or put the restaurant on the boat."

"Or open a gym."

And then they went off on a new tangent while I ate the rest of my lunch in shocked happiness. Their enthusiasm was contagious, and I found myself actually enjoying the experience and spending time with them all, dreaming away about the possibilities of my life.

After endless ideas shared at the table, we finished our meal and decided to move on to go feed the lorikeets. Telling everyone to relax, I cleaned up the plates and trash, joking that it would help me on my new career path.

Trays loaded up, I walked toward the garbage can, and I heard a voice a little louder than the rest. "He's super hot. You should totally try to tap that."

"Emily!" several other voices said at once.

Literally, I had to bite my tongue to keep from laughing too loudly. Yeah, to anyone watching, I looked like a total idiot, grinning and chuckling to myself. But this day had turned out to be more than I could have ever imagined.

THIRTEEN

Olivia

Exhausted after a long day of story times plus a DIY hot cocoa bomb teen event, I checked my mail before heading up the stairs. Tonight was a definite leftover night. Or maybe delivery. All I wanted to do was put my aching feet up, eat, and read.

As the doors started to close, a hand reached in, giving me a start. But thank goodness it was just Luke.

"Hey," he said with a big grin on his face. "Happy hump day."

That smile was really something else. "Happy hump day to you. Still haven't been fired?"

He laughed. "Nope. Not yet anyway."

A delicious aroma permeated the small space, making me glance at the plastic bag he carried. "What do you have that smells so good?"

Luke held up the bag. "This? It's Chinese...

Want some?"

Did I want some? Was the Pope Catholic? "No. No. I can't steal your food."

"I have tons." My traitorous stomach rumbled loudly, making Luke laugh. "Come on," he argued. "I insist."

With absolutely no willpower left in me, I easily relented. "Your place or mine?"

Luke chuckled. "How about mine this time? You can check out the ol' bachelor pad."

"Oh, God. I'm seriously scared."

"You should be. It's disgusting." As we exited the elevator and started down the hall together, I had to wonder if he was kidding or not. "Hey, why don't you go change and get more comfortable, then come over? That'll give me time to pick up all my dirty socks."

I wasn't sure whether to laugh or groan as I keyed into my place, so I did a little of both while Luke laughed.

Minutes later, dressed completely for comfort, I knocked on his door which was slightly ajar, the legendary sounds of Johnny Cash spilling into the hallway.

"Yeah. Just come on in," he called from somewhere inside.

So I did, my eyes wide with anticipation at what I might find. The layout was opposite of mine, but that was the only similarity. Every single thing in Luke's place was black, white, or gray. Stunned, I quickly scanned the room.

Yep, black couch, black chair, gray and white patterned rug, black TV and coffee table, all of it spotless.

Wow. It was cool, crisp, and totally unexpected.

"I'm just getting the food together." Luke's head appeared around the corner of the kitchen, his eyes going up and down my body. "Nice pajamas."

"Hey, I've had a long day. Okay? And you said to get comfy." Maybe pajama pants and a tank top were taking it a bit too far. But I didn't care. Something about Luke made me comfortable, like I didn't have to try to impress him. And I did still have my bra on. So there was that.

He disappeared back into the kitchen. "Have a seat. Let me take care of you then."

That was seriously sweet. Luke was turning out to be prime boyfriend material. Or my so-called lessons were actually working. Maybe it was a bit of both?

I did as he said, finding a spot on the couch which was more comfortable than it looked. Not as great as mine but pretty good still. The music caught my attention again, and I noticed an actual old-school record player with rows and rows of vinyl lined up neatly beneath it in shelves. How cool was that?

Arms loaded down, Luke brought out a bunch of stuff, filling up the coffee table as I helped him arrange everything. It didn't take long before our plates were practically overflowing with chow mein noodles, steamed vegetables, and orange chicken along with some chilled Sauvignon Blanc in beautiful wine glasses.

"Thanks for sharing," I said between bites.

"No problem. See? Told you I had enough."

I had to admit there was something really nice about it all, and Luke's place was actually pretty cool. For such a single SoCal dude. To my surprise, Luke was genuinely starting to grow on me.

The song changed, nudging my thoughts in a different direction. "Hey, are you a vinyl person?" I asked.

After swallowing his bite, he turned slightly to face me. "Yeah. Something a college roommate got me into."

"That's really cool. I've always wondered, what's the big deal? Like how is it different? Why do some people get so into it?"

His eyes glinting with humor, he stared at me, slowly shaking his head. "You have no idea what you've started."

With a giggle, I grimaced. "No? I guess not?"

And then he talked endlessly about the quality and richness of the sound, how you could hear the depth the artist intended rather than the compressed sound of digital. Part of it went over my head, but what I did soak in was his passion and excitement. The animation in his face was incredible to see, and I loved the way his dark eyes seemed to get even deeper than usual as he spoke.

It was mesmerizing, and I couldn't look away. Shoveling in the food, I stared at Luke in amazement as he came alive in front of my eyes. As if he had suddenly come into sharp focus, I could really see what these girls saw in him and why they couldn't stay away. He was ridiculously attractive, all that dark hair, perfectly messed up, that devilish way his eyes gleamed, like you just didn't quite know what he'd do.

Sure, he was commitment-shy. But damn, I could see why a woman would give it a shot.

Not me, of course. We were just friends, and I intended to keep it that way. I'd finally gotten over a heartbreak, and the last thing I needed was another one courtesy of Luke. No, thank you.

Trying to get back to the topic, I attempted to pay more attention to his words, truly listening to "Ring of Fire" as he pointed out the differences.

After we made a huge dent in the food, I helped Luke clean up, and I settled back on the couch, watching Luke as he shoved on a baseball cap and proceeded to show me a bunch of his records. Putting on some Fleetwood Mac, he eventually took a seat beside me as I yawned, a post-dinner food coma washing over me.

"I'm sorry," I said, "but I don't have it in me to have a boyfriend lesson."

"No worries. And who says we can't just hang

out as friends, Livs?"

Hearing him say my nickname in his signature deep voice caused a fluttering sensation deep in my stomach. "Livs? Did you just call me Livs?"

"Yeah, I like it." He wiggled my knee. "And I really liked your family too."

I should have known he'd pick up on that from my family this past weekend. Of course.

"So?" he asked. "How'd I do? Did I pass whatever test you were throwing at me by meeting the parents?"

A smile filled my face at his unexpected question. Did Luke actually care what my family and I thought of him? "You totally passed. They loved you."

His brows raised in shock. "They did? For real?"

"Absolutely. They thought you were fun and very nice too."

He nodded. "Fun and nice. Well, all right. That's pretty good."

His tone gave me pause, causing a swell of curiosity inside me. "What's happened in the past when you've met parents of girlfriends? I mean, not that I'm your girlfriend. Obviously. But I just wanted to see how it all went, you know, like a practice run."

"To see if I was a total asshole, you mean, with no people skills whatsoever?"

Underneath the teasing, I could sense something deeper. I just didn't know what. "No. No. That's not what I meant. Please don't take anything I say seriously tonight."

He relaxed his shoulders, leaning back into the couch. "Yeah, I know. So in the past, it's gone just fine. I've met exactly two sets of parents. One dad was a real butthead, but other than that, it was okay. But nothing like your family. They were actually... fun."

And there it was again—that something else. Like he couldn't believe my family was fun. "Did you think they wouldn't be fun? Because I'm not very fun?" What *did* Luke think of me? I'd never really cared before. But suddenly, I did now.

"What? You think you're not fun? Why would you think that at all?"

There was no way I was going there with Luke, so I simply shrugged. "Because of my job. Because of my quiet lifestyle I guess."

Luke leaned closer to me. "Stop. Okay? That's ridiculous. That doesn't make you any less fun to be around. You know that, right?"

Again, he pushed against my knee, his hand lingering a little longer this time, something about it really nice, distracting me from our topic of conversation. "What were we talking about again?" I asked.

With a laugh, Luke pulled my feet up onto his lap, my body turning automatically on the couch. "Come on. Clearly, you've had a long day. Why don't you tell me about it, and I'll give you a foot massage?"

Was he kidding me? Was he trying to make me

swoon or something? "Are you serious?"

"Wait just a sec." Putting my feet aside gently, he stood up and disappeared, quickly returning with a bottle in his hand. "This was a gag gift at work once, but I kept it."

Leaning forward, I strained to read the words peppermint foot lotion. "Oh, my gosh, that sounds like heaven."

"Good. I've never tried it. So you'll have to let me know."

Suddenly, my feet were back in his lap, and the refreshing scent of peppermint filled the air. The second his hands touched me, I let my head fall back against the armrest of the couch. Heaven was no exaggeration, especially when he began to work strong fingers into the arches of my feet.

"Oh, God," I groaned, not even caring how needy I sounded.

Luke's husky laugh met my ear. "So tell me, if you can, how your day was."

With a dreamy sigh, I began to tell him about work—how it started with double story time and ended with cocoa powder all over my clothes. He paused for a second to turn his hat backward, something about that gesture giving me a little tingle deep in my belly. What on earth was that?

His hands returned to massaging, and my eyes might have rolled to the back of my head. Boy, it was hard to worry about library stuff when his magical fingers were at work. "Um, so yeah, and there was a meeting with my boss in the middle where she wanted me to come up with another program, a really big one that will bring in tons of readers. No pressure or anything."

"Man, she really pushes you, doesn't she?"

"Mm-hmm. Sure does."

"So did you think of one?" he asked.

Again, I couldn't focus. "One what?"

"You know what? Let's talk after," Luke suggested.

I couldn't have agreed more. With his strong hands caressing and massaging, it was impossible to think, impossible to stress. What had been bothering me anyway?

As he gently stretched my foot forward and back, I savored the feel of his touch, something I'd been missing for a very long time. In the year since my break-up, I hadn't been with anyone, and wow, did I crave it.

My thoughts drifted to Jared, but I couldn't quite envision his face at the moment. Maybe that was because all I could see was Luke, the way his dark brows were pulled together in concentration, the set of his full lips serious, contrasting how cute and boyish he looked with his hat like that.

Stevie Nicks began to sing "Dreams," and I closed my eyes, the peacefulness of the moment stealing through me. This was nice. I could definitely get used to this.

But it was also dangerous. I couldn't risk getting hurt again, and Luke had heartbreaker written all over him. At this point, after getting to know him better, I actually didn't think he did it on purpose, and I didn't think he was necessarily a bad boyfriend either.

It really did seem like the obvious—that he just hadn't met the right person. But when he did? She'd be a very lucky girl, especially if she received foot massages like this one. Holy cow.

I might have drifted because sometime later, my eyes opened to find Luke studying my face. "Hey," he said softly, jostling my feet. "You awake?"

"I'm a big blob of jello right now."

Throwing his head back, he laughed. "Well, good. Mission accomplished."

My feet still in his lap, I wondered if I should move. But his hands held me there, resting on my ankles, warming me in his cool apartment. Luke was bigger on AC than I was.

"So I still want to hear about work," he said. "What happened with Nikki? Do I need to come in there and rough her up?"

God, he made me laugh. "No. Please don't. It'll be fine. What I really wish..."

He wiggled my ankles. "What?"

Despite my relaxed haze, I still had trouble with my words. Why was it so tough to admit this?

"What?" he said again.

I needed to get it out, and for some reason, Luke seemed safe. He'd never once made me feel less than. "I'd love to start some kind of romance book club at work," I admitted.

"That'd be amazing. Why wouldn't you?"

"Because of Nikki. Because of most people at work really, with the exception of Nadia."

He still looked confused. "What do you mean?"

"There's a huge stigma about romance," I tried to explain. "Readers of other genres look down on us. They think it's the lowest of the low."

"That's crazy. Why do people have to be so rude? Why can't they just let people enjoy what they want to enjoy?" The vehemence in his voice surprised me, making me smile like crazy. "And you know what? I think your idea is amazing. You should totally mention it to Nikki. What's the worst thing that could happen?"

What *was* the worst thing that could happen? She'd be snobby about my love of romance. But why should I care? Why did her opinion matter at all to me? Well, it did matter a little because she was my boss. But could she fire me over romance books? I seriously doubted it.

What the heck? Luke was right. I was going to do it.

FOURTEEN

Luke

Being able to walk to and from work was the only good thing about my job. Dealing with parking downtown was annoying, and every day I was glad I didn't have to bother.

Loosening my shirt and tie, I took a deep breath, finally able to relax. I remembered to turn left instead of walking straight home. Yup, I'd changed my route in the last week so I could happen to walk by the library on the way to my apartment.

Not sly. Not cool. But if I had the opportunity to run into Olivia, I was going to grab it. I was working damn hard to earn her trust. I knew she thought I was some kind of playboy womanizer, but hopefully, her opinion of me was changing for the better the more she actually got to know me.

She was all I could think about lately. Even at

night, she'd invaded my dreams and not just the sexual kind. I could hear her laughter, see her glowing face, and even smell her sweet scent. Fuck me, but I had it bad. Like a teenage boy with his first crush.

Walking past the amazing architecture, I slowed my pace. Jesus. Could I be any more of a stalker? If I did run into her, it wouldn't take much for her to figure out this was a very indirect way for me to get home. And Olivia was one of the smartest people I'd ever known. At this realization, I put my head down and moved faster.

"Luke?" a voice asked. A voice that sounded like sweet honey.

Rolling my eyes at myself, I whirled around, and there she was, instantly drawing a smile from my face. "Hey."

"What are you doing here?" Her brows creased as she pointed in the other direction. "You work way over there, don't you?"

Damn. Took her less than a second. "Um, I... I..." You know what? Fuck it. Might as well grab the bull by the horns. "Want to grab a drink or something to eat? Celebrate a Friday night?"

The line between her eyebrows disappeared, only to be replaced by a soft smile. "Sure. That sounds nice."

Nice? Was that a good thing? "All right. Where do you want to go?"

She thought for a minute, people streaming

past us, going in and out of the library. "I have no clue," she finally said. "You're Mr. Restaurant Man. You decide."

I knew exactly where to go. "Come on. It's not far. But we can catch a ride if you want."

"Nah, it's cool. I know a guy who gives great foot massages."

We both laughed as we headed out. Yeah, about that foot massage from a couple of nights ago... it might have appeared in my dreams as well.

Together, we dodged all the crazy people filling the sidewalk. Friday nights in the Gaslamp were no joke, a hot destination, and the Crescent Moon Lounge proved to be the same. But because I was somewhat of a regular, we at least got two seats at the bar.

After I texted Aiden to let him know we were here, Olivia and I ordered our drinks. I turned toward her, our legs touching in the crowded space. "So how was your day?" I asked her, resisting the urge to grab onto her bare knee. Did she have to look so hot in her little pencil skirt? She definitely had that sexy librarian vibe going on today.

"It sucked."

The sour look on her face quickly cooled the lust in my body. "No. What happened?"

She huffed out an annoyed breath. "So I talked to Nikki about the whole romance book club idea, and she totally looked down her nose at me, saying we couldn't entertain anything of the sort in the library."

"What the fuck?"

"Right?" Olivia agreed, indignation lacing her voice. "And that she was surprised I would read that kind of filth."

My blood pressure spiked in a sudden flash of anger that someone would say that to this incredible girl sitting next to me. "Okay. Seriously, I'm ready to kill her."

"Who are we killing?" Aiden made an appearance behind the bar, handing me my Jack and Coke and Olivia her strawberry margarita.

An alarmed Olivia whirled around then heaved a sigh of relief when she recognized Aiden.

"We're killing Olivia's boss."

"Ahh, maybe we could add mine to the mix," Aiden joked.

"Mine too," I added.

"Wait," Olivia chimed in. "Wasn't this a movie?"

We all laughed before Olivia and I both took a long drink. She eyed Aiden still standing behind the bar. "So do you work here?"

"Yeah. I'm the sous chef. And the head chef is brilliant but a prick of the highest order."

"That's the worst kind," Olivia said, raising her drink. "To the shittiest bosses' club."

I clinked my glass to hers while Aiden looked on. "I'm raising a virtual glass, you know, drinking on the job and all, although my boss doesn't hesitate to do it on occasion. But apparently, he walks on water, and the owners don't care that he sleeps it off in his car sometimes because he's such a genius."

Yeah, Aiden kind of despised this place.

He looked behind him toward the kitchen. "Hey, I gotta go. I just wanted to say a quick hello before it gets too insane in here."

"Thanks, man."

We ended up ordering a bunch of appetizers and sharing them, chatting easily about our days, Olivia filling me in on the exact conversation she'd had with Nikki. I couldn't believe the bullshit that she'd spouted, and I was furious on Olivia's behalf.

But the more she talked it out, the calmer she became, until she was her usual happy, light-hearted self again. And even though she wasn't sure what to do or how to move forward, I was happy to be her sounding board, and the conversation eventually turned to some of the more interesting people that lived in our building, something that amused us both.

Olivia suddenly scooted closer to me, moving her plate and drink also. Our thighs were pushed together, and it was pretty much all I could think about.

"You okay?" I asked her.

She leaned in. "Yeah. Just this guy on the other side of me keeps bumping into me, and it's annoying."

Looking over her, I shot the dude a glare before a hand landed on my leg.

"Calm down, Hercules," Olivia said. "I took care of it."

I busted out laughing while she squeezed in tighter to my side. Goddamn, she felt good. She went back to eating, and so did I, the food too fantastic to ignore.

"Well, I don't know who made this fine cuisine, if it was Aiden or not, but it's *so* good," Olivia gushed, echoing my thoughts.

"Right? It always is."

"How long has Aiden worked here?" Olivia asked around a mouthful of food.

"For three years. He went to culinary school then worked his way up to where he is now. I keep telling him he needs to be head chef somewhere. He's good enough to do it."

"Why doesn't he?"

"I have no idea." At the funny smile on her face, I nudged her shoulder with mine. "What?"

"So Aiden doesn't share all of his deepest feelings with you?"

"God, no," I scoffed. "Why would he?"

Her eyes drifted to the ceiling, and she finished off her drink before slamming it back down on the bar. "I'm gonna need another."

We flagged down the bartender for refills, and while we waited, I decided to go out on a limb and ask Olivia something I'd been stewing about recently.

"So I don't know if you remember," I began, "but I'm going to Boston next week. And then when I get back, it's Trevor's wedding."

Olivia nodded. "Of course, I remember."

"Well, I'd love it if you went with me, you know, just for a good time, good meal, free drinks, a little people-watching," I added, trying to keep it casual.

"Isn't it too late? Didn't you RSVP already?"

"Um, was I supposed to RSVP? I'm kind of in the wedding party?"

She laughed. "I think so?"

"Whoops. I'm sure they'll be okay with it, and of course, I'd like you to meet Krystal too."

"Okay, yeah, that sounds nice... as long as it's fine with them."

The obnoxious guy behind Olivia was getting sloppy and dropped his knife on his plate, making a loud noise. Olivia jumped, and I noticed a shudder go through her body.

"Do you want to switch spots?" I asked her, sizing the guy up. I could definitely take him. Easy.

"No. No. I'm fine. I just hate that noise."

Confused, I looked around for a second. "What noise?"

"The clanking of silverware." She shivered again, wrapping her arms around herself. "It reminds me of this guy I dated before Henry, and he used to bite down on... oh, God, I can't even think about it."

That sentence could end in a million different ways, and I needed to know. "Bite down on *what*?"

With big eyes, Olivia leaned in and whispered, "His fork."

I nearly laughed at the way she said it, like it was some kind of crime to bite silverware.

Deadly serious, she held my gaze and said, "And I had to break up with him because of it."

I couldn't hold it in anymore, and I burst into laughter. "You did? Why?"

"Because it gave me *chills*," she said, like it was the absolute worst thing in the world.

"Chills? What's wrong with chills?"

"I. Hate. Them."

Leaning back in surprise, I stared at her. Was she joking? I'd never heard of someone hating the chills, and I wasn't quite sure how to respond. But I didn't have to worry about it because Olivia was knocking back that margarita, looking like she was ready to spill all.

"And the worst thing is when guys touch me so lightly, giving me goosebumps, like that's a good thing." Eyes wide, she shook her head at me. "And I despise it. Hate it with a passion. Like no guy can ever touch me the way I want them to."

Holy shit. This was gold here. "How do you want them to touch you?"

"I don't know." She shrugged. "There's no perfect formula, you know?"

That wasn't nearly good enough. "I totally disagree. I'm sure there *is* a perfect formula. Just say it. What exactly do you want?"

Pushing her side into mine, she grabbed my bicep. "Like this. None of that tickly, light touching, scratching stuff. I want hard grasping. Grip my arms. My legs. Squeeze tight. Almost to the point of bruising, but just short of it. I want a guy to grab onto me like he *wants* me."

"You want passion."

"I want passion."

For God's sake, she had no idea what she was doing to me. She finally let go of my bicep, and I hated it. I wanted her hands on me.

"But it's more than that," she continued. "I just want a guy to listen to me, to care about what I want. Or maybe one who instinctually does it without me even having to ask. And it's so frustrating to not be able to find somebody that touches me the right way."

Oh, I'll touch you the right way, baby, if you ever give me a shot. I came so close to saying that ridiculous cheesy line, but of course, I bit my tongue. "What about your ex-fiancé? Didn't he touch you the way you wanted?"

Her sigh spoke volumes. "I had to remind him. A lot. He forgot."

"He forgot? How is that even possible?"

"I have no idea." She shook her head like she didn't want to even think about it. "And when I did speak up and say something, he called me the

Goldilocks of touching, like it was my fault that I asked for certain things."

Man, I hated this douchebag. "Asshole."

Those gorgeous eyes of hers widened, and I could practically see into her soul. "You think so? You don't think I was being selfish?"

"Did he say that?" I growled.

She looked down at her empty plate. "He might have."

Grasping her chin with my hand, I forced her gaze back up to me. "That's total and complete bullshit. You have every right to ask for what you want in bed *and* in a relationship. And if a guy says the opposite, then he's a dick. And you should run away as fast as you can."

The smile that transformed her face surprised me. "Maybe we have this all backward."

"Have what backward?" *And why the hell is your skin so soft?*

"Maybe *you* should be giving the relationship lessons."

"Now that would be interesting."

Both of us laughed, and with reluctance, I eventually let my hand fall away from her face. She looked past me, deep in thought while I took a sip of my drink.

"I just have this feeling," she said, "that Jared will, you know? Like he'll have the magic touch."

A dagger sunk into my gut at those words. What if the dipshit did have the magic touch? I couldn't make any sort of comment on that, so I just grunted.

"What?" Olivia asked.

"One of you needs to ask the other out first."

She grabbed her phone from the counter. "You're right. You're absolutely right. I'm tired of all this. I'm just going to do it."

Great. Why the fuck had I said that? "Do what exactly?"

"Ask him to meet me for coffee. I think that's better than drinks. Don't you think?"

"Yes, absolutely." It definitely seemed the lesser of two evils. No way did I want a tipsy Olivia hanging out with Jared.

"I can always save face and pretend like it was more of a friends thing if I need to."

While I sat there in disbelief, she tapped away on her phone, every letter sucking more life out of me.

After she finished typing, she read it out loud. "Hey, Jared. Just wanted to see if you'd like to grab a coffee sometime." Her bright eyes met mine. "What do you think?"

"It's good."

Fuck that. I didn't like this one bit. I needed to make a move before that idiot had a chance. And I knew exactly what to do.

FIFTEEN

Luke

"Aaaand send," she said, putting her phone back down with a satisfied smile. "I'm proud of myself."

"Me too." I literally lied between my teeth. I mean, of course I was proud of her. I just hated the actual thing she was proud of.

She kept staring at her phone, and I wondered if I'd lost her for the night, or at least until Jared responded. But the seconds, then minutes, ticked past with no answer. Olivia's enthusiasm and confidence were fading right in front of me, and I knew I had to kick this night into gear.

A good song came on right then, and I touched Olivia's arm. "All right. Put the phone away and come dance with me."

Her head whirled around so quickly, some of her hair hit me in the face. "What?"

"You heard me. No sense obsessing. So come

on."

"But—but what about our stuff?"

After grabbing our bags, I asked the bartender to stash them behind the bar, slipping him a fifty. Nothing a little money couldn't handle, and I wasn't going to let anything stop me.

I clasped her hand and led us to the far corner of the bar where a few other people danced, the music blasting from the speaker above us. Good. It was too loud to talk or even think. All we could do was feel.

Finding an empty space, I whirled her around and held her firmly in my arms, crushing our bodies together. Her startled gasp hit me square in the chest, and then the way she looked up at me, her lips slightly apart, her eyes big and vulnerable behind her glasses... fuck me. It took everything in me not to lean in and kiss the hell out of her.

I needed to take it slow with Olivia. For a few long seconds, she stared at my mouth, and I wondered if I was misreading the situation. But then she turned her head to the side and carefully let her cheek rest against me.

Our hips began to move, finding the beat of the song. Closing my eyes, I inhaled the scent of her, the scent that haunted my dreams, like I knew it would even more so tonight. Her palm was still in mine, again her skin so damn soft, her hand so delicate compared to my big rough one.

The way she fit against me was so fucking

perfect. I let my free hand roam up her back until I reached her head, and I couldn't help it. I clasped her against me, tucking the top of her head under my chin, every part of us touching. Yeah, every part.

I was lying if I said I'd never noticed Olivia's breasts. Because I had. They always seemed like the perfect handful to me. Fuck her ex and the Goldilocks comparison. Olivia was *just right* in every possible way. I'd already known that, but the way her chest pressed into me was incredible.

At first, she seemed a little stiff in my arms, and I wondered why... if she was nervous about the way I'd touch her, if it'd be off and make her shudder. It definitely crossed my mind. That was the last thing I wanted, the exact opposite of what I was trying to do.

But she didn't shudder. Not even a little shiver from this beauty in my arms. She relaxed into me, and holy hell, the way we moved together made me hot. Like hotter than reading about Christine. What was it they said about dancing? That it was the perpendicular expression of a horizontal desire?

Yup, that about summed it up.

The song ended, and I let up on my grip, wondering what Olivia was thinking or feeling. But she didn't budge. She kept her head right where it was on my chest, our hands together, fingers interlaced.

Okay. So apparently, we were going to keep on

dancing. I was more than happy to... as long as Olivia was into it. I'd hold her all night if she'd let me.

And that's just about what happened. We danced for a very long time, the music shifting between slower songs and faster tempos. There was zero mention of Jared or checking of cell phones. We were in the moment—drinking, laughing, and moving our bodies together. I'd never had so much fun in my life.

Hours later, we walked home, our hands swinging together loosely between us, both of our bags on my shoulder. Yeah, I was a gentleman, and I wasn't even close to being done with my full-court press.

The streets were quieter now, the soft light from the lamps making Olivia's face glow more than usual. After holding her in my arms, there was no going back for me, and I wanted more. Taking advantage of the lack of people, I paused, our joined hands causing her to slow down as well.

"What is it?" she asked.

Taking a breath, I decided to just go for it. "So I've been meaning to ask you... part of being a good boyfriend is being a great kisser, right?"

Her laughter rang out in the empty street. "Where exactly are you going with this?"

"You know exactly what I want. I want to kiss you."

My directness surprised her into silence, and

I edged closer to her, the tension rising around us. She stepped backward, right into a building. I took the opportunity to close the distance between us, her chest rising and falling rapidly. I liked that I had that effect on her.

I reached up to grasp her face in my palm. With my thumb, I stroked her cheek. "Livs."

Our breaths mingled as she studied my expression, her eyes slowly drifting downwards. Dropping my head, I pressed my lips to her forehead, letting them linger, wondering at this moment.

Her palms flattened against my chest, making me think she might push me away. I went still, waiting, my heart pounding underneath her touch. Would she give me a good shove?

To my shock, she grabbed me by the shirt and pulled me right into her body. Holy fucking shit. That was unexpected. And a definite greenlight for that kiss, especially when her arms moved up to my shoulders and wrapped themselves around my neck.

I nudged her nose with mine, moving ever so closer to that luscious mouth I'd been admiring for weeks. I fought between wanting to be gentle and my raging desire. In the end, desire won, and I crashed my lips against hers, passion for this woman overtaking all else.

And my God, she tasted like a dream, her lips so soft, so fucking perfect as I slanted my mouth over hers again and again, wanting to devour every part of her. I clutched her head between my hands, her hair tangled in my fingers, our bodies crushed together.

With a moan that made me hot as hell, she deepened the kiss, her tongue touching mine, sending fire through my veins. Why the hell did she taste so good? Somehow, the passion flamed even higher between us, our mouths taking all from each other, exploring, greedy, hungry.

My hips ground into her, craving more, craving everything. Fuck. The desire pummeling me right now was unreal. Like a million times stronger than anything I'd ever felt. Everything in me wanted to keep this going. I imagined tossing Olivia over my shoulder, carrying her home, and throwing her on the bed, ripping her clothes off and fucking her raw.

Jesus. I needed to slow down. Gripping her arms, I tore myself away from her mouth, my lungs heaving for oxygen, Olivia doing the same.

At that exact moment, a booming sound went off, startling Olivia.

Another loud noise, then we both smiled as we realized what it was. The Padres must have won. Olivia's eyes took in the fireworks going off behind me over the baseball stadium. But I wasn't done. I needed to know something.

Still with my hands around her biceps, I stared at her, willing her to look at me again. "I want to ask you something."

"Sure," she said, her voice slightly wobbly.

"What is it?"

I leaned in close. "Did I give you chills?"

"No."

Zero hesitation. Only a smile. A sweet smile that stole my breath.

"And what about the rest of the kiss? Did I pass the test?" I asked, beyond curious and needing to know.

"Um, yes, you did. You definitely did."

The booming fireworks played out on her face, as if reinforcing her answer. And like the cocky son-of-a-bitch I was at the moment, I flashed her a smug grin before turning around to watch the colorful explosions going off over downtown.

They didn't last long, and with her hand in mine, we soon started down the street for the short walk home. Her phone made a loud noise suddenly, and I just knew it was Jared. Great timing. Thanks, asswipe.

She hesitated, but for some reason, I wanted her to check her phone. A weird part of me wanted to go head-to-head with Jared. Olivia was worth fighting for.

I held her bag out to her. "I know you want to check if it's Jared. Go for it."

Several emotions flashed over her features, and I caught confusion the most. Maybe after our night, after dancing and kissing, she wasn't one-hundred percent sold on Jared anymore. Maybe I was slowly creeping in there.

Grabbing her phone from the side pocket,

the light illuminated her face as she read. A second later, she shoved it into the bag without answering back and continued walking.

"So? Was it him?" I had to ask, didn't I?

"Yeah, he wants to meet for coffee on Sunday."

"Ah, that's cool."

And there was that hesitation again. "Yeah. It'll be nice."

Hmm, interesting response.

As we entered our building, I thought about how to play this. Subtlety usually wasn't my game. Riding up in the elevator with another couple, we were both quiet, and I had to wonder what Olivia had on her mind.

And she was still silent walking down the hall. Part of me thought about extending the evening, asking her over, but it was pretty late, and maybe it was a good idea to call it a night.

We reached our doors, and I turned to her as she did the same. It was now or never. "One more kiss?" I asked. "You didn't sound so sure the last time, so I think I need to try it again."

The way she giggled and looked up at me didn't help the lust pounding through every cell in my body. It was definitely a flirty move from her.

"One more," she finally answered.

Dropping my bag, I grasped her shoulders, bringing our bodies flush together. This time, I was gentle, kissing the corners of her mouth first before laying one on her. Sweet and lingering.

Soft and tender. That'd give her something to think about while she had her damn coffee with Jim.

When I pulled away, she sighed, her eyes fluttering open. "Well, good night. Thanks for taking me out."

"Any time." I keyed into my place, the feel of her eyes on my back. "Good night, Livs."

Man, I hoped I'd done the right thing, leaving her hopefully wanting more.

SIXTEEN

Olivia

That kiss. Wow, that kiss. I couldn't possibly have feelings for Luke, could I? No. That'd be crazy. I didn't want feelings for Luke. He was all sorts of wrong for me.

Of course, he was fun to hang out with, and surprisingly, I *really* enjoyed spending time with him. He was becoming a good friend. But that was all. A friend.

But damn... that kiss. It was all I'd thought about since Friday night. How pathetic was I? Swooning like crazy all over a kiss. Who knew Luke had it in him?

I couldn't think about that at the moment, though. It was completely unfair to think of one man when I was about to meet another. Opening the door to the coffee shop, the aroma hit me right away, causing a flurry of excitement in my chest. Oh, boy, I hadn't even had any caffeine yet, and here we were, heart beating wildly.

But this was it. Months of pining. Months of dreaming. And it was finally happening.

My eyes scanned the crowded room, catching someone waving from the back. Jared! I rushed forward then remembered to play it cool. I couldn't seem too desperate. So I walked slowly, aware of Jared's gaze on me, and tried to swing my hips a little.

Oh, no. That was not me, and I saw Jared's eyes widen slightly. Why did I have to be such a dork?

What I needed to be was myself. Completely myself. And he could take it or leave it.

He rose up as I approached, and we had the world's awkwardest half hug, kissy cheek thing before I sat down. And then the awkwardest silence as we stared at each other a beat too long.

"So how are you?" I asked as he took a drink from his mug.

"Good. Good. How about you?"

"Good. Yeah. Great."

"Well, good."

Could we say the word good one more time?

"Did you, um, want some coffee?" he asked.

The stupidest laugh in the world came out of my mouth. "Oh, right. Yes, of course. Of course. I'll be right back. Oh, did you want anything?"

"Nope. No. I'm good."

And there it was. Another good. I stifled my giggles as I ordered my drink and waited. Why was this so weird? Part of me thought about texting Nadia. Or maybe Luke. Oh, no. Why had I thought of him? *Stop it, brain.*

Thank goodness the baristas were all hopped up on caffeine because my drink was ready in a flash. Taking a cleansing breath, I realized I needed to hit the reset button on this "date."

Walking back, I gave myself a pep talk to relax and let the conversation flow. This was no big deal. Just because I hadn't been on a date in years didn't mean anything. I could always fall back on my go-to social skill—asking questions and getting the other person to talk.

And that's exactly what I did. Taking a seat across from Jared, I asked him all about his music, and that's what we discussed for hours. And hours. And hours. More like one hour. It just felt longer for some reason.

Listening to him talk about his latest lyrics, that's when it hit me. Jared was still a beautiful man. I mean, look at that hair. Look at those eyes. But he wasn't for me anymore.

When on earth had that changed? How could my obsession fizzle out like that?

In stunned silence, I nodded at all the right places, only partially listening at this point, totally annoyed at myself.

What a dingbat I'd been. Nadia had been right. I'd been in a love triangle and hadn't even realized it.

But had it even been a love triangle really? Once Luke and I had started hanging out, Jared hadn't stood a chance. I'd just been stubbornly clinging onto that crush because it was safe. *He* was safe. Especially since nothing would have come of it most likely if I hadn't pushed it.

But I had pushed it. So had Nadia. And I had to wonder why.

Twisting my napkin, I kept my eyes on Jared, a forced smile on my face as my world slowly tilted out of balance with an insane realization.

I'd known it for a while really. I just pushed it down because it was unsafe, rocky, and sure to be a disaster of epic proportions, making Henry seem insignificant. But I now had to admit it to myself.

I had feelings for Luke. Major feelings.

And I wasn't exactly happy about it because they were strong. So incredibly strong. I didn't want to like Luke. There was only one way it'd end, and that'd be heartbreak for me. I was sure of it.

Unease growing in my gut, I tried to return my focus to Jared, and I mostly succeeded. When he asked me questions about my job and my family, I was drawn back in. After all, I didn't want to be rude. I'd been the one who'd suggested this whole thing in the first place.

Gosh, I was an idiot. And suddenly, I felt even worse because subconsciously I'd used Jared to try to distract myself from my stupid growing feelings for Luke. I expected better from myself.

And now, I had a new problem. As quickly as

this thing with Jared had begun, I had to end it. And it was made all the more awkward because of my job and the fact that he was a regular. What had I been thinking?

I needed Nadia. I just had to get through this as kindly and noncommittally as possible. Was that a word? Did that even make sense?

"Well, I had a really nice time," Jared said, gathering up his phone and empty cup.

"Yeah. Yeah. Me too."

"Maybe we could go for a walk if you're up to it," he suggested.

Whew, boy. Trying to think on my feet, not my specialty, I grasped onto the first thing that popped into my head. "Oh, I can't really. It's my friend's wedding and I need to get going."

His brows shot up. "Wedding? You have a wedding to go to?"

Why hadn't I just said birthday? What was wrong with me? I blamed it all on Luke. Him and his panty-melting kisses. It was all his fault. He was totally and completely messing with my brain.

"Um, yeah. Later I do. But I need to start getting ready. You know, hair, make-up, ironing, polishing jewelry, shaving, finding my earholes since I haven't worn earrings in forever, um, all that stuff, you know."

Those eyebrows went up even more. "Right. Right. Of course."

Earholes? Please, someone save me from myself.

"Okay, well, then, this was fun. Thanks. Thanks for meeting me."

"Yeah, it was fun."

We both stood up, making our way through the crowd, walking to the exit and heading outside. And here we were again. Another awkward hug and quick peck on the cheek.

Jared put his hand on my arm, lightly trailing his fingers down my skin. "All right. See you at the library probably this week," he said.

"Mmkay. Sounds good." I whirled around in the opposite direction, trying to hide the shiver that went through me because that touch had given me *goosebumps*.

Ugh. Why? Why? Why?

Rubbing my arms, trying to get rid of the dreaded chills, I realized I was going the wrong way. But I didn't care. I'd just go around the block. All I could think about was putting on my pajamas and crawling back into bed for the day. Call Nadia. Grab a book. Read the entire rest of the day away.

Sounded like heaven. And you know who I wouldn't think about? Luke. Nope. Not even a little.

But as luck would have it, that wasn't meant to be. Because right as I tried to creep down the hallway, Luke's door burst open, and he came out, dragging his suitcase.

Perfect timing. Couldn't have been a minute earlier or later. Had to be right now? *Thanks, universe. Thanks a lot.*

That was cool. I could handle it. But looking up at his bright smile, nope, I definitely couldn't handle it. Because now I knew. I knew I liked him, and all I could think about was that kiss.

"Hey," he said. "Just heading down to wait for my ride to the airport."

At that reminder, my stupid heart sunk. "Oh, okay. Well, have a great trip."

"Thanks." He paused, his too handsome eyes drilling into me. "Are you just getting back from your coffee date?"

"Yes." I resisted the urge to fidget.

"And? How was it?"

"Good," I lied.

"Yeah? Everything you dreamed of? Did he give you..." He leaned in closer, totally invading my space. "...the chills?"

Bastard. How could he possibly know that?

"No response, huh? So I take it that's a yes?" The smirk on his face was downright obnoxious.

"Ugh." I shoved him away. "You're so annoying."

His laughter filled the empty hallway. "Thanks. I try."

I turned to go, but his heavy hand on my arm stopped me.

"Wait."

Something about the deep and husky way he'd said that made my knees a little shaky. That one small word held meaning, a meaning I didn't quite understand but definitely something I felt.

"What?" I asked, spinning around to face him, his eyes searching mine before dropping down to my mouth.

I knew what he wanted. And damn it, I wanted it too.

"I'm going to miss you," he said softly.

Oh, I was officially a goner. And even more so when he pressed into me, lowering his forehead to mine. "I'll miss you too," I admitted.

Like a dam had been broken, his lips captured my own in a scorching hot kiss. One hand grabbed onto my hair, tilting my head, his tongue massaging mine. His other arm went around me, clasping me tightly against him, my deceitful body dissolving into his.

I didn't hesitate to kiss him right back, my fingers digging into his biceps, holding on for the wild ride Luke insisted on. Holy smokes, I couldn't even imagine how Luke would be in bed, how intense and passionate he'd be if this moment was any indication.

By far, Luke had the most talented mouth I'd ever known. His kisses melted me completely.

A buzzing sounded, and he pulled back, muttering a curse. After checking his phone, our eyes met. "My ride's here. Sorry."

"No problem."

"I'll call you," he said. "I promise."

And with that, he was gone.

Where was I? Who was I? Luke's kiss had

sent me into an utter daze, and all the sudden, I dreaded this week without him.

SEVENTEEN

Luke

The more the days dragged on with endless, pointless, soul-sucking meetings, the more I realized I needed to make some changes in my life—two things, specifically.

Number one... Olivia. I wanted her. And I wouldn't stop until she was mine. It was as simple as that.

And number two... I had to quit my job. Why hadn't I done it already? I had plenty of money. So that wasn't it. Maybe it was because I just didn't know what else to do.

As the week wore on, a seed of an idea formed in my head. Well, the seed had actually been planted by Olivia's family, maybe even Olivia herself that day. But the only thing I looked forward to during this godawful business trip was eating.

In Boston, there was a plethora of fine dining options, and I became obsessed with their online menus, looking for the perfect place to try each night.

Sometimes, I went with other people, but I enjoyed it more by myself to be honest... because this wasn't just a meal to me. It'd become research and development, a possible dream in the making.

Really, if I thought about it, I'd done this forever... ever since that first time I'd gone out to eat with Aiden and his family as a kid.

My parents didn't go out to eat. Ever. And I knew now exactly why. I hadn't realized what I'd been missing as Aiden's mom ushered his sisters and us out the door that night.

So at age eight, a simple rib place had seemed like heaven. Maybe it was the fact that I didn't have to listen to my mom cursing in the kitchen or sit at the table full of shame and anxiety about whatever argument was about to happen.

But whatever it was, that tiny rib joint lit something up inside me, something I'd downplayed forever because I needed stability. I needed a good job with benefits that paid well. Well, I'd had it and I was sick to death of it.

Man, I couldn't wait to get back home to Olivia and put all this into action. By the time Friday morning rolled around, I swear impatience flowed through my veins.

For years, I'd been complacent, not caring,

not giving a shit about anything, just coasting through life, numb and dull, waiting for something to wake me up. Now I was awake. And I had a sexy little librarian to thank for it.

We'd talked some on the phone and texted a bit, but there was nothing like being together in person, and I couldn't wait to spend time with her this weekend, especially in a romantic setting like a wedding. Besides, I was more than excited to see Trevor and Krystal finally tie the knot.

So when my flight got delayed for mechanical reasons, I was thoroughly pissed off and a little freaked out. And even more panicked when that delay caused me to miss my connecting flight, and I had to spend the night in Atlanta, missing the rehearsal. And then when I didn't think I could get any more annoyed, they couldn't get me on a flight out till later in the day on Saturday, the day of the actual wedding.

Fucking hell. I'd already missed the whole rehearsal dinner for one of my best friends, and now I'd barely make it in time for his wedding. Part of me wanted to rent a car and floor it all the way. At least I'd be moving. But of course I wouldn't make it in time.

So I tried to keep it together, driving the guy next to me crazy with my jiggling knee as I kept checking the clock on my phone over and over once I finally got on a goddamn plane.

Shit. Shit. Shit. I didn't even have enough time

to go home. Aiden would need to bring my tux to the church to change into, and Olivia would have to meet me there.

Not exactly the way I'd planned it. I'd wanted to make it a big event, wooing her, showing up at her door in my tux, maybe with flowers in my hand. But instead I'd make her go all by herself to a wedding where she didn't know a soul.

What an asshole.

Jumping up as soon as the plane pulled into the gate—yeah, I was that guy—I charged down the aisle, practically running to the airport exit, carry-on suitcase in hand. Catching a cab was the fastest way to go, so I didn't hesitate. And I told the guy I'd give him an extra fifty if he'd floor it.

Checking my messages, I saw that all was good, thank God. I'd only be fifteen minutes later than I was supposed to be. And we still had about thirty minutes to go until the actual ceremony started. Of course I'd need a run-through of what the hell I was supposed to be doing. But how hard could it be to walk down an aisle and stand behind the groom?

When I got there, Aiden met me out front and led me to the room where the guys were getting ready. Besides us, there were a few cousins in there as well as Trevor's dad.

Shedding my travel clothes and shoving on my tux, I glanced around for Trevor. "Where's the groom?"

"Right here, dipshit." He came around the

corner then. "Thanks for showing up."

"You know how sorry I am." Walking forward, I gave him a one-armed hug. "You're looking good, my man. How you doing?"

Taking a step back, Trevor took a deep breath. "Nervous as hell."

"Why?"

He shrugged. "I have no idea. I guess I just want everything to go right. For Krystal. You know?"

I gave him a pat on the shoulder. "I'm sure it'll all be great. And if it isn't, well, that's what the open bar is for, right?"

Laughing, he nodded like he was trying to convince himself. "Right. You got it."

Aiden came over, and we talked about logistics for a few minutes, then shot the breeze with the cousins. Part of me wanted to go check and see how Olivia was doing, but I didn't want to abandon the groom. I was the co-best man after all.

Plus, I'd texted her, and she assured me she was fine, sitting next to an older lady who was chatting her ear off. She said little old ladies always liked her. Why was I not surprised? God, I couldn't wait to see her again.

Aiden, Trevor, his dad, and I were each knocking back a shot of whiskey when there was a knock on the door. A woman poked her head in. "Game time, gentlemen."

Anxiety washed through me. Damn. Why

was *I* nervous? What was it about weddings? It wasn't like the bride was going to run away or anything. The two of them had been together for fifteen years or something ridiculous like that. If anyone was a sure thing, it was Trevor and Krystal.

The group of us, looking sharp I might add, followed the woman down the hall and lined up just the way we were supposed to in the church's vestibule. I wanted desperately to poke my head in and see if I could spot Olivia, but that probably wasn't cool. So I just stood there, shoving my hands in my pockets, trying to be there for my buddy who was pacing in front of us.

Trevor's dad escorted his mom in first. And then Krystal's mom showed up for Trevor to take in. Now it was only us five groomsmen waiting for the bridesmaids.

Inside, I could hear the string quartet finishing up one piece and moving into another. I had no clue what. Of course Krystal had planned everything down to the exact second.

She was a really cool girl, someone I'd grown up with since high school... smart, organized, and completely kept Trevor in line. From my perspective, they just about had the perfect lives—a nice house in La Jolla, two dogs, great careers, all of it. We didn't exactly talk about our feelings and shit, but I knew Trevor was happy.

Trevor and Krystal were an institution. And they were finally getting hitched.

We'd teased him about it forever. Like what was the big holdup all these years? Trevor would just shrug and say they were fine the way they were. But for whatever reason, they'd decided to take the plunge now.

The three cousins, Aiden, and I stood there it seemed like forever. What was taking so long? Had I missed something from the rehearsal?

"Is this the way it's supposed to be?" I asked Aiden. "This long wait?"

"I don't think so. They didn't say anything about this last night."

The cousins came over, obviously concerned as well, the tension in the air rising. Not able to resist, I opened the door a little and poked my head in. Trevor stood at the front of the church, facing me, immediately spotting me. After nearly twenty years of friendship, I could instantly read the look on his face. It was "what the hell is going on?"

Oh, shit.

Something was up. That same edginess filled the church, people whispering to each other, glancing all around. I needed to do something... anything. Giving Trevor a swift nod, I held up a finger, indicating to give me a minute, and he nodded back.

"Come on," I said to Aiden. "We're gonna go find the bride."

The church wasn't that big. Chances were they were down the hall from where we'd been getting ready. And that's where we started.

It was eerily quiet. At first.

As we continued on, a couple of bad-asses in tuxes, determined to help their friend, I picked up on a whisper of voices that grew louder and louder the farther we walked. And then it became frantic, hurried tones, mixed in with... fuck. Was that crying?

This wasn't good. At all.

Dread filled my body as we walked up to the closed door, Aiden and I giving each other a look. This was seriously scary shit, knocking on the door of a bridal suite with sobbing going on inside. But I did it anyway.

Any noise died instantly at my knock. I didn't wait for an answer. My friend was waiting up there, and he needed his bride. Now.

Stunned, tear-stained faces turned my way.

"What is going on?" I asked, not able to hide the impatience in my tone.

Krystal was surrounded by a sea of blue dresses, and I could barely catch a glimpse of her. But when the sea parted, I could see her clearly.

My heart fucking caved in at the expression on her face. The red eyes set off by streaming mascara were not a good sign.

"I'll go get Trevor," Aiden said in a steely voice.

Great. So I was stuck with the bride?

"She's having second thoughts," one of the bridesmaids said.

I couldn't have been more stunned at this

news. Second thoughts after all these years? "You are?" I managed to ask her. "Why?"

She didn't answer me, just broke down in sobs, the sea of blue rushing back in. I felt utterly helpless. Totally useless. I'd never seen her this way. She was always so confident and sure. And while she was my friend and I'd known her since high school as well, Trevor was like a brother to me. The thought of him getting stood up today hurt like hell.

"Krystal!" Trevor shouted from the hallway.

All of us froze. That one word said everything. Disbelief, worry, fear, pain. Every swear word I knew flashed through my mind. And then Trevor stepped into the room, his eyes zeroing in on his hesitant bride.

"Everybody out."

Damn. I'd never heard that tone from Trevor before in my life. Never.

It was a tone that no one dared argue with. All of us rushed out of there, only to be met by half the church, Trevor's obviously concerned parents leading the way. Tears in her eyes, Trevor's mom clutched my bicep. "What's happening?"

I put my arm around her shoulder, first glancing at her and then the whole crowd. "The bride and groom need some time. Why don't we all go back inside and give them some space?"

There were mumbled murmurs of agreement, and everyone slowly turned around, except for

Mrs. Hines who didn't budge.

"I need to know what's going on with my son," she demanded.

Oh, boy. Mama bear was coming out, and she needed the truth, I decided. "Krystal's having doubts," I said in a low voice.

She swore and looked away, glaring at Krystal's mom who seemed on the verge of hysterical. Things were definitely bad if I didn't even flinch at Mrs. Hines swearing, a woman who had the sweetest soul in the world and never said an unkind word.

"No matter what happens, I know Trevor will be okay," I reassured her.

And I meant it. Kind of. To be honest, I didn't remember what Trevor was like pre-Krystal. It'd been so long, their identities had merged. But I hoped to God that Trevor would be all right if Krystal pulled out of this wedding and marriage.

As Mr. Hines took over steering his shocked wife, we followed the crowd, slowly shuffling back down the hall. Exhaustion hit me, and all I wanted to do was find Olivia. So when I was finally able to get inside the church, I immediately scanned the crowd, absolutely dying to see her gorgeous face, to be with her and soak her in.

EIGHTEEN

Olivia

The crowd's restlessness washed over me, anxiety and worry combining for a nauseous mix. The lady next to me, Tina, kept swiveling her head around, occasionally even standing, to see what was going on. Thank goodness for her, or I'd be sitting here completely alone.

An old neighbor and former piano teacher of Trevor's, she was by herself today too. Well, I supposed technically, I wasn't all alone. I was with Luke.

Wow, I liked the way that sounded. *I'm with Luke.*

Tina interrupted my moment. "And there goes the groom."

Stunned, I watched as the groom stalked down the aisle, a stormy look on his face, not meeting anyone's eyes.

Oh, my. This couldn't be good. Tina held my arm as we watched both sets of parents soon follow, a bunch of other people also rushing out behind them. This was crazy! I had no idea what to do.

"Just stay here, hon," Tina advised. "Let's see how this plays out."

Releasing a tense breath, I nodded. She was right. What else could we do anyway?

So the two of us sat there in our nice dresses, observing the room, the air conditioning a little too cool. Music continued to swirl around us, the string quartet still softly playing their instruments in the front corner of the sanctuary.

The day was gorgeous, the sun's rays lighting up the stained glass, making patterns on the carpet next to me. I focused on my breathing, trying not to let the nervous vibe affect me. Right after a deep exhale, the violins screeched to a halt, catching everyone's attention.

Luke stood at the back of the church, all eyes turning to him. My word, he looked incredibly handsome in his tux, towering over Trevor's mom who stood next to him.

"There's been a slight delay," he announced. "So if everyone could please hang tight, we'll keep you updated. And don't forget, there'll be an open bar later."

Relieved titters of laughter echoed through the room before everyone started whispering again, Tina grabbing my hand. "Oh, I hope

Trevor's okay."

"Me too. Me too." I hoped they were *both* okay. Whatever was happening, I felt for the bride too. The whole family. Heartbreak was the worst, and I didn't wish it on anyone.

My eyes still on Luke, I watched as he strode forward, heading to the front where the musicians were. Talking to them for a moment, he slipped the violinist something—money?—and they picked up their instruments, immediately starting a new song. The music had a calming effect, reminding me of the movie *Titanic* and how the musicians kept playing even amidst disaster as the ship went down.

Still at the front, Luke's gaze scanned the crowd, and I wondered if he was looking for me or someone else. After all, he probably knew tons of people here today. I thought about standing up and waving him down, but that seemed like a dorky move. So I just sat there staring, admiring, remembering the last time I'd seen him and that kiss.

Our eyes suddenly connected, a jolt of energy shooting through me. But that was nothing compared to the electric shock his smile gave me. While my heart jumped around like an excited puppy, Luke started to head straight toward me, resembling some ultra-handsome supermodel walking the runway.

My body drawn to him, without even

thinking, I rose up as he neared. And then I was in his arms, his embrace wrapping around me like home, like a safe harbor in this strange storm. Squeezing my eyes shut, I inhaled him, all masculine and spice with a hint of mint, our chests moving together as I tried to draw in air.

The way he was hugging me, holding me so tightly, made me think he'd missed me just as much as I'd missed him. His lips were in my hair when I heard a voice behind me say, "Lord have mercy."

With a giggle, I leaned back, and he slowly let me go, his hands grasping my shoulders, his eyes boring into mine. "Are you okay?" he asked.

"Of course. Are *you*?"

Looking away, he blew out a giant sigh. "I've been better." Realizing he had an audience, he gestured to my chair. "Have a seat, gorgeous."

Smiling to myself, I sat back down and he knelt beside me, trying his best to be more inconspicuous. At least we were off to one side of the room.

"So what's going on?" I whispered.

"They're talking." Luke shook his head. "I guess Krystal's not sure about the wedding."

I couldn't help gasping. "Oh, my God. That's terrible."

"This will destroy him." He rubbed his brow as if he had a migraine. "I feel so awful for him."

"So do I," Tina chimed in.

There were ears listening all around us that I'd

forgotten about. "Luke," I said, "this is Miss Tina. She used to live next door to Trevor and taught him the piano."

"I knew you looked familiar," Luke said. "Good to see you, even under the circumstances."

"You too, dear."

A loud noise in the back caught everyone's attention, and Luke returned to standing, every single person looking backward as a group of young men in tuxes entered. But no Trevor.

Aiden stepped forward. "I'm sorry to tell you all this. But the wedding is off."

Shocked gasps echoed throughout the room, and then the murmuring took over until Aiden cleared his throat and moved farther up the aisle.

"I talked to Trevor, though, and he wants everyone to still go to the reception. It's bought and paid for, so we all should at least go eat a good meal and enjoy some drinks." There was an awkward pause. "So I'll hopefully see you all there," Aiden added.

I glanced at Luke whose attention seemed torn between me and his friend. I touched his hand. "Don't worry about me. Go ahead."

Relief was written across his face. "I'll be right back."

And he was true to his word. After talking to Aiden for a minute, he returned to my side. "Come on, ladies. I'll take you across the street. I don't know about you. But I could use a drink. Or two. Or five."

"Definitely," Miss Tina agreed.

Luke held out both elbows while we each took a side. This was unreal. I could see the same hesitant, unsure expression playing out on everyone else's face as well. But most people seemed to stand up and follow Luke and Aiden, who led the way to the reception hall opposite the church.

"The former bride and groom are both with their parents right now," Luke said, answering my unasked question.

"How's Trevor? Do you know?" As soon as the words left my mouth, I knew how ridiculous they sounded. How would any person feel after being stood up at the altar on their wedding day?

"I don't know. I imagine he's pretty devastated."

Giving Luke's elbow a squeeze, he shot me a soft smile, and something inside my chest swelled. This couldn't be easy for him either.

Not only was it hot to see him take charge like he had, but it was a big crack in that veneer of his, the supposedly uncaring, selfish man-boy. Maybe I'd been wrong with my initial thoughts about Luke that I'd stubbornly held onto. Watching him today, it became totally obvious that he *did* care. He cared deeply about his friends.

After we crossed the street safely, we entered the stately old building to be greeted by a beautifully decorated hall—flowers and candles everywhere, a DJ playing soft tunes. I helped

Luke, Aiden, and the other groomsmen gather up place cards so people could sit wherever they wanted.

Luke spent a few minutes talking to the DJ, telling him to *not* play anything on the list that he'd been given, while Aiden helped the catering staff quickly break down the head table at the front.

Once we were finally seated with drinks in front of us, I studied the room, realizing that it was only half full. Tina had found someone else to sit with, an older gentleman who couldn't take his eyes off her. *Go, Miss Tina.*

All heads suddenly turned as Trevor came in, his parents on either side of him like a protective shield, his younger sister trailing behind in her bridesmaid dress like she didn't quite know where to go or what to do.

Of course, I didn't know Trevor hardly at all. I'd only met him that one time at Javi's birthday dinner. But the look on his face was enough to crush the hardest of hearts.

Honestly, it was amazing that he'd shown up at all. Luke, Aiden, and the cousins surrounded him in a flash, arms around his back, leading him to our table. Seeing he was in good hands, his parents and sister walked away to go talk to some other people, probably family if I had to guess by the resemblance.

They all sat Trevor down, Aiden taking a seat on one side of him and Luke the other. The waiter brought over a bottle of whiskey plus a bunch of glasses that were filled almost as swiftly as he unloaded them.

I couldn't help thinking this was like a scene in a movie, the jilted groom, the reception that had turned into some kind of odd funeral, the crazy amount of booze being consumed.

As the dinner was served and people began to eat, my eyes couldn't stay away from Luke who sat on the other side of the table now. Along with the other guys, his coat had been shed and his tie loosened. All formality had left the room, and Luke looked like the definition of sin, the bare skin of his chest evident at the top of his unbuttoned shirt. I'd felt that chest under my hands, and even with material between us, it'd been magnificent.

Although Luke was purely focused on his friend, his eyes found mine throughout our strange meal, and I could tell he was still divided about where to put his attention. But each time our gazes caught, I gave him a reassuring smile. I didn't need him right now. His friend did.

And I was more than happy to watch him, weirdly, my mind still processing who Luke really seemed to be. Of course, my heart hurt for Trevor, but at the same time, this night had been more than illuminating about my neighbor.

Hushed voices carried on conversations around the room while eating the delicious food. And poor Trevor spoke exactly once, when he requested a second helping of dinner, saying he'd paid for this celebration and he'd damn well eat as much as he wanted.

Amen to that.

One spot that was never quiet was the open bar, a steady stream of traffic flowing back and forth between the tables and the busy bartenders. And everyone around our table made sure that Trevor's glass was never empty. I had to wonder how long it'd be before he passed out. That'd be the only relief he'd get from this awful day.

The DJ kept the music quiet and chill, definitely reading the mood in the room. If any dancing happened tonight, I'd be absolutely shocked.

After eating a big slice of cake, which had been discreetly cut up in the kitchen, I headed to the ladies' room, wondering if it was time for me to go soon. I'd noticed a few people leaving, and I figured that Luke would be here for a while, staying with Trevor.

Once I freshened up, I found a quiet corner in the hallway and texted Nadia, telling her about all the craziness, taking longer than I intended.

"Hey, there you are," a familiar voice said.

I looked up to see Luke walking toward me, taking my breath away with his holy hotness. His hands reached out to me, and he pulled me up in a flash, straight into his body. Wow, he felt incredible. And even more incredible when his strong arms closed around me.

"Thanks for being here," he said against the top of my head.

"Of course." But I wasn't sure he heard me because my face was buried in his chest, pure lust rising up in me. "You're a good friend to Trevor."

His grip loosened and our eyes met, his brows creasing with concern. "I'm trying. I don't know what else to do."

"You're doing your best. And I doubt there's really anything anyone can do to make him feel better."

He nodded. "It just sucks. Completely sucks. For them to be together for so long, and then this? It doesn't even make sense."

"It doesn't. It really doesn't. Do you know why or what happened?"

"Not a clue," he admitted with a grimace. "And I don't want to ask. I'm sure Trevor will tell us if he's ever able to talk about it."

I shook my head in sympathy, not sure what to say.

"And I'm really sorry too," Luke continued. "For you."

"For me?"

"Yeah. I promised you a fun night of dancing and drinking. And then this..."

"Don't even worry about me," I said with a light caress against his chest for emphasis. "I'm fine. Just worried about you."

His lips curved up in a slight smile. "You're

worried about *me*?"

Reaching up, I touched his cheek gently before dropping my hand to his shoulder. "Yeah. It can't be easy for you either."

He didn't reply, but that smile grew. And I noticed his gaze moving lower to my mouth. "I really missed you last week."

My heart skipped a beat at those words and the raspy way he'd said them. "I missed you too."

One of his brows shot up. "You did? For real? Your asshole neighbor?"

"You're the worst," I teased.

"Well, it's a good thing you're the best because we balance each other out."

At the sincerity in his eyes, I went speechless. But it didn't matter because apparently Luke was done talking. His arms squeezed me tighter, and his mouth came down on mine in a passionate kiss that left me spinning. How were his lips so soft yet unyielding and demanding?

"You feel so good," he whispered against my mouth.

"So do you."

He glanced around quickly. "Come here."

"Where?"

He grabbed my hand and led me down the hallway, away from everyone else and the sounds of the wedding. Opening a random door, he backed me inside, kicked the door shut, and pushed me against the wall, his lips hard as they captured mine once more.

Wow. Luke meant business, and I was all for it.

His mouth swept across my cheek and toward my ear. "You look so fucking hot in this dress."

Hands gripped my bare arms. Lips devoured my neck. Words and thoughts escaped me as I held onto Luke, stunned at this passion sweeping through us.

"The whole time I was gone, I thought about you. Thought about this."

He did?

His hands moved to my waist, stroking up and down my sides, and I had the feeling Luke was holding himself back. Somewhere in the recesses of my mind, I knew this was absolutely the wrong time and the wrong place.

"Shouldn't you be with Trevor right now?" I managed to ask.

"He's with his dad. They went outside to talk, and they'll probably be a while."

"Ohhh," I said as Luke practically made love to my neck. Well, in that case. I yanked his shirt up and slid my hands under the cool material.

Luke's breath hissed out against my skin at the contact. "*Jesus.*"

His muscles tensed and flexed beneath my fingers. It'd been so long since I'd touched another man that he felt like pure heaven to me. Or maybe it was just Luke. I couldn't think about that too much right now. I let need guide me, and my needy ass was hungry for this man in front of me.

Our mouths met for more kisses, hands exploring all over each other's bodies, the hard planes of Luke's chest pure fire under my touch. I pushed my hips forward, needing friction, desperate for some action. And Luke didn't disappoint. My legs spread around one of his, and I found myself practically riding his muscular thigh.

I didn't have time to be embarrassed. Besides, if anything, it turned Luke on even more, judging by the groan that came out of his mouth. His hands moved from my waist to my breasts as he palmed me hard through the material of my thin dress, my head falling back against the wall at the erotic sensation.

And when his thumbs brushed my nipples, they responded immediately, hardening beneath his caresses.

"Livs," he whispered, "you're so damn sexy."

I opened my eyes to see his face so close to mine, his gaze beyond intense, his breathing ragged. Our eyes locked together, I kept touching him, grasping, scratching, wanting to tear his shirt off.

Luke inched up the bottom of my dress until it was no longer impeding me, his warm fingers reaching back to grab handfuls of my ass. "You're wearing a thong?" he asked in a gravelly voice.

Biting my lip, I nodded. I had no idea anyone would be seeing or touching my underwear today. It'd strictly been a fashion decision, the best choice with this particular dress.

His Adam's apple moved up and down as he swallowed hard, the gleam in his eyes turning downright wicked. "The things I want to do to you," he said.

I gulped. "What, um, things?"

"This." With one finger, he touched the center of my underwear, making a small circle that had me gasping. "Oh, God," he groaned. "You're so wet."

I didn't know who was more affected by that. "It's all your fault."

"Oh, yeah?" He grinned. "Wanna see if I can make you even wetter?"

With my own smile, I nodded, any words stuck in my throat at the way he was looking at me, like he was hungry, and I was a tasty snack in front of him. And then he was on me, his lips taking mine in a sensual kiss that had me breathless. His hand cupped my underwear, his heat and the soft pressure turning me on, bringing fire into my veins.

I pushed my hips forward, wanting more from him, impatient, and I knew he got the message when he pulled my wet panties to the side, his fingers beginning to explore me. He hissed a breath out against my face, his eyes intent on mine.

To have him touching me like this felt like a door had been shoved open between us. This wasn't pretend. This wasn't a lesson. This was intimacy with a man that I hadn't experienced in a long while.

"Spread your legs, Livs. Let me really feel you."

Oh, this man. Impatient as hell, he hitched one of my legs over his, spreading me apart, making me vulnerable and open to his caresses. I couldn't help wondering if Luke was one of those guys who'd need a map.

But just as the thought entered my mind, he found my clit, circling it softly, making me moan against his shoulder. Nope. Luke most definitely didn't need an ounce of guidance. He knew exactly what to do.

His other hand returned to my breasts, my nipples straining for his touch, achy and throbbing. I wished I could somehow free myself of the dress and my bra. But Luke literally took things into his own hands when his fingers drifted to my collarbone then began to move beneath the neckline of my dress.

What an awkward angle it had to be for him. But he managed. God, did he manage. One thumb rubbing my clit, the other stroking my nipple.

"You like that?" he asked.

"Mmmmm."

Words wouldn't come out, not when I was complete putty in his capable hands. I hadn't felt this good in a long time. Maybe forever. Luke knew just what to do to drive me right to the edge.

And when he inserted one long finger into

me and then another, I almost collapsed. Thank goodness for the wall behind me and Luke's leg practically holding me up. His lips found mine again, his tongue massaging and caressing. All the while, his fingers pumped inside me, his thumb teasing my clit faster and harder, again and again.

He teased my lower lip with his teeth, pulling, the sensual act enough to make me snap. And then I felt it, the first tingles of my impending orgasm, starting deep in my core and spreading. It hit me fast, coursing from my throbbing pussy all the way to the tips of my fingers and toes.

"Oh, my God," I cried out, squeezing my eyes shut at the pure intensity of pleasure racking my entire being.

His body crushed into me as he kissed me passionately, my knees weak and my legs wobbly. As if he knew, his arm went around me, keeping me steady and upright.

The relentless waves finally subsiding, I opened my eyes to see him watching me, and I suddenly felt a little embarrassed.

"You're so fucking beautiful," he said.

Those words and the way he was looking at me soothed away the blossoming vulnerability. And then when he cradled my cheek in his hand, the need to touch him nearly overwhelmed me. My hands returned to his chest, and I slowly lowered them to his waist, reaching for his belt.

His sudden intake of breath told me I was on

the right track. Biting my lip, I slowly unbuckled the belt, determined to make him feel the same way I'd just felt. I wanted to make this man walk out of here with shaky legs, and I knew exactly what to do.

NINETEEN

Luke

"Yo! Luke!" Aiden's voice echoed down the hall.

I rested my head against Olivia's in frustration, trying to catch my breath.

"Where you at, man?" Aiden's voice moved closer.

Everything in me wanted to hide, wanted to do anything to avoid the outside world, but if I didn't answer, there was a chance he'd barge in here and embarrass Olivia. "Hold up. I'll be out in a minute," I called.

There was a tense pause as I kept my eyes on Olivia who was busy fixing her underwear and pulling down her dress.

A shuffling noise sounded at the closed door. "Uh, sorry, brother. It's just that Trevor's back and wants to talk to us, something about his wedding night and honeymoon."

Shit. "Okay, yeah. Be right there."

After I shoved my shirt back in my pants, I adjusted my straining bulge as best I could. Olivia surprised me by putting her hands in my hair and straightening it, something about her movements incredibly calming. "You should go," she said quietly.

"I hate leaving like this."

She raised a single brow. "Your friend needs you."

"But I need *you*."

Laughing, she shoved me away. But I took one more second and leaned in closer. "We're not finished here."

"Yes, sir," she replied, her gorgeous lips turned up in a teasing smile. She pushed me once more. "Go. Go. Don't leave poor Trevor hanging."

She was right. The guy was in the middle of the worst day of his life and I needed to be there for him. With one last kiss, I headed toward the door and slid out, wanting to give Olivia some privacy if she needed it.

Aiden took one look at me, his eyes squinting with suspicion. "Who was in there with you? Olivia?"

I put an arm around him, guiding him away. Normally, I wasn't one to kiss and tell, at least not since I was a teenage horndog, and at this particular moment, no way was I going to say anything more than a simple yeah. It was a testament to how much we'd grown that Aiden didn't pry.

With a nod of his head, he said, "Cool," and let it drop.

"So what's going on with Trevor?" I asked.

"I'm not sure. But I think we might have to call out for work next week."

And that's exactly what happened.

After gathering in a quiet corner of the reception hall, Trevor, Aiden, and I decided to go on a bro-moon together. Trevor barely got out the words, but in the end, he asked us to keep him company the night of his wedding and to go on his honeymoon with him.

It took nothing to persuade Aiden and I to drop everything else in our lives. Of course, we'd be there for him during this insane time, plus an impromptu trip to Mexico sounded pretty damn good.

Except for this thing happening with Olivia. That I'd miss. Too damn much.

But Trevor needed a crutch right now, and Olivia had more than encouraged me to go when I'd explained the situation to her briefly before she caught a ride home.

So after a shitty "wedding" night where we worked out all the travel details, we woke up hungover Sunday morning to get on the plane to Cabo. Before heading to the airport, I made a quick call to my boss, using his personal number that I had for emergencies.

Only, of course, the dickhead wasn't cool with

me being gone last minute for an entire five days of work and told me if I went, I wouldn't have a job when I came back. And I told him to fucking shove it. The time I'd put in there. Jesus Christ. The asshole couldn't understand that I needed some personal time? I had taken exactly one sick day since I'd started.

The whole situation was unbelievable.

Deciding I'd try not to worry about it until I got back, I also opted not to tell Trevor or even Aiden because we already had enough on our plate, what with the jilted groom who was so weirdly quiet... which I supposed was normal for the situation he'd found himself in.

And it pretty much continued that way through the rest of the week, Aiden and I doing our best to pick up the conversation as we lay around on the beach and at the pool, checking out the best restaurants and tourist spots.

Most of the time, we were surrounded by damn couples. Couples everywhere. Disgustingly happy and handsy all over the place. Trevor kept his sunglasses on all day, so I couldn't see what he was taking in. But I tried my best to distract him by pointing something out in the opposite direction whenever yet another stupid couple engaged in PDA near us.

At night, we'd drink ourselves into oblivion, passing out in our big suite until we decided to join the living once more for a late breakfast. During all that time, Trevor didn't breathe a word about Krystal or the wedding, but I knew it had to be constantly on his mind. Obviously. And fuck if I didn't know what to do about it.

Aiden and I had our own text conversation going on and decided not to ask. Hopefully, Trevor would bring it up when or if he was ever ready.

Before I knew it, the days had flown past and we sat down for our last dinner at a Mexican restaurant of course. Margaritas in front of us, we chowed down on chips and salsa, all of us pretty good with the spice level from growing up in San Diego.

"Damn it all, I'm still just so pissed off," Trevor said completely out of the blue.

Whoa. Aiden and I shared a surprised look. "I can imagine," Aiden ventured to say.

"How could she do that to me?" The look on his face was tortured. "After all that time together? Like it didn't mean shit to her, you know?"

Oh, man, here we go. Aiden and I both nodded.

"And why couldn't she have broken it off with me earlier? Even the morning of the wedding?" A storm brewed in his eyes as he shook his head. "On top of all that, she had to embarrass me in front of everyone important in my life."

"Dude, you have nothing to be embarrassed about," Aiden said around a mouthful of chips. "*She's* the one who should be embarrassed."

"Yeah. Exactly right," I agreed.

Trevor ran a hand through his hair, tugging at

it in the process. "I just feel like my whole life is ruined. I don't even know what to do now. I've got to move out, find a new place. I've never even lived by myself."

I had forgotten that he'd gone from high school, to rooming with us in college, to living with Krystal. "You know you can live with me or Aiden until you figure it all out," I said, trying to reassure him.

Aiden nodded. "Yeah. Come crash with me. I've got lots of spare room."

Trevor looked up, a tiny glimmer of hope evident in his expression. "You sure?"

"Absolutely."

"That'd be great because I don't even want to spend a minute at my place. I mean, my *old* place." With a groan, he buried his face in his hands. "Shit."

I had no idea what to say. How on earth did you make a jilted groom feel better? And apparently, Aiden was the same, judging by the anxious glance he gave me.

What would Olivia do? I thought for a second, then came up with something. "Think of all the things you can do now," I said, trying to focus on the positive, the proverbial silver lining. "You can grow your hair out, maybe grow a beard, change jobs."

Although Krystal had been cool, or so I had thought, there were certain things she wasn't into, like facial hair or risky careers.

Trevor removed his head from his hands, his suddenly gleaming eyes darting between the two of us. "You're fucking right. She always wanted to see my jawline, so she liked me clean-shaven. But that's the first thing I'm going to do... stop shaving. And then I'm getting some tattoos."

"Yeah, man. Do it," agreed Aiden.

We paused as the waiter brought us our food, my fajitas sizzling on a piping hot platter, and we soon began to dig in. After shoveling our meals for a few minutes, the mood suddenly shifted and became lighter.

Trevor set down his fork, swiping his lips aggressively with a napkin. "And you know what? While I'm at it, I might quit my job."

"No way," Aiden said.

"Yes way. I fucking hate it," he spit out. "And Luke's right. Maybe it's time to change everything up."

"What would you do?" I asked him.

"I don't know." Trevor glanced around the restaurant, taking in the crowded tables and the lively band in the corner. "I'll have to think about that. I've been thinking as half a person for so long, I don't even know what I want anymore."

Huh, maybe their relationship hadn't been as great as I'd always thought. I wondered about asking, but I had the feeling Trevor just wanted to move on and think about the future and not dwell on the past.

"I have an idea," I blurted out instead.

Two heads swiveled toward me. "What's that?" Aiden asked.

It was the moment of truth... time to bring up something that had been whirling around in my head for a long time now, ever since that eye-opening trip to the Safari Park with Olivia and her family.

Maybe they'd been joking around that day, but it'd stayed in my mind, something I kept thinking about late at night when I couldn't sleep. Or early in the morning when I'd crawl out of bed for another day of drudgery. And now that I'd lost my fucking job, I had absolutely nothing to lose.

"What if we started a restaurant together?" I finally asked. "The three of us?"

Aiden stopped eating his enchiladas which meant he was all business. "Are you serious?"

"Jesus. Wow," Trevor said. "What a crazy idea."

"You think so? Hear me out." All eyes were on me, and I felt my excitement level grow, something I'd never in my life experienced about job or career shit. "So I got fired, or maybe I quit—I'm not really sure how we ended things—but I have no job when I get back."

Trevor swore. "Because of me?"

"Nah, man. It's been a long time coming. You know I hated my job."

"Same," they both said.

Sales weren't my strong suit, but now was the time to sell my heart out and push hard for this dream in the making. "So what the hell are we doing right now? Life is short. I know it's cliché, but it's true. And we're wasting too much time at jobs we don't like while the years fly by. We're not getting any younger."

"You've got a point," Trevor agreed. "So what are you thinking?"

"I'm thinking we split it in thirds so we all have equal control. Any time we disagree, it would just be majority rules. And Aiden can be the head chef."

I glanced at Aiden to see what he thought and realized he looked torn. "I mean, that would be great and all," he said. "But opening a restaurant is crazy expensive, and I don't have the funds you guys have."

"Yeah, I've thought about that, though." It was no secret that Trevor and I had done pretty well financially, although who knew what Trevor was up against at the moment with the house in La Jolla. "And that doesn't matter. We can work out the finances and all still be equal partners."

There was a long pause around the table as they both thought, the only sound the music blasting through the place. I took the moment to stuff down some more chips and salsa, washing it down with half my margarita.

Voicing this all for the first time did something to me—it made me want it more. I hoped like hell my two brothers from another mother would join me because we'd have an absolute blast. But if they didn't? I'd do it on my own. I'd make it happen... no matter what.

Trevor cleared his throat, focusing in on me. "You know what? I'm in. Let's do this fucking thing."

"Yes!"

We shared a fist bump, then both turned to Aiden. I wasn't sure what the hold-up with him was about, except for the financial aspect. Aiden had wanted a head chef position since he'd started in the culinary field. I thought that was the dream, the end goal.

A slow grin took over his face as he glanced between us. "All right, man. But I get final say on the menu."

I laughed. "And so it begins."

"And so it begins," Aiden repeated.

The three of us sat there for hours brainstorming, stuffing ourselves, writing things down, having a serious blast as we dreamed big. Why the hell not? Drink after drink, we talked about all the possibilities—where, when, what kind of vibe and theme, and most importantly, the food.

By the time we hopped on a plane the next morning, we were beyond hyped, the complete opposite of the way this bro-moon had started. Not only was I glad that we'd turned things around for Trevor, but I could hardly wait to get back and share everything with Olivia.

TWENTY

Olivia

The week went by so incredibly slowly, and all I could think about was Luke. Yeah, I was that girl. But how could I not think about him every second of the day after that crazy intense experience we'd had, plus the out-of-this-world orgasm he'd given me.

All I wanted to do was return the favor. I was obsessed with getting into Luke's pants. I'd felt that humongous bulge against me. What would it be like to actually touch him?

Rubbing my legs together, trying to make the ache go away, I returned my attention to my friends. It was my birthday after all, and they were determined to make this a girls' night I wouldn't forget. My sister and Nadia had acted as the ringleaders, getting everyone together for the evening.

First, we'd gone out for Italian, Emily and

I doing our best while ordering to practice the language for our upcoming trip, the waiter politely going along with us and even giving us a few pointers about our accents.

And then, to my shock, we'd ended up at a naughty paint and sip event, something I hadn't even known existed and something that certainly didn't help my non-stop horniness for Luke. Staring at the naked models at the front of the room and trying to recreate them was, um, a challenge. I opted to just paint a male chest, not going for the full monty displayed so artfully for us.

As I did my best attempt at painting the man's nipples, I knocked back the wine, loving the music, the vibe, and hearing my friends laugh their asses off at the crude jokes flying around the room. Leave it to Emily and Nadia to discover this kind of event.

Right when our instructor began to walk us through shading the nipples with the exact colors to use, my phone buzzed on the table and I saw it was Luke, back from his impromptu honeymoon.

He'd kept in touch during the week, keeping me up-to-date on Trevor and what all they were doing. No mention of our tiny hook-up. So I didn't mention it either. Really mature. Or maybe texting wasn't the place to have that conversation.

Besides, I kept coming back to that same

nagging little issue about what was going on between us. Were Luke and I heading toward an actual full-blown relationship? Or was this just a casual, hooking up type of thing?

Finishing off my wine, I also completed the nipples which ended up being way too pointy. Still giggling, I picked up my phone to respond, telling Luke that I was out for my birthday, something I'd mentioned to him earlier in the week.

To my surprise, he asked me if I'd stop by when I got home because he had a gift to give me. I told him it might be late, but he said he didn't care what time it was. He wanted to see me.

I might have let out a squeal of excitement, making all heads turn my way.

"What's that for?" Nadia asked as she poured me more sauvignon blanc.

At the moment, with the wine flowing and naked men in the vicinity, I didn't have it in me to be coy. "Luke said to come over later, that he has a gift and wants to see me tonight."

Emily, whose cheeks were pink like mine, poked my shoulder. "Oooh, someone's going to get that big d."

"Oh, my gosh. Why do I tell you anything?"

It might have slipped that we'd had a little, teensy, tiny, casual thing occur at the "wedding." But I couldn't help it. How could I not share something that had totally wrecked me. In a good way.

"You know you love us," Nadia said. "And because I know you're still stewing about it all, I think you should go for it. No one says your heart has to be involved."

"Exactly," Emily agreed from the other side of me. "And you've been celibate for like a year. Don't let the memory of that asshole Henry stop you from getting some."

"Why are you both assuming this is about sex?" My narrowed eyes altered between the two of them.

And narrowed eyes were returned, especially from Emily. "Do you really think he's asking you over for a nice, warm hug?"

We all burst into laughter at that, catching the attention of our friends and everyone else in the place.

"Okay. You have a good point."

Dipping my brush in the brown color, I resumed painting, all the sudden in a hurry to finish. We were close anyway, thank goodness, because the last thing I wanted to do was ditch my girls.

My thoughts buzzing around in circles, I had to wonder if Nadia and Emily were right—if Luke was simply setting up a booty call. And more importantly, if that indeed was it, how did I feel about that? I *did* really want Luke. Desperately. Was it possible for me to keep it physical, leaving my mind and heart out of it?

A while later, after showering me with

presents as we let our masterpieces dry, I found myself in my elevator, arms loaded down with gift bags, juggling a rather embarrassing bare man's chest painting. I already knew I would stash this thing in the back of my closet. Not only did it clash with my décor, but it was horribly done with the weirdest looking nips ever. Being an artist was definitely not my calling.

Giggling at myself, making tons of noise as I tried to balance everything, I attempted to key into my apartment. The door behind me opened, and in my surprise, a bunch of things fell onto the ground.

Luke's laughter rang out in the empty hallway. "Put that shit down and come here, birthday girl."

He didn't give me much of a choice as he wrapped his arms around me, and I dropped it all as he whirled me into the air, spinning me in circles. Oh, wow, he smelled delicious, fresh from the shower, his hair still damp.

To my shock, he peppered my face with kisses, then landed his mouth on my lips, slowly letting me slide down his body when he stopped moving. In that moment, I decided to stop thinking and worrying so much.

No one said Luke and I were getting married. We were both single. We both had needs. Clearly. And for once, maybe it'd be fine to let myself get some without trying to push for more.

He let go of me, pulling back to stare into my

eyes. "I've got something for you... something you really need."

I raised a brow at the blatant come-on. "Seriously? And is it perhaps six inches of pure pleasure?"

His quick laughter rang out. "What? Are you kidding? First off, try more than six inches."

"*More than six inches?*" I gasped.

He shot me a cocky smirk but didn't answer. "And secondly, exactly how much did you have to drink at your paint thing?"

"You're implying I'm drunk." Crossing my arms over my chest, I watched his face contort as he stifled a smile. "So where's this gift then?"

Still not answering, he reached down to gather all of my scattered belongings, while I quickly snatched up the painting and turned it away from his eyes. If Luke saw this thing, he'd never stop teasing me about it.

"Let me help you with this, and then I'll get your present, little miss impatient."

I gave him a little nudge before I opened the door and scrambled inside, tossing the huge canvas in my coat closet. *Whew. No harm done.* Luke followed me, carefully setting all of my stuff down on a side table by the door.

"All right. I'll be right back," he said.

Once he disappeared, I turned on the twinkly curtain, then rushed to the bathroom, brushing my teeth in a flash while checking out my reflection. Not too bad for thirty-one. Pretty much the same as thirty. Giggling to myself, I rinsed my mouth, ready for this night, ready to attack this man.

Really, I shouldn't be allowed to drink the vino. It made me super horny. And Luke was definitely in trouble tonight.

Hearing a noise at the front door, I rushed to finish primping and headed back to the living room. And there was Luke, holding what was obviously a lamp behind his back.

"Impossible to hide this," he said with a laugh, bringing it out and setting it beside him.

My breath halted in my throat. "Oh, my gosh. What is this?"

"It's a lamp," was his dry answer.

I huffed out some air. "I know that. Obviously. But... but why?"

"For when you read. You need better light for your eyes."

Something warm and liquid exploded in my chest. Luke had bought me a lamp? He was thinking about my eye health? Rushing forward, I threw my arms around him, smashing my mouth to his in a sloppy kiss. So much for no damn feelings.

The feelings were there. Undeniable. Growing. Spiraling. Pulling at my heart.

And then I was lost, drunk on the taste of him, relentless with my lips, showing this man how much I wanted him. He answered my silent plea, giving me back everything I gave him...

and more. His arms wound tightly around me, crushing our chests together.

Impatient to finish this thing that we'd started at the non-wedding, my hands moved down to the hem of his soft t-shirt, wanting it off, dying to see what Luke looked like. I began to edge the material upwards, but his hands suddenly stopped me.

Luke pulled back, the endless pools of his eyes piercing me. "Exactly how much did you have to drink tonight?"

"A drink and a half," I lied. Drunk or not, I was going to have my way with Luke tonight. Of course, that was if he was willing. Consent and all. Besides, I wasn't really drunk. Just a little tipsy.

A long pause strained the atmosphere, the only sound our breathing while we stared at each other.

"Are you going to deny a girl a little fun on her birthday?" I finally asked, biting down on my lip.

"Ah, hell," Luke groaned, reaching for his shirt and whipping it off, my eyes widening in disbelief at the spectacular sight in front of me.

Luke was perfection. When he'd mentioned working out a lot, I thought maybe he'd been exaggerating. But he definitely wasn't. His broad shoulders and hard chest led to defined abs and an absolutely mouth-watering V at his hips. My fingers itched to touch him, trace that V with my tongue, and drive him to the brink of insanity.

After picking up my jaw, I stepped forward, one determined birthday girl.

TWENTY-ONE

Luke

Shit. All the blood in my body rushed to my dick at the way she was looking at me. And when she literally licked her lips, fire pulsed through me. I had to wonder what my sexy little librarian would be like in bed. Would she be soft and sweet? Or would she turn into a tigress?

I guided her backward until we stood in front of the couch, and I kissed the fuck out of her, intending to get her on the couch, tear off that hot dress, and dive head-first into her sweet pussy.

But fuck me, her hands were all over me, making me weak in the damn knees as her fingers explored my chest, pressing into me, her mouth soon breaking away from mine to follow her caresses. Olivia actually licked me, moaning as those luscious lips of hers swept ever south.

My bulge strained in my boxers, uncomfortable as hell, but I didn't dare let myself loose, not wanting to assume anything with Olivia. Trying to rein in my pounding lust, Olivia didn't help matters when her teeth nipped my abs, followed by a gentle kiss.

Tigress. Definitely tigress.

And I loved every second of it. Even more so when her hands reached for my shorts, edging them down over my hips and my legs, leaving me in only my boxers. As I stepped out of them, she looked up at me, her eyes dark in the dimness of the room. Part of me wanted to plug in the light so I could see her, see every inch of her beauty.

But she'd cast a spell over me, and I could barely breathe, let alone move, especially when she sat on the edge of the couch and began to lay down kisses along my hips, her fingers trailing the ridge there.

I hissed in some air, the only thing in the world the feel of this girl's lips on my body. My God, she was amazing. But that was nothing compared to when her fingers found the edge of my boxers and she slowly pulled them down, releasing my hard cock right in front of her face.

My heart pounded as she stared at it for a long second. What the hell was she thinking? Too big? Not enough? What on earth did Olivia like? I had no fucking clue, and it drove me crazy, the not knowing.

Again, she glanced up at me, her lips

curving into a soft smile. "You're enormous. You weren't joking about more than six inches," she whispered.

Yeah, that felt good. Incredible actually. Male pride swelled in my chest, especially when her tongue darted out again to moisten her lips. Jesus. When she did that...

Her hands moved up and down my thighs, giving me the very thing she hated. Chills. But of course, I absolutely loved it. Touch was my love language as I now knew. Thanks to Olivia.

Something else took over in my chest just before guilt flooded me. Reaching for her arms, I pulled her up roughly to look me in the face. "This isn't right."

"What isn't right?" she asked, the hint of hurt in her tone.

"It's *your* fucking birthday. Not mine."

She heaved out a sigh, her worried frown disappearing to be replaced by a mischievous grin. "Then let me do what I want."

Standing completely naked before her, I felt powerless to resist her, and damn it, I didn't want to resist her. I'd do anything she said right now. "Then do it."

As soon as the words left my mouth, I knew I was in for it. Her smile turned downright wicked, and she grabbed onto my biceps, turning me around with a whole lot of force for someone so much smaller than me. Or maybe I wanted to be bossed around by this girl.

But whatever she was about to do, I wanted it with all my soul.

"Sit," she demanded.

Goddamn.

I sat. And she knelt down between my thighs, my cock standing at full mast. That's what Olivia did to me, just the thought of her, let alone the sight of her, hair flowing down her shoulders, eyes gleaming in the sparkly light, her dress riding up to reveal her gorgeous thighs.

She started with her hands, rubbing up and down my legs. Oh, shit. She was going to drag this out, wasn't she, and torture me to death. Yep, definitely. Because then she leaned forward, pressing her body into me, slowly kissing her way up my chest until our lips connected once more.

I couldn't help it, I grabbed onto her—hard—my hands soon roaming down to that lush ass of hers that was barely contained by her dress anymore. And there was a thong again. I groaned as her stomach pressed into my erection. More than anything, I was dying for her to touch me there. Touch me. Taste me. Suck me into her mouth. Her teasing drove me insane.

Our tongues dueling, she then bit down on my lip and pulled back. God, I couldn't even take it. Her soft breasts crushed into my bare chest as she dragged her body back down. My breathing picked up in anticipation. Was this it? Was she finally going to touch me?

Right when she was in the perfect position between my knees, she paused, glancing up at me. "So I can do what I want, right?"

"Any fucking thing you want. *Anything*." I hoped she understood that. I was down for anything with Olivia.

Once again, she moved her hands along my thighs, slowly working her way upwards. Every part of me fought for control as I forced myself to sit still, to not shove my hips in her face. My patience was rewarded when, my God, she finally wrapped her soft fingers around the base of my dick.

Our eyes caught as she lowered her mouth, gently licking my tip in a slow, sensual movement that made me shudder. "*Fuck*," I groaned. Just by that alone, I knew I was in for a wild ride.

"You taste good," she whispered, her breath hot against me.

My fingers dug into the couch cushions as I watched her licking and kissing her way up and down the length of me. With full-on eye contact, she sucked on my balls. Good fucking God. Olivia knew what she was doing. And even better, she seemed to like it. That was the biggest turn-on of all, enthusiasm, and I was living for it.

When she finished, she licked her way back up my rock-hard cock, then flicked her tongue back and forth on that ultra-sensitive spot just under my tip. What the fucking hell? She was like a blow-job queen, and I suddenly felt like the luckiest man in the entire universe.

I let my head fall back on the couch, shivers overtaking my whole body, the pleasure almost too much to take. Squeezing my eyes shut, I let myself feel everything, soaking in the mind-blowing sensations all from Olivia's skillful mouth.

The warm salty breeze coming through the window above me, the sounds of traffic below, and the music pulsing from a car seemed like they were all in another dimension, far away, the only thing in the world Olivia's lips and tongue on me.

Fire filled my veins. Pure bliss in my chest. This was heaven.

Olivia paused, causing me to glance down at her. Was she still enjoying this?

Her smile told me yes. Yes, she was. Thank fuck.

"Hold my hair," she said. "I want you to come in my mouth."

Sweet Jesus. "Are you—are you sure?" I breathed.

Nodding, she wet her lips and kissed away the pre-cum still beading from my tip before going down completely on me. "*Oh, God,*" I groaned as she slowly sucked me into her mouth.

Clutching onto her hair, I moved it to one side, absolutely needing to see her face, her eyes, while she practically swallowed me whole. Holy shit.

I knew I was big, but Olivia handled me like a fucking rock star, using one hand to stroke what wouldn't fit into her mouth.

I didn't know what would make me come faster—the incredible feeling of her lips around my cock or the visual of her deep-throating me. She made a small gagging noise, and while it felt so fucking good, I didn't want her to hurt herself over me.

With my hand grasping her hair, I stopped her. "Livs, you don't—you don't have to—"

She somehow managed to smile at me, the light reflecting back in her eyes, making the breath catch in my throat. Olivia was quickly becoming my dream girl. More than that. I'd never dared to even dream about someone like her. That someone this amazing would come into my life and make me feel this way.

With her free hand, she clutched onto my thigh and continued on, sucking me even harder, her cheeks hollowing out. What could I do? The girl was stubborn. And hot. And crazy hot. Did I say that already?

Her head bobbing up and down, she kept catching my eyes, watching me, seeing what I liked, how I responded. But to be honest, everything she did was pure ecstasy. Everything. But especially the way the ultra-sensitive head of my cock felt against the back of her throat. My fucking God.

I knew I wouldn't last much longer, the base

of my spine already tightening, my muscles starting to clench in anticipation of this epic release I knew was coming. And she didn't let up, her movements increasing in speed, every sensation making me shake.

"Livs... *Livs*."

The pressure inside me built to insane heights, and I wondered if she really was okay with me exploding in her mouth. But she'd already said that's what she wanted. And Olivia didn't seem like the kind of person to say one thing and mean another.

She gagged again, and the sound, the idea that she was working so hard to get me off... I couldn't hold back anymore. My hips jerked, one hand in her hair, the other clutching a pillow.

"Fuck. *Fuck*," I gasped as my orgasm ripped through me, almost to the point of pain from the sheer intensity of it.

My whole body shuddered, my eyes rolled into the back of my head as my cum spurted into Olivia's warm, wet mouth. The uncontrollable spasms started in my cock then shot through the rest of me, blood rushing past my ears, every cell inside of me buzzing with electricity.

My God, Olivia had stolen my soul.

I lay there completely blissed out and dumb-struck, my muscles weak and shaky, a peaceful satisfaction stealing through my limbs. What had this girl done to me?

Lifting my weak-ass head, I glanced down at

her to see her wiping the corner of her mouth with her wrist, her brows raised and a hesitant smile on her face that quickly changed to one of smugness when I tried to speak and nothing but gibberish came out.

Instead of attempting to talk again, I let my head fall back, enjoying this complete feeling of relaxation that hijacked me—body, soul, and mind.

I sensed movement next to me and then Olivia settled into my side, her hand on my chest stroking softly, chills forming on my skin.

"You like that, right?" she whispered.

"Mmmm. Heaven."

And when she used her nails to scratch me gently, I couldn't imagine any greater satisfaction than this here right now. The most amazing orgasm of my life followed by Olivia's touch.

My heartrate slowly returned to normal as well as my breathing. And it suddenly struck me that I couldn't just lie here and soak up this feeling. It was Olivia's birthday, and I needed to do something about that, something that would hopefully blow her mind like mine had been blown. No pun intended. A lazy smile formed on my face.

"What's so funny?" Olivia asked.

"Hmm? Oh, um, uh..."

Olivia's light laugh hit me, along with a warm drowsiness. I'd get up in a minute. I really would. I had to. I opened my eyes and our gazes connected, instantly sending a jolt through my chest.

I summoned up every ounce of willpower inside me to sit upright again, Olivia's brows raising in surprise. "What's up? Are you leaving?"

"Hell no. Not unless you kick me out."

We stared at each other in silence, something intangible passing between us.

"Of course I'm not kicking you out," she said.

"Good. Because you have no idea what I want to do to you."

TWENTY-TWO

Luke

The sound she made brought me completely back to life again.

"What—what's that?" she gulped.

"I want you to sit on my face."

Her widening eyes made me smile. I had no clue what she was thinking. Was it a good thing? Or bad thing? Just in case, I didn't want to give her too much time to think, to psych herself out. So I kissed her, tasting myself on her lips, making me think of her mouth around my cock.

For as long as I lived, I'd never forget the sight of her on her knees before me, the feel of her sucking, her hair wrapped in my fingers.

I crushed her to me, realizing that she had way too many clothes on while I was completely naked. We needed to fix this situation. Stat.

My hands reached for the bottom of her dress, palming the soft skin of her thighs, edging her hem up higher and higher. Every second, I grew more and more desperate to see Olivia's glorious body, to feel her smooth skin against me.

Leaning forward, practically devouring her mouth, I lifted her dress higher and higher, fanning my fingers out, pressing into every inch of delicious flesh revealed along the way.

She hesitated, and I pulled back. "What?" I asked. "What is it?"

Gnawing at her lower lip, she studied my face before casting her eyes downward. "I have a birthmark on my stomach."

"So?"

"So it's ugly," she said in a disgusted tone.

None too gently, I lifted her face up with my hand, forcing her to look at me. "Your whole body could be covered in a birthmark, and do you think I would care?"

When she didn't answer, I decided to answer for her.

"No. No, I wouldn't give a shit. Because you're hot as hell just the way you are."

I swore she melted into me, and the vulnerability she showed struck me hard, making me even more determined to do this right, to give Olivia the most phenomenal experience of her life.

We kissed for a long moment, my hands roaming all over her body. Goddamn, I wanted this dress off.

My mind on one thing and one thing only, I

tried again, and this time Olivia didn't hesitate. She even helped me, our hands working together to lift the stretchy material up her waist, her chest, and then over her head, leaving Olivia in nothing but her bra and underwear, the soft lights making her skin glow.

She was the most beautiful girl I'd ever seen, and I let my eyes soak in all of her before I attacked her. Honestly, I didn't even notice the birthmark she'd mentioned.

"Right here," she said, pointing at something on her stomach.

"What? I don't even see anything. All I see is perfection in front of me."

Her lips curved into a smile. "You're such a liar."

"I'm fucking serious. What?" I moved my face against her stomach, nudging her with my nose. "I don't see *anything*."

"This. Right here." She poked her abdomen with her finger. "It's like splotchy and gets darker than the rest of my skin in the summer."

"Jesus, Livs. You think I even notice that?" I pulled back, shaking my head. "All I want to do is bury my face in your tits. All right?"

She laughed, her cleavage jiggling with every movement. Fuck me.

At the wedding that wasn't, I'd felt her up like a teenage boy in awe while grasping his first breast. And tonight? I didn't feel any differently. Seeing Livs in her black bra took me back, way back, and a shot of nerves pulsed through me.

A shaky breath escaped me as I stared. *Nice, dude. Maybe try to act like a grown-up, experienced male?*

And then she really took me back to feeling like a damn virgin when she reached behind her and unclasped her bra, revealing the most perfect breasts I'd ever seen in my life. Holy shit.

Like a wet dream happening before my very awake eyes, she palmed her cleavage. "What are you waiting for?" she asked.

My fucking God. She didn't have to tell me twice. I dove right into that mouth-watering chest displayed so appetizingly in front of me. *Wow*. Totally groping all the delicious softness, I kissed every inch of her, tasting her, licking her, not able to get enough. She clasped my head to her, her sweet sighs encouraging me to keep it up.

When I flicked her hard nipple with my tongue, she moaned, and I did it again. And again. Worshipping her body, moving from one side to the other, then sucking that nipple right into my eager mouth. The real-life Olivia surpassed even my wildest fantasies. This girl was *it*.

Hunger overtook me. My engines revved up again, my cock stiffening already at this most delectable woman in my arms. I couldn't wait for her to ride my face and taste that sweet pussy that I'd explored with only my fingers before.

But I took it slow, relishing every sigh, every moan. Olivia made me come alive. And not just when I'd exploded in her mouth. No. Giving was just as pleasurable for me. Maybe more so.

I liked it. Truly. I wanted it. I *ached* for it. Like some kind of drug, I was quickly becoming addicted to Olivia. I didn't want to just get her off, though. It was somehow deeper than that.

Her hands grasping my shoulders, I feasted and feasted until we were both breathless with desire. And then I moved to her neck, leaving scorching kisses from her collarbone to the base of her ear. Something told me she wouldn't like me touching her there much. That was a total chill-inducing zone for most people. So I moved on. Back to her pouty mouth, her wicked tongue pushing into my own, making me hotter than hot.

With her bare leg draped over mine, I grabbed her thigh hard, my greedy palm traipsing upward, wanting to find paradise, dying to take her to the peak of ecstasy. When she'd fallen apart up against that wall, when I'd felt her dripping wet for *me*, it'd done something to me.

I wanted to experience that again. Needed it. Craved it with everything in me. And I wasn't going to stop until we got there.

Grabbing her arms, I lifted her body up against me, her bare breasts pushing into my chest, her hard nipples making me salivate. The only thing left between us was her black thong. And I wanted it off.

She didn't protest as I practically tore the damn thing off her, then placed her where I wanted her, high up on my chest, while I lay down flat on my back.

"Right here, Livs," I ordered, "on my mouth."

Our eyes connected while she hesitated yet again, making me wonder if she didn't like this. I knew some girls weren't into getting eaten out. Or they were self-conscious. Which was it?

"What's going on?" I asked, trying to ignore her gorgeous tits on display from this angle. "Do you not want to?"

"I—I've never done this before."

"Done what? Sat on a man's face?"

Biting her lip, she nodded, all of her confidence from before fading, giving me a glimpse of that hidden vulnerability again. I couldn't help thinking of her ex, wondering if it was because she hadn't been into it or because he hadn't offered.

I clutched her shoulders, needing to know the answer. "Do you want to, though?"

Again, she moved her head up and down in a slight nod.

"Then what are you waiting for? My God, I want it so much. You have no idea."

That did the trick, her face changing from uncertainty to smiling in a flash. Thank fuck. I wasn't lying when I'd said how much I wanted this.

This time, I put her *exactly* where I needed her, her thighs on either side of my head. For a long moment, I stared up at her, taking a second to admire the absolutely stunning view, my entire field of vision full of Olivia.

My hands followed, wrapping my arms around her legs first, massaging the soft skin there. I breathed her in, the scent of her arousal filling my nostrils.

"Do you know how sexy you are?" I said, my voice raspy.

Her smile lit up her face above me, and she began to move her hips, not quite meeting my mouth. I couldn't help grinning at this small sign of eagerness from her, my cue to dig right in to this delicious feast literally before my eyes.

Wow, her pussy was pretty. Absolutely perfect. And for a second, I forgot what I was doing, I was so lost in her.

But when she wiggled her hips again, I remembered, and I gave her a gentle swipe with my tongue, tasting her for the first time. The primal grunt that came out of me couldn't be helped. Fuck, she tasted so damn good.

For the life of me, I tried to go slowly, tried to remember to tease her into a frenzy until she was actually so needy that she'd fuck my face. But I had no clue if I succeeded because I was totally lost in this girl... experiencing Olivia in all her glory.

With broad, flat strokes, I worked my way

inward, exploring every part of her that I could reach with my mouth, with my lips and especially my tongue while avoiding her clit, trying my best to wait till she was so turned on that she'd relax completely against me.

I stuck my tongue deep inside her and swirled, her loud groan filling the air above me. My hands going back to her luscious ass, I grasped her tightly to me, impatient, hungry, need rising up in me like a starving man.

Kneading all that soft flesh, I worked her over with my mouth, scratched her with my beard, taking note of every whimper, grunt, and moan she made, listening for what she liked the most, then did that again and again.

When she was practically gushing, her body became heavier against me, gravity crushing me to the couch, making me hot as hell that Olivia was finally letting herself go. I could feel *all* of her, nothing held back between us. She was completely open to me.

And I loved every damn second of it.

Everything became magnified as she started to move faster, more insistent... instinct and desire taking over as she chased her release.

Determined to work her up to the very edge, I pushed the tip of my tongue right under her clit, wanting her to practically beg me for it.

"Fuck my tongue, Livs. I'm dying for you to come on my face."

A deep groan came from low in her throat

as she began to grind her hips down on my mouth, intense, demanding, every smash of her dripping pussy pinning me down harder. My cock stiffened almost to the point of pain at the sight of Olivia's blazing need and wild abandon, riding me with zero inhibitions, trusting me like this, giving herself over to the moment and me.

I finally gave her exactly what I knew she needed and worked her swollen clit, first circling then flicking back and forth, seeing what drove her crazier... harder, faster, more and more pressure.

There was no place in this universe I'd rather be than the two of us working together like this.

When her head rolled back, a loud moan escaped her beautiful mouth, and I knew she was close. I didn't let up. I wouldn't let up. My forearms clenched around her, tongue swishing and licking with everything in me, my hot breath on her even hotter pussy.

Her hips rotated against me, my muffled groans urging her on to her peak. Our eyes connected, her hands in my hair, and I felt something foreign tug in my chest.

There was a quickening, a heady moment of anticipation between us right before the big moment. My heart pounded. My lungs worked tirelessly. And suddenly, Olivia came... hard, urgent, her whole body shaking.

The look on her face, of pure pleasure, of pure bliss, sent me straight to heaven. And the feel of her coming right against my mouth? I was on top of the world. Nothing could ever compare to this.

Her climax came in waves as I watched her, taking in her wild hair, half-lidded eyes, and gorgeous breasts. She was the most beautiful soul I'd ever seen.

Once she finally stilled, she slowly scooted down my body, wiping some of that wetness and proof of what I'd done to her on my chest, pride filling me at the sensation. Then she promptly collapsed on top of me, her spine putty, her bones jelly, sweaty skin on sweaty skin.

"Oh, my God, Luke, that was the best orgasm I've ever had," she mumbled breathlessly against my neck. "Happy freaking birthday to me."

My chuckles made her bounce, but she didn't move, not even a little. I clasped my arms tightly around her, amazed at the feel of our naked bodies together, vowing to savor this moment and never go to sleep.

TWENTY-THREE

Olivia

I woke up buck naked on the couch, Luke's arms wrapped around me. Our bodies melded together, I moved up and down gently with his every slow, relaxed breath. He felt incredible beneath me, both hard and soft at the same time, his skin surprisingly smooth.

Lifting my head slightly, I took in his gorgeous face, his long lashes and full lips, his cut jaw and stubble, the same stubble that had...

Oh, my. The events of last night came crashing over me, the oral sex marathon that had taken place playing out in slow-motion in my mind. Holy crap. I couldn't believe what had happened between us. Had I actually sat on his face?

Suddenly feeling flush, I remembered every electrifying sensation, every movement of his mouth and incredibly talented tongue. Luke had zero inhibitions, and he'd treated my body with such reverence, such awe and admiration, that I'd responded in kind and completely let myself go in a way I never had before.

Luke was clearly a god in bed. And we hadn't even had sex. Yet. Sheesh. That might actually kill me. Like seriously. The thought made me nervous because I had an inkling I'd be a complete and total goner if that happened. And as much as I liked Luke, *really* liked Luke, a part of me wanted to keep this casual. The last thing I wanted was to lose my heart.

But I didn't get much time to think about it because, before I could even wake Luke up, craziness descended upon us.

A loud pounding startled me upright, Luke jumping up as well, his eyes darting around like he was unsure of his whereabouts.

"Livs! Hurry! Open up!" Emily's voice said from the other side of my door.

Adrenaline took off through my limbs at the urgency in her tone, and I grabbed a blanket off the couch, quickly wrapping it around me. Without even thinking about Luke and his nakedness, I flung the door open, worry for my little sister engulfing me.

Her face deathly white, she rushed in, slamming the door shut behind her, whirling around to lock the deadbolt and chain with shaky hands.

"Oh, my God. What is it?" I asked.

She grasped my shoulders, her fingers digging in. "I need to lay low for a while."

"Lay low?" My heart pounded so hard, I thought I might be having a heart attack. "What on earth are you talking about? Why?"

Luke rose up from the couch, a blanket around his waist, drawing Emily's attention. She clasped a hand over her mouth. "Oh, shit. I'm sorry. I'll just—I'll just—"

Emily stepped toward the door, but I grabbed her in time. "Wait. You're not going anywhere until you talk to me and tell me what's going on."

I noticed her trembling then, and my older sibling instincts kicked in. Steering her toward the couch, I suddenly remembered what had occurred there last night, so I made a course correction and forced her to sit in the one chair I had.

Turning to Luke, I asked, "Will you make her some chamomile tea, please? It's already out on my counter."

"Sure. Yeah."

Sitting on the corner of the couch, I clasped my blanket tighter around me, facing Emily. "So what is it?"

She surprised me by shaking her head, her eyes darting from the messed-up couch pillows and scattered clothes on the floor to the sounds in the kitchen. "Did you two...?"

"No. No, we didn't. Not that it's any of your business. But who cares about me right now?

What's going on with *you*?" At this point, I was frantic to know.

Leaning closer, she inhaled deeply before blowing it out. "I, um, kind of got mixed up with the wrong guy."

"What?" I exploded. "What does that mean? Did he hurt you? Are you okay?" I searched her face, her arms, every piece of exposed skin, for bruises or marks.

"He didn't hurt me. It's nothing like that. *He's* the one in trouble, and... and..." She buried her face in her hands. "This is gonna sound awful," she mumbled.

"You can tell me anything. *Anything.*"

Glancing back up at me, she visibly cringed. "I was just fooling around with him. He's really, really good in bed." Her eyes went to the window. "Like he does this thing with his tongue where he —"

I bumped her leg with my foot, determined to get to the bottom of this. "Please. I don't want to know that right now. Could you just tell me what happened?"

Her attention returned to me, the dreamy look in her eyes fading. "Right. Right. So anyway, he's going through some stuff, and I don't want anything to do with it. I am literally running away from him, and I feel a little bit bad about it."

At that moment, Luke came into the living room, a steaming mug in his free hand that he placed on the coffee table near Emily. I wondered what he'd do, if he'd make a run for the door or stick around. But without a second of hesitation, he plopped himself down on the couch next to me, still holding the blanket around himself.

"What kind of trouble are we talking about?" he asked, obviously overhearing most of the conversation from the kitchen.

A beat passed as Emily's lips clamped together. "He owes some people money. A lot of money."

"Oh, God," I moaned.

Luke whistled. "And how bad are these people exactly?"

"Bad. Really bad."

"How so?" I needed details. "Have they hurt you? Threatened you?"

Luke and I both watched as Emily's trembling fingers reached for the mug of tea. She took a slurpy sip, testing the heat, before taking a longer drink. With both hands wrapped around the cup, she leaned back into her chair again.

This suspense was not good for my blood pressure, and I fought the urge to yell at her and hurry her along. For as long as I could remember, Emily hated being rushed. And it'd caused more than a few fights when we'd been growing up because I despised being late.

So I sat there, biting my tongue, on edge that these bad guys would find their way here and bust down my door. But having Luke sitting next to me was somehow a reassurance. Strange. But nice. Very nice. And even better when he put a firm hand on my covered knee as if to offer me support.

"His name's Evan," she finally began. "And he has a bit of a, um, gambling problem."

Beside me, Luke made a frustrated noise, but I didn't spare him a glance, fear for Emily consuming me. "So he borrowed money or something?"

"Exactly. From some guys in Vegas."

"Wow," Luke said. "Not a good idea. At all."

I completely agreed. But I didn't care about Evan one bit, only Emily. "So how are *you* involved?"

"I wasn't. I didn't even know about it until he showed up at my door in the middle of the night."

"Oh, my God." I clutched onto Luke's hand. "So what happened? What'd he want?"

"He said he needed a place to hide out for the night."

"Asshole," Luke growled. "He had no right to drag you into his shit."

While I completely agreed with Luke, I didn't want to waste time badmouthing Evan, even though he deserved it. We needed answers. "So then what?"

"Well, he told me the gist of it. We stayed up till dawn talking about it. Then when I went out for my morning run, I noticed some guys in a car watching my place. And it's like they weren't even trying to be subtle. They didn't care in the least if I noticed them. Almost like they wanted me to see and be scared." A shudder went through her small frame.

"That's terrifying."

"Right? I turned right back around and told Evan he had to leave. I grabbed my purse and came here. Is that bad that I totally ditched Evan? I feel so horrible."

"No, you shouldn't feel bad. Not even a little. You needed to get the hell out," Luke said, his tone forceful. "He should never have involved you."

"Exactly," I agreed, Luke and I one-hundred percent on the same page. "How well did you know this guy anyway?"

Emily shrugged. "Not very well apparently. We only met a few weeks ago and didn't even talk much. Just screwed a lot."

I couldn't help rolling my eyes at this lovely tidbit. But in this moment, I decided to spare her any kind of lecture. Because really, even people you knew very well could surprise you. All I had to do was think about Henry and how he'd shocked me after four years.

Putting her tea down, she began to rock back and forth. "What should I do? What should I do?"

"Maybe go to the police?" I said cautiously.

"No." Emily's rocking became more vigorous. "It's so flimsy. What would I even say? Two guys sitting in a car were maybe watching me? And some guy I slept with a few times is super sketchy with a gambling addiction. What could they even do?"

I supposed she had a point. "So what do you want to do?"

"Can I stay with you?" she asked quietly, her shoulders up near her ears.

"Of course, you can." Inwardly, I sighed. The timing was truly terrible, right when things were heating up with this man beside me. Luke's fingers tightened on my leg, making me wonder if he was thinking the same thing.

Just then, Emily's phone rang, and her eyes widened after she retrieved it from her pocket. "It's him."

"Don't answer," Luke and I said at the same time.

But did she listen to her older, wiser big sister? Nope. Of course not.

"Hello?" she said, gingerly holding her cell to her ear like she wasn't sure she wanted to hear what he had to say.

For a long moment, she was quiet, her eyes darting around the room, but suddenly, she sat up straight, her chin jutting out as she interrupted. "You know what? You're on your own. I want nothing to do with this, and honestly, we're done. I don't want to talk to you ever again."

And with that, she hung up, shut her phone off, and stuffed it down the side of the chair.

"What did he want?" I asked.

"Money. Which I don't have anyway."

"Fucker," Luke grumbled.

"Right?" Emily rubbed her hands repeatedly on her thighs. "He said he's going to Vegas to straighten everything out. And I really think he means to keep gambling to try to get himself out of this mess."

Luke groaned beside me. "Oh, God."

"But I'm done. I shouldn't feel bad, right?"

"No. You absolutely should not," Luke said before I had a chance. "You just met this guy. Even if you were married, you owe him nothing. *Nothing*."

Hearing Luke speak this way, well, it stirred something in me, setting off little flutters in my chest. Being protective of my sister, reassuring her, helping in his own way... it was incredibly sexy to witness.

Emily's eyes welled up, making my heart tug with sympathy, and then the crying really began. Standing up, I went over to hug her as best I could while trying to keep my blanket up with one hand.

Behind me, I heard Luke clear his throat. "I'm gonna head out. Unless you want me to stay," he added.

I couldn't help shooting him a quick smile. "We're good. But thanks."

As Emily really started to sob, I watched while Luke quickly gathered up his clothes and bolted for the door, inwardly laughing at his hasty retreat in the face of Emily's tears. Once he reached the exit, though, he paused and turned. "Hey, don't hesitate to knock on my door. If you need *anything*, let me know. I'll be home."

"Thank you," I said as Emily sputtered something that sounded like thanks as well.

With that, he was off. And all sense of our incredible night ended.

"I'm sorry I'm messing up your b-b-birthday weekend," Emily cried. "I'm *so* sorry."

I patted her back gently. "Oh, sweetie, it's fine. No big deal. That's what family is for."

"I'm so lucky to have you," she blubbered.

"Aw, same."

Still holding her shaky shoulders, I let her cry and get it all out. She'd mentioned being up all night, and I knew from experience that a tired Emily could get even more emotional. I supposed we all did. But for some reason, sleep was even more precious for Emily.

So once she finally stopped sobbing, I led her toward the bed, helped her remove her shoes, then covered her with my soft comforter. "Sleep. You're safe now. Okay?"

Her only answer was sniffling as she rolled her face into the pillows. But while I tiptoed toward the bathroom, desperate for a hot shower, I heard a muffled thank you.

Holy cow. How did Emily manage to get herself into these situations? While I let the water warm up, memories of her getting into weird scenarios cascaded through my mind.

Who could forget her frantic phone call to me when she'd been locked in a frat house basement on Halloween night? Or what about the time she'd been stuck in the back of some guy's truck as he took off down the highway for God knew where? Both times, she'd managed to save herself. Thank goodness.

But it didn't change the fact that ever since we were little, I'd had to take care of her, checking in on her even in elementary school to make sure the boys weren't picking on her or that she hadn't forgotten her lunch. Not that I was complaining.

Like I'd said to her earlier, that's what family did for each other, if you were lucky enough to have a decent family. I knew Emily would do the same. In fact, she'd been there for me completely when Henry had dumped me and I'd been a complete mess. I couldn't forget that. I'd even stayed at her place for a while until I'd found this new apartment.

I did think about calling my parents, but Emily and I had a sister code of sorts where we didn't like to tell them everything, especially scenarios where we'd possibly screwed up. So maybe I'd confide that Emily was living here but not tell them exactly why.

Shedding the blanket, I stepped into the hot stream of water, the remaining scent of Luke on my body—that indescribable delicious hint of spice and all masculinity—rising up in the steam, giving me a pang of sadness.

Now that Emily was crashing here, I had no idea what the future held. How long would she need my help? And when could I be alone with Luke again?

TWENTY-FOUR

Olivia

Well, my poor sister. As if her life wasn't shaky enough, she lost her job as an administrative assistant the very next day. When I came home exhausted from work, once she removed the chair she had blocking the door, there she was in tears again. The drama in her life.

"It's not like I did anything wrong," she complained while stuffing her face with the Thai take-out I'd brought home. "They were cutting back anyway, and I guess I didn't make the cut."

"Oh, God, Em, I'm so sorry."

"No. I'm sorry." She wiped her mouth on her sleeve, all pretense of civility gone as she sat there hunched over, eye make-up smeared and hair up in a falling-apart bun. "I'm a mess right now."

"It's temporary. All temporary. We all hit

rough patches sometimes. That's life."

She nodded like she didn't quite believe me. "I've already applied at a temp agency."

"Good for you. Who knows? You could be working again tomorrow."

But as the week wore on, those words rang through my head, mocking me relentlessly because jobs were scarce at the moment and competition fierce.

As the days passed by, Emily became almost a permanent fixture on my couch. She ate there, she slept there, she spent hours on her phone there. My apartment grew messier and messier, dishes piling up in the sink and on the counter, clothes overflowing from the chair in the living room, and shoes everywhere.

With Luke accompanying us, we'd paid a visit to Emily's apartment and brought over several suitcases of her belongings. Seeing her place made her sick with anxiety.

And then, she began to worry about next month's rent since she lived paycheck to paycheck. But at the same time, instead of pounding the pavement looking for a job, she barely moved from her spot on the couch, only slightly lifting her head to say hello to me whenever I came home.

Frankly, it was exhausting. And I knew at some point, I'd have to give her some tough love. How long did I let her wallow in self-pity? Should I pay her rent so she'd have a place to go back to? Or should I just let her stay here until our big Italy trip, then figure it all out afterwards?

The whole thing really brought me down too. Especially because I barely saw Luke. Well, I did see him some, for brief moments when he stopped by to check on us or bring food over. But whenever I even thought about going over to his place, Emily said something about being scared or sad or depressed.

So Luke and I had zero time alone, and it made me crazy. This was a good reminder of why my sister and I had never been roommates and why I preferred to live alone.

After several weeks, my nerves were completely frazzled, and I knew that something had to give. I just didn't know *how*. After yet another patronizing conversation with my boss, I came home all fired up. My life needed some changes. A person could only take so much.

Kicking off my shoes, I stomped toward a sleeping Emily, making as much noise as possible. I threw all the clothes off the chair, and shoved aside the sprawled-open suitcase which made an awful screeching sound.

Sorry, downstairs neighbor.

Emily rose up to a sitting position on the couch, her expression clouded. "What's going on?"

"What's going on? I don't know. Why don't you tell me?"

She rubbed at her eyes, yawning. "What do you

mean?"

I watched as she stretched and let her head fall back. "What I mean is... how is the job search going?"

"Oh, that. Not so great."

Ignoring her defeated tone, I plowed onward. "May I ask when the last time you actually looked was?"

Silence filled the air, and I knew I had my answer. Sighing, I leaned back in my chair, resting my head as well.

"Why haven't you been looking?" I asked.

"Because I didn't even like my job. Why should I find another one just like it? What's the freaking point?"

"To make money. To pay bills. To pay rent *somewhere else*." I couldn't help emphasizing those last two words.

She sat up straight, truly meeting my eyes for the first time since I'd sat down. "I'm so sorry, Livs. I know I'm being a total freeloader right now. I'm just scared to go back home, to even live on my own. What if those guys come looking for *me*, thinking I know where Evan is or something?"

That was a valid concern, and I understood. "What about staying with some of your friends?"

Emily groaned. "I can't crash with any of them. They're all married or in long-term relationships, and you know Kirsten and Isabella even have babies. I can't put myself in the middle of that. You know what I mean?"

"I get it," I admitted with a defeated sigh. "I do."

"I'm just single, jobless, pathetic Emily who got mixed up with the wrong guy."

At those words, my heart softened, all the fight leaving my body. "You're not pathetic. You're just—you're just going through something right now."

"To be honest, I'm scared the entire time you're at work and I'm terrified to even leave your apartment. What if those guys track me down? It wouldn't be too hard for them to figure out where my sister lives."

Oh, God. She was right, and now I was frightened too. Great. I made a mental note to prop the chair under the door tonight and put my pepper spray beneath my pillow.

A sudden loud knock made us both jump.

"It's me... Luke."

"Oh, thank goodness," Emily muttered.

Thank goodness was right, I thought as I rushed to the door, whipping it open to find a grinning Luke. "Don't worry. I'm not the evil henchman coming to break your knees."

Glaring at him, I began to shut the door in his face, but with a faux hurt look and a strong arm, he stopped me.

"Joking," he said. "Or is it too soon?"

"Too soon," Emily called from her well-worn spot on the couch.

Back to smiling, Luke came in like he lived

here, somehow filling up the room with life and vibrancy again, and plopped down on the chair. "So I wanted to ask you something," he said, turning his full attention to me. "Will you go on a date with me?"

"A date?" He had to be kidding. With all the things going on in my life right now, going out on a date seemed completely frivolous. "Are you serious?"

"Yes, I'm serious," he scoffed. "A date. You know, I get dressed up. You get dressed up. We go somewhere nice, maybe eat dinner—"

"I know what a date is."

The corners of his mouth curved up with the hint of a grin. "Well, good. Then it's a date."

"I didn't agree."

"Yet."

"You're awfully confident."

Biting down on his lower lip, he gave me a smoldering look that told me exactly what he was thinking. "I am," he said in a husky tone.

Oh, boy. That panty-melting half-smile with that voice, not to mention that ridiculously handsome face. He was definitely hard to resist. But I needed to stay put... for my sister. "I can't leave Emily alone at night."

"Yes, you can," she countered. "I'm fine. Don't miss out on a free dinner because of me."

Luke laughed. "Exactly. What she said."

Smiling, I paused for a moment, really needing to think this through before agreeing. Personal wants versus familial obligation... that's what it boiled down to in the end. Family always came first, though. At least in my case.

Two sets of eyes on me, I opened my mouth to speak, but Luke beat me to it. "What if some friends came over and hung out with Emily? Would that work?"

"I don't want to bother my friends with this," Emily protested.

Luke's attention turned to my sister. "What if you hung out with *my* friends?"

Emily's eyes rolled to the ceiling. "I don't need a babysitter."

"I know. But they do."

"That's ridiculous," Emily said with a groan before focusing back on me. "Come on, Livs. Just go."

In the end, I ignored the uneasy feeling in my gut and agreed to go. Emily, despite telling me minutes before how scared she was to be alone, became adamant that I had to go on this date, and there was really no way to argue with that since she was the only reason not to. Besides, I *did* want to go.

I tapped Luke's arm and nodded my head toward my bedroom. "Hey, can I speak to you for a second?"

His brows raised, but he didn't say anything, just followed me down the hall.

"Don't talk about me," Emily yelled after us.

Yeah, right.

Once we were safely in my room and I'd closed the door behind us, I whirled around to face a distracted Luke who was more interested in checking out my bed than anything I had to say. He sat down on the edge, bouncing up and down, making it squeak slightly.

"I like it," he said.

I poked him in the shoulder. "Would you be serious? I have something I need to talk about."

"What? What is it?"

Sitting down beside him, I leaned in close to his ear. I wouldn't put it past Emily to eavesdrop by the door. "I'm worried about my sister. She's like a shell of herself. And she told me she's really freaked out and scared."

"She is? But she doesn't even know for sure that those guys were watching her place. You know?"

"I know." Ignoring how freaking good he smelled, I whispered some of the things she'd told me, choosing to confide in Luke and tell him all about our conversation.

Luke stared at the wall for a moment, rubbing his chin, before turning to me. "I don't know the answer. I really don't. Maybe it'll just take time for her to get back to her normal life and feel safe again."

"Maybe. I just don't know what to do for her. The only time she moves from the couch is when she needs food or the bathroom. I don't even think she's showering anymore."

"It does kind of smell in your place."

Nudging him with my body, he barely moved. "Thanks for that. You've been very helpful," I mumbled.

He nudged back gently. "Any time."

I smiled at him, enjoying this light moment. There was something nice about sharing my worries with him, something I hadn't experienced with a man in a very long time. Confiding in my family or friends was different somehow. I couldn't put my finger on it, but this was easier for some reason.

Luke put his large hand on mine, squeezing. "Look, I don't think there's much you can do that you're not already doing. Maybe go outside with her, take her to some of her favorite places, let her interact with actual real-life people to remind her that the world isn't such a bad place. Most of the time."

"That's actually a pretty good idea."

"I'm not all brawn," he teased, that gleam in his eye downright infectious. "Feel better?"

"I do." And I really did. Who knew that Luke could be so comforting?

"So you'll go out with me then?"

Nodding, I had to smile at his eagerness and his one-track mind. "As long as Emily is okay with it." A glimmer of excitement shimmied through my chest at the idea. "When are you thinking?"

"Tomorrow."

Oh, wow, I hadn't been expecting that. And I hadn't been expecting him to look at me the way he was looking at me now. Staring at my lips, an invisible strand of heat pulling us together, the intimacy and warmth of my bedroom seemed to close in on us.

I heard a noise from the living room and instantly pulled away. "Tomorrow it is," I answered, my voice coming out lower than expected as a thrill of anticipation shot through me.

A date with Luke? What exactly would that involve? I had no idea, but I couldn't wait to find out.

TWENTY-FIVE

Luke

Reaching out my hand to knock on her door, I was surprised to realize how nervous I was. What the hell was that about? By this point, we'd hung out so much. The girl had even sat on my fucking face.

But tonight? It felt like something more, like we had the chance to really take this thing between us beyond boyfriend lessons, beyond an incredible birthday night hook-up.

Inhaling deeply, I did it. I knocked, hoping the two jackasses behind me at my place were paying attention. They had an important job to do tonight... if I wanted Olivia to fully relax and have fun. The girl needed it. They both did actually.

After a moment of hesitation when I knew I was being observed through the peephole, the door swung open, Emily giving me the up and down. "You actually look nice," she said.

"Thanks?" I chuckled, wondering how to reply because... well, she didn't look so great at the moment, not even close to the confident, well-dressed girl I first met at the Safari Park.

Her hair stuck out all over and appeared matted on one side, making me wonder when she'd last combed it. And honestly, there was an earthy scent wafting toward me, confirming that she might not have showered in recent days. Olivia was right to be concerned.

As if on cue, the door behind me opened, and I held my breath, praying that these two guys possessed even a tiny amount of acting skills. Emily looked over my shoulder at Aiden and Trevor.

"Hey, man, where are you hiding the good wine?" Aiden asked.

I rolled my eyes. "That wasn't part of the deal. You're here for my AC only."

"AC? What's going on?" the familiar voice of Olivia asked.

Whirling back around, I almost couldn't breathe. She looked hotter than I'd ever seen her. Even hotter than she'd been at Trevor's "wedding." I took in her dark dress, her miles-long legs, my eyes eventually moving upward to her sexy, amused smile.

"You look amazing," I said, remembering the flowers in my hand and handing them to her.

Her smile growing, she accepted the bouquet,

lifting it to her nose and sniffing. "Thank you."

There was a long moment of silence where I thought about all I wanted to do to her, until some doofus behind me cleared his throat. "So where's the wine?"

I gave up. "In the cupboard all the way to the left."

Someone patted me on the back. "Thanks, man."

"Uh, can I ask what's going on?" Olivia said.

I pointed my thumb at them. "Aiden's AC went out, so these guys are hanging out here."

Olivia's gaze darted back and forth between Aiden, Trevor, and her sister. "You should go over there for the night," she suggested, pulling on Emily's dirty sleeve.

And this was why I liked this girl so much. She hadn't even been in on the plan, and she'd played into the bit perfectly.

We all watched as Emily thought for a minute. When the guys and I had discussed it beforehand, we were all sure that Emily would resist and need persuading. But to my shock, she nodded. "You have lots of wine?"

"Yeah, unfortunately." I tried my best to sound slightly annoyed, hoping she'd buy it.

And miraculously, she did. "All right. I'm in."

Take that, high school drama teacher who said I wasn't made for the stage.

She moved into the hallway as Aiden, Trevor, and I exchanged a quick triumphant look. I thought about introducing them all, but Emily didn't even pause. She walked right into my place and straight to the couch.

Aiden shoved me in the shoulder. "Have fun, bro."

They went in, shutting the door behind them, leaving Olivia and me all alone. Thank God. That was the whole point here tonight.

Olivia's lips trembled like she was holding in her laughter. "Did you plan that?"

Smug ass that I was, I didn't even try to deny it. "Yep. Pretty smooth, right?"

And now she giggled, making her even more irresistible. I pulled her to me, careful not to mess up her dress or makeup, but my phone buzzing interrupted the moment before it began.

Giving her a quick peck on the head, I pulled back. "Come on. Let's forget about them and all of their issues and go have some fun."

"I couldn't agree more."

With that, I grabbed her hand and led her downstairs toward the waiting car, where we settled into the back seat. Putting my arm around her, she leaned into my side like she belonged there.

She turned to me, placing her hand on my knee and wiggling it impatiently. "So where are we going?"

"Nice try."

After giving my leg a good squeeze, Olivia looked out the windows, obviously trying to figure out where the driver was headed. Truthfully, it wouldn't take a rocket scientist to realize we were literally driving down the street to the harbor. My plan was maybe a little bit cheesy, but I hoped she wouldn't mind too much.

From the front seat, soft music played, adding to the ambience as anticipation filled the air between us. Traffic was surprisingly light, and we made it to our destination in only a few minutes.

Olivia's eyes lit up. "The water? Please tell me I'm dressed right."

I chuckled. "Of course. As hot as it is, we're not going swimming." Although that wasn't a bad idea, something I'd have to remember for another time.

As we walked the short distance to the departure area, I could practically hear Olivia's brain at work. "A dinner cruise! That has to be it. Is that it?" she asked.

"You got it, genius."

Her sharp elbow met my side. "I can't tell if you're teasing or not."

"Never," I deflected. "You really are a genius. Smartest woman... Wait. Let me correct that. Smartest *person* I've ever met."

Even though I was serious, she gave me an eye-roll as we waited in line to board, the heat of the day beginning to fade with the breeze coming off the water. I kind of regretted wearing this suit coat... until I noticed Olivia actually checking me out.

"You look really handsome, by the way," she said, reaching up to trace the skin beneath my open collar with her fingers.

Okay. Maybe I didn't regret the extra effort I'd put in for this date.

"And I like your haircut." Her smile was all for me, making me realize I was the luckiest dude here tonight.

"Thanks," I said, drawing her into my side. Heat be damned.

The wait wasn't too long, and soon, we were seated in a quiet corner of the dining area, cold glasses of champagne in our hands.

I clinked my glass to hers. "To taking out the most beautiful woman in the world."

"Stop," she said, smiling as she took a sip of her drink.

"Don't tell me to stop. It's the damn truth."

Her cheeks pinkened at the praise while we stared at each other, oblivious to our surroundings, but when the server brought out some bread, it broke the spell, and I took a second to glance around and soak in the vibe of the place. Low lights, classical music, and huge windows that showed off the beautiful scenery. Not to mention the delicious smell of food everywhere.

Man, I was in foodie heaven, made all the more amazing by having Olivia by my side. With a happy sigh, I broke apart some of the warm, crusty bread.

This was something I could get used to, something I hadn't experienced before—contentment, happiness, a feeling that I could be totally myself with a woman and that she might be okay with it.

"So," I began, "I have something important to tell you. But first, maybe we should talk about the kids and get that out of the way."

Olivia's laugh washed over me. "The kids first. And then we'll vow not to talk about them the rest of the night, right?"

"Exactly." I loved that Olivia actually got my sense of humor. "So any changes with your sister since we talked yesterday?"

"None. Zero. Except I did pay her rent for next month just in case. Plus, I'm going to listen to your advice and take her out for ice cream soon." Spreading some butter on her bread, Olivia scooted closer to me. "And what about Trevor? I haven't really seen him since *that* day. How's he doing?"

I shrugged because I really wasn't sure myself since Trevor was so tight-lipped about it all. "Well, he's moved in with Aiden for now. We helped him pack up his stuff. And I think he's trying to figure out where he wants to go, what he wants to do."

"I can't even imagine what he's going through."

"Yeah, he's a mess. That's for sure."

"Poor Aiden. Now he's got to look after two hot messes tonight."

"Hey, at least Trevor doesn't smell," I pointed out.

She giggled. "Well, let's hope they all get along okay."

"I'm sure they will. Trevor probably won't even talk to your sister. He's sworn off women forever. He's done. Especially since Krystal kept the dogs."

"Ouch, that must have hurt." Her brows lowered in confusion. "Why couldn't he have them, though?"

"I have no idea. He wouldn't really say much about the conversation between them, and he's not exactly the most talkative guy at the moment. Aiden and I are trying our best not to pry and just be there for him when he needs us. You know?"

Olivia took a long sip of her drink then nodded, and I wondered if now would be the right time to bring up all that I had on my mind, if we'd had enough chatting about everyone else and their problems.

I'd been waiting for the perfect moment to talk to her, to tell her about my dreams and hopes for my future, but we hadn't had any time alone lately and it never seemed like something that we could really discuss in depth like I wanted to.

Finishing off my champagne, I cleared my throat, deciding to dive right in. "So I mentioned that I have some big news for you."

"Oh, yeah? What is it?" she asked with wide eyes.

I wanted to start at the beginning and be completely honest about where all this had come from. "You've inspired me."

Her eyes appeared even larger, her gorgeous lips parted in surprise. "I have?"

"Absolutely yes," I admitted. "I don't know if you remember that day I met your family at the Safari Park and the conversation we had over lunch."

She was quiet for a second, clearly thinking. "About restaurants?"

Grinning, I simply stared at her, wondering how long it would take for her to connect the dots.

Suddenly, she gasped. "What? You're going to open a restaurant? Are you serious?"

Nodding slowly, I soaked in her reaction, the happiness and wonder written all over her stunning face. "Dead serious," I answered.

"Oh, my God. That's amazing. Wow." In her excitement, she grasped onto my forearm and didn't let go. "How on earth did that come about?"

She already knew that I'd left my old job, something I had mentioned in passing when I'd brought her and her sister dinner one night. But now, I told her all about the bro-moon, every detail, everything Aiden, Trevor, and I had discussed, how we all wanted and needed changes in our lives at this exact moment in time. I mentioned how we'd even gone to scout out locations, spending every minute of our free time hashing out our plans.

The look on her face, like she was actually impressed, kept me going and going as a strange sense of pride filled me. I wanted her to keep looking at me like that. All the fucking time. It felt like I meant something to her, and for the first time in my life, I'd found a girl who meant something to *me*.

Not just something. She meant the world to me. Somehow, some way, during these last few months, she'd become something more to me.

I cared about her. I wanted to please her, make her happy, make her smile all day, every damn day. And not only that, I liked who I became when she was around. I didn't feel like that piece-of-shit loser who hated my life. She made me a better man. More importantly, I *wanted* to be a better man because of her.

The way she asked question after question and took an honest, genuine interest in my new venture made my chest tight. No one had ever cared about my dreams or hopes for life. Maybe that was because I hadn't had any before. But now I did. Thanks to her.

For the rest of our meal, we discussed all the details, Olivia offering opinions and her thoughts, her passion shining through, making her more beautiful than ever before to me.

"If you keep looking at me like that," I said, watching her lick some chocolate off her lips from the molten lava cake, "I'm going to..."

"Going to what?" Her tongue flickered out again, and I knew she was now teasing me on purpose.

"You know what I want to do?" I leaned in closer, my nose against her cheek, inhaling her, my hand falling to grip her thigh. "I want to fuck you."

She inhaled sharply, her face flushing instantly, whether from the alcohol or my words, I wasn't sure.

"I'm absolutely dying to," I added for emphasis so she'd know I meant it.

Olivia quickly recovered from her surprise, her eyes taking on a dark, sultry look that made my dick come alive instantly.

"Well, what are you waiting for?" she asked in a sexy, whispery voice.

Good fucking grief. That was it. Desperate now, I glanced around, scoping out the scene. Where on earth could we go? I needed to be alone with this girl. Right now.

With a frustrated growl, I shoved my chair away from the table and stood up, determined to make this happen. To my shock, Olivia stood up as well, like she was just as into it, and something about that made me want it even more—if that was even possible.

Grabbing her hand, I led her through the busy dining room and out the door to the quickly darkening deck area, the hot air not doing anything to cool the blood pounding through my body.

Come hell or high water, I would make this happen... right here, right now, even on this goddamn boat.

TWENTY-SIX

Olivia

Luke was like a man possessed, the way he clutched my hand, the intense look on his face as he searched our surroundings.

I spotted the narrow set of stairs a split second before he did, and then our eyes caught in a moment of mutual understanding and desire.

Then Luke was off, practically dragging me behind him as we rushed up the steps, coming out on an open deck with a scene that took my breath away.

The sun had set, leaving splashes of orange and pink painted across the wispy clouds over our stunning downtown. As if that wasn't enough, the lights of the tall buildings reflected back in the water like something from a postcard.

"Stop admiring the view and admire me," Luke said.

I giggled at his ridiculous command, but he certainly grabbed my attention. And then, I truly looked at him, the smirk on his handsome face, the way his broad shoulders filled out his suit, and most especially the way his dark eyes seemed to devour me.

Flashes of the last time we were together went off like fireworks in my mind, a sexy montage of Luke naked on the couch, me kneeling between his muscular legs, his head back like he couldn't even hold it up. Thinking about what was under his suit made me want to jump him.

Glancing around, I noticed we were all alone. Thank goodness.

"Come here," Luke said.

"Yes, sir."

Our bodies came together in a heated embrace, his arms tight around me, his lips quickly capturing mine in a scorching hot kiss. Luke was a phenomenal kisser, alternating between sweet, almost gentle, then turning feral and rough, like he couldn't make up his mind.

And I couldn't either, especially in this setting. The excitement of being with Luke outdoors like this made me feel truly alive. We were out in the open air, cool breezes blowing from the water, surrounded by both nature and the heartbeat of the city.

His hands began to roam down the bare skin of my arms, the feel of his rough fingers making me wonder if that love languages quiz had been wrong. Because touch was it for me. Or maybe no one had ever touched me the way Luke did.

Against my stomach, I could feel the evidence of his growing desire, the passion quickly igniting between us into a wildfire. Nothing else mattered at the moment. All thoughts, all my worries, fled my mind.

Luke filled my entire existence.

I started to grind my hips against him, and he groaned before grabbing my ass. Hard. "You have no idea how much I want you," he said softly.

"Oh, I have an idea." Reaching between our bodies, I palmed his erection, slowly moving my hand along the length of him.

He hissed, his eyes narrowing at me, his expression unreadable against the night sky. But I could guess what it was. It had to be the same as mine.

Desire. Deep, hot desire. And now desperation.

I had no idea where this could go in our current situation. I'd never dared do anything like this. I'd only ever done it on a bed, in private, with the front door firmly shut and locked.

But this? I could hardly believe what we were doing. It was terrifying, but also thrilling. And maybe I was reading too much into it, but it also felt like we were a team, in this together, both of us carried away by this crazy passion we shared.

Luke didn't give me much time to think, his lips coming down on mine again, his tongue sweeping into my mouth, possessive, hungry.

His hands reached for my breasts, cupping them roughly, my nipples tightening at his heated touch.

All I could do was hold onto his arms, my knees suddenly weak, Luke's passion and the unsteady boat not helping. I already knew in the depths of my heart that Luke would hold me up. He'd never let me fall.

Something about that thought connected with me, connected the physical desire with the emotional. And I gave Luke everything I had, kissing him back thoroughly, his groan in my mouth like kindling to the fire.

He stepped backward and sunk down onto a large bench, pulling me with him, settling me sideways on his lap. And now his hands were everywhere, the heat erupting into a blazing inferno as he stroked my bare upper thigh, my dress riding up indecently.

My heart beat wildly, our heavy breathing lost to the sounds of the night surrounding us.

He brushed his thumb over my lips, our eyes meeting. "Sometimes I think you're a dream. That you're too good to be true."

Oh, my heart. With those words, with his intense caresses, I felt safe, secure, and truly cared for, a dangerous little tugging in my chest. But I wouldn't think about that now.

His greedy hands demanded my full attention as he explored my body. Even though I was covered by my dress, I felt completely at his mercy.

Raw need vibrated between us, an overwhelming ache growing between my legs. I was so drenched, he had to feel it, just like I could feel his rock-hard erection beneath me. My dress rode up, exposing my thong, my bare ass to him.

I wiggled in his lap, and his primal groan sounded right in my ear. I loved that sound, the fact that I could do that to him. So I moved again. And again. I spread my legs a little, absolutely loving the feel of his cock right where I wanted him.

He gripped the hot flesh of my hips, moving his body with me, his heated, ragged breaths against my neck.

"I can feel you, you know," he whispered. "Feel how wet you are."

I stilled, a little embarrassed. Was that a turn-on for him? Or was he grossed out?

He took my earlobe between his teeth, pulling then releasing it. "And it's so *fucking hot*."

Oh, thank God.

At those words, that Luke actually liked what I was doing, relief washed through me, and something else... pure lust. Grinding my hips even more, I wanted him so much. The night of my birthday had been amazing. But right now? I wanted him inside me. I wanted that massive cock of his deep in me, and I wanted to climax around him.

My movements became more and more

urgent, need consuming me, every cell in my body working toward one thing. Luke's hand on my hip tightened while his other hand moved across the top of my thigh.

"Please," I begged.

He knew exactly what I wanted, and his fingers edged inside my panties, teasing me at first. Wiggling my hips, I tried for more pressure, and Luke's low chuckle sounded by my ear.

"What do you want, Livs?"

"The same thing you want... your cock inside my pussy."

"*Jesus,*" he hissed.

And that was the end of his laughter. I ground my hips, his hard-on and his fingers so close to everything I needed so desperately. His finger finally connected with my clit, and we both made a noise, the feeling shaking me to my core.

He made lazy circles to the soundtrack of my shallow, breathy moans. "Oh, God," I whimpered.

I was so close to shattering. But it wasn't enough. I wanted to feel him. I *needed* to feel him. And the urgency of time hit me. We might not be alone out here forever.

"Luke. Wait."

"What?" he grumbled.

Reaching for his belt buckle, I made quick work of undoing his pants and zipper, and he quickly adjusted himself to free his dick. I might have salivated a little at the sight of all that hardness straining for *me*, to be inside *me*.

"I don't have a goddamn condom," he said, drawing my attention back to his face. "*Please* tell me you're on birth control."

"I'm on it," I answered, beyond relieved that I hadn't taken out my implant.

"Thank fuck."

He grabbed me again, and with one swift movement, he swept my drenched underwear to the side. My head turned, I watched as he held his hard cock, ready for me. I could hardly believe I was here, about to have sex with Luke. In public, no less.

My heart pounding, the blood rushing through my veins, I slowly lowered myself, his swollen tip nudging my entrance from behind. He rubbed himself back and forth, making me gasp when he reached my clit.

"Oh, God."

I couldn't take it any more. And apparently, neither could Luke. He lined himself up, and I sunk down, sitting on him, my ass to his hips. My breath hitched as he eased inside of me, filling me, stretching me.

"You're so damn tight," he groaned.

Speech eluded me, the only thing existing in this universe the feel of him. Wrapping his arms tightly around me, he began to flex his hips, every movement setting off a cascade of incredible sensations.

"Luke," I whispered, beginning to move with him, searching for that rhythm only we could find together.

"Does that—" he started but suddenly stopped.

The sound of laughter hit me, jarring me back to reality, that we were out in the open up here, having sex under the stars, where anyone on this boat could find us.

In the space of a heartbeat, Luke took off his suit jacket and threw it over our laps, covering our connected bodies. And then they appeared. Not just one couple, but person after person arrived at the top of the stairs, maybe the whole boatload of passengers.

I could hardly breathe at the panic shooting through me. Not to mention the immense amount of frustration that Luke and I hadn't been able to finish this insanity that we'd started.

The only hope I had was that they would go away soon.

But nope. More couples showed up, spreading out and taking over the entire space, not even realizing that a woman was sitting here bare-assed with a man inside her.

Luke's forehead hit my shoulder with a grunt. "I fucking hate people."

I couldn't help giggling. If I let my annoyance go, I could see the comedy in the situation. But something told me Luke didn't find it so funny.

Holding his coat in place, he slid out of me and we both adjusted ourselves as I looked around to make sure no one saw us. But everyone was taking in the scenery, and at least the darkness would hopefully hide us if anyone glanced our way.

With a sigh, I scooted next to him, and he took my hand in his, quiet, stewing probably.

While we sat there in misery, waiting for our blood to cool, it dawned on me that despite the simmering frustration, Luke was by far the best lover I'd ever had. During my *years* with Henry, he'd never caused that soul-deep sexual craving like Luke did so effortlessly.

And he'd certainly never been capable of touching me the way I wanted to be touched, and even worse, he hadn't even tried, which raised a question in my mind.

I reached my body up toward Luke's ear. "I have something I want to ask."

"Hmmm," he grunted.

I ignored his obvious irritation. I knew it wasn't aimed at me, just the blue balls talking. "So I never get the chills with you. Do you have to work really hard at that?"

He shrugged. "Honestly, I don't even think about it."

Despite our current, beyond awkward situation, a wistful sigh escaped me. Luke had something I never knew existed, something I'd been made to feel shameful about.

He had the magic touch.

TWENTY-SEVEN

Olivia

All I thought about after that night was Luke, Luke, and more Luke... Luke's smile, Luke's deep laugh, Luke's eyes lighting up, Luke's passionate grip on my arms, Luke inside me. Luke inside me.

I was positively bewitched by him. More than bewitched. But I still didn't want to admit it, didn't want to be under his spell, even though I clearly was, because I didn't know how he felt.

Was he attracted to me? Yes, he made that pretty obvious. But did he like me more than that? I had no clue. Maybe this was how he'd behaved with all the exes, and once he'd had his fill of them in the bedroom, then he just got bored and let their relationship die off.

Whatever happened, I'd be fine. Of course, I'd be fine. Maybe I was just in it for the amazing orgasms as well. Two could play that game, right?

"Ow!" Emily complained.

"Oh, sorry. My bad."

Whirling around, Emily grabbed the brush from my hand. "I'll do it myself."

And with that, she plowed through her hair, pulling out clumps and dumping them on the floor. Gritting my teeth, I left the room to finish getting ready, ignoring the curses coming from the living room.

My sister was going through a hard time, I reminded myself. She was scared about both her past and her future. And she was taking a big step today... in only a few minutes.

We planned to go out. Emily was officially leaving the walls of my apartment. Finally. Not for good or anything. Just to go for a walk around the Gaslamp area and grab an ice cream cone or something.

And after many moments of dragging things out—going to the bathroom, getting another sip of water, changing shoes—we finally made it out the door, Emily silent beside me. Glancing at her while we waited at a stoplight, I noticed her shoulders were practically to her ears with tension.

"See?" I said. "It's not so bad out here. Right?"

A car squealed around the corner, loud and annoying as it took off down the street. *Thanks, mister.*

"No. No. Not so bad," Emily agreed, her voice

unsteady.

Hey, at least she was trying. Putting my arm around her, I guided her to our favorite ice cream shop where we placed our orders and quickly went back outside to avoid the crowded interior. Right as Emily exited the door, she bumped into someone, toppling her double scoop of cookies and cream to the ground.

"Damn it!" With a fierce glare, she met the offending person's eyes. "*You*."

My heart stopped at the thought of Evan or the big bad men, and I quickly peered around Emily's body blocking the doorway to see Luke's friend Trevor.

Oh, dear, that was almost as bad as the henchmen. The day after my date with Luke, all Emily could talk about was how much she despised Trevor. I still didn't understand why, but I knew I needed to do something before this nice afternoon out took a terrible turn.

I squeezed past my sister to face a steely-eyed Trevor. "Hey, how ya doing?" I said, my voice a bit too cheery even to my own ears.

"I'm fine."

An awkward pause occurred as I waited for the usual follow-up question... for him to ask how we were doing. But he didn't.

How strange. When I'd met him before, he'd been so friendly. Even at the wedding that wasn't, most likely the worst day of his life so far, he'd smiled at me.

Staring at his face, I tried to discern why, and after a beat, I realized he was returning my sister's glare. So the feeling was mutual?

Shaking my head, I realized I couldn't dwell on it at the moment. "Emily, you go in and get another cone, and I'll clean this up."

She mumbled an annoyed reply that I ignored, and Trevor reached for the napkins in my hand. "I'll get it," he grunted.

In a flash, the two scoops went into the nearby trash can, and another uneasy silence passed while Trevor knelt down to wipe up the last remnants.

Emily returned to my side, already eating her fresh ice cream. "Let's go," she said, her eyes narrowed at Luke's friend.

What in the world was I caught between? Feeling the open hostility, all I wanted to do was escape, so I followed her, saying a quick goodbye to Trevor who didn't respond.

Needing to eat my ice cream fast so it didn't drip down my hand, I refrained from asking the many questions forming in my mind. But once my cone was in satisfactory condition, I couldn't hold back any longer. "What was all that about?" I asked while we slowly walked down the wide sidewalk.

"All what?"

I groaned. "Um, you know, all the animosity between you two. What exactly happened the other night?"

"Trevor's a misogynistic asshole," she answered with zero hesitation.

"Whoa. Wow. Okay. That's a pretty big accusation."

"It's not an accusation if it's the truth."

Stunned into silence, I kept working on my ice cream while Emily did the same. We turned the corner, narrowly avoiding a couple of skateboarders.

"I didn't tell you the whole story because you were in such a good mood and I didn't want to spoil it," Emily eventually admitted.

"That was thoughtful of you."

"I have my moments."

We both laughed, the tone lightening for a second before becoming cloudy again. "So tell me now."

Emily's eyes studied my face. "Well, you're still glowing, but I'm gonna tell you anyway."

I was glowing?

"So the three of us were hanging out in the living room, making small talk I guess, and Aiden asked me why I'd been staying with you." Emily paused to bite into her cone. "Even though I really didn't want to talk at all, I gave them the very short version. And you know what Trevor said?"

"What?"

"He said that it was *weak*—" Her tone turned glacial. "—that I'd bailed on Evan when the times got tough."

A loud gasp escaped me. "He did not."

"He sure did."

"What a dick!"

"Right?" Emily aggressively balled up her napkins and hurled them into a trash bin at a bus stop. "And then we argued and argued and argued about it. Would you believe he thought I should be trying to help Evan get through a *tough time*?"

"That is ridiculous. He's one-hundred percent dead wrong."

"He is *absolutely* wrong, and of course, I told him that. It's so obviously projection."

"It's totally projection. Did you say that to him?"

"I might have," she said sheepishly. "But you know what? If he can talk like that to me, well, I can give it right back."

"You tell him."

"And wow, he did not like that one little bit, saying if I wasn't loyal to the guy I was with that that said a lot about my personality and character."

My blood pressure began to rise. "Excuse me? You weren't even with the guy really. And also, you have to draw a line somewhere with every single person in your life. And if they cross that line, like—oh, I don't know—they have a severe gambling problem and pull you into some Las Vegas crime family drama, well, it might be time to pull the plug."

"Exactly! I'm not some disloyal cheater or something. I don't owe Evan anything. We were just fuck buddies. And obviously, Trevor's lumping me in with his ex-fiancée which is wrong on so many levels."

"It's so wrong."

She paused to look at me, and I spotted remorse in her eyes. "I might have crossed the line with Trevor, though, when I said I could see why his fiancée left him if he, um, had that kind of attitude."

"Oh, my," I muttered with a grimace.

Her expression mirrored my own with some added hand-wringing. "I know. I know." An obstinate look took over her face. "But I refuse to apologize."

I didn't know what to say to that. My only hope was that Trevor and Emily would hardly ever have to see each other in the future. I mean, why would they? Even if something crazy happened, like Luke and I getting married, that didn't mean my sister and his best friend would have to hang out. Except maybe a little at the wedding. Or at an engagement party. Or holidays maybe?

"Oh, look at that." Emily's voice cut into my meandering thoughts. "Foxxy's is hiring."

Glancing up, I noticed we had somehow traced the familiar path to one of our favorite clothing stores. Emily's finger pointed to the blinged-out sign in the window that they were looking for help.

I grabbed her shoulders, excitement pulsing through me at the possibility of Emily finally getting a job and moving out. "Yes. Yes. That would be perfect for you."

"Would it, though?"

"Of course it would. Think of the discount you'd get."

She sighed. "Besides paying minimum wage, which we both know isn't enough to support myself in this city, I'd always want to spend half my paycheck on clothes."

Unfortunately, she did have a point.

"And also," she continued, "we leave for Italy in a week. It's not like I can say, 'Oh, thanks for the job offer, but I can't start for a month.'"

My excitement began to diminish as I felt this opportunity slipping through our fingers. But I couldn't let it. Despite her previous anger at Trevor, or maybe because of it, this was the most alive I'd seen Emily act in weeks. I had to make the most of it.

"It can't hurt to try," I suggested. "You should check it out at least. And even if they're okay with you not starting for a month and you do get it, you don't have to keep working here forever. It could be a fun temporary job to have while you figure your life out. You know?"

Emily thought for a long moment, staring at the door as someone exited, the booming music spilling out to our spot on the sidewalk. "All right. You know what? I'm going to go for it."

And with that, she was off... much quicker than I would have expected for a girl who'd just combed her hair for the first time in weeks. And she looked pretty cute too. Thank goodness.

Not sure what to do with myself, I stood outside, finding a place to lean against the wall and watch people go by, my mind mulling over all the craziness in my life lately—this thing with Luke, Emily moving in, the upcoming trip to Italy, and now all the drama between my sister and Trevor, a topic I couldn't wait to discuss with Luke.

Before long, Emily came bursting out the door, a smile on her face.

"Did you get the job?" I asked hopefully.

"Kind of? They said to come in right away when I get back, and it should all be fine. They need several people."

"That's promising."

"It is. It's not the ideal job, for sure, but I need to get my ass off your couch. It's really uncomfortable."

The nudge I gave her wasn't gentle, and she laughed, her eyes filled with the old Emily's merriment. There was my sister! She was joking with me, and it filled my heart with relief that she appeared to be climbing back to her usual self.

"Seriously, though," Emily said, "I can't even tell you how much I appreciate all you've done for me lately. I don't know what I'd do without you."

"Aww. Well, you'd do the same for me. You *have*. Remember what a mess I was after Henry?"

She rolled her eyes. "How could I forget? I had to go to the froyo place every single night for like a whole month."

Oops, I'd conveniently forgotten all about that.

For the rest of the walk, we laughed and teased each other just like old times, Emily occasionally attempting to learn more about my "relationship" with Luke, or at least the juicy details.

But I couldn't tell her much. I didn't want to. What happened between Luke and me felt private—the steamy stuff, the talks, and especially the boyfriend lessons that had started the whole thing.

Sure, I'd told Nadia, but that had been in the beginning, before any feelings had ignited. Stupid, stupid feelings.

Quickly grabbing the mail, Emily and I headed upstairs as we chatted about what to do the rest of the afternoon and evening, debating whether to actually cook or order delivery instead. Not paying any attention, I opened an envelope and sliced into my finger.

"Ouch," I said.

Walking down our hallway, Emily glanced over at my paper cut. "Ew, why do those always hurt so much?"

"I have no idea," I mumbled, in a hurry to get

inside and take care of it.

Emily's loud gasp startled me, her arm flinging out in front of me to abruptly stop me. My eyes took in her expression first, her mouth agape, and I slowly turned my head to see that my apartment door was wide open.

"Did you—did you forget to lock it?" Emily asked.

"I don't think so." I pushed her arm away and tiptoed ahead, keeping a good distance from my door.

My eyes couldn't quite believe what was in front of me. Books littered the floor, couch cushions had been thrown to the ground, my cluttered coffee table completely cleared.

"My God," I whispered.

Emily clutched onto my arm, her expression dazed.

Wrapping my fingers around her wrist, I started to retrace my steps back down the hall. "We should go."

She didn't hesitate, and we rushed to the elevator where I punched the call button repeatedly. Part of me wanted to turn back and pound on Luke's door. Was he okay? I imagined him sprawled out on his floor, a pool of blood growing around his still body.

Stop it, crazy imagination!

My buzzing brain remembered he was out for the day. Thank goodness.

"Oh, God," Emily moaned, her eyes darting

between the empty hallway behind us and the elevator doors. "Fucking hurry."

"The stairs."

Rarely did I use the stairs, but I didn't hesitate today. We ran down the stairwell, our feet pounding on each step, making enough noise to wake the dead.

Belatedly, I wondered if the bad guys were in the stairwell. Weren't they always hiding out around the corner in every scary movie I'd ever seen?

I couldn't think about that right now. At least we could exit onto any floor. For some reason, it seemed safer than the elevator.

So we kept on going, Emily right on my heels as we raced down and busted through to the lobby, both of us panting. We ran up to the security guard at the front who stared at us with wide eyes.

"Someone's been in my apartment," I gasped. "And I don't know if they're still there."

His eyes narrowed. "Stay right here."

And he was off, reaching for his phone as he walked away with a determined stride, leaving Emily and I to stare after him, a million thoughts whirling around like a cyclone in my mind.

"See?" Emily said. "Look what happens when you leave your apartment."

TWENTY-EIGHT

Luke

I came home from an incredibly successful day, bursting to see Olivia and tell her all about my good news. When I walked into the lobby, I was shocked to find Olivia and Emily talking to a police officer.

What the hell?

Not sure whether to interrupt them or not, Olivia turned to catch my eye, quickly waving me over. As soon as I walked up, she threw her arms around me, burying her face in my chest.

"What's going on?" I asked.

"Evan broke into our apartment," Emily said. "Or I mean, *Olivia's* apartment."

For a moment, I was speechless, my gaze going to the policeman scribbling on his pad, still jotting down notes.

Another officer walked up, and Olivia turned to face her, although she kept her arm firmly around my waist. "We're all done," the officer said to Olivia. "Before you clean up, you should take more photos and notes about any damage so you can contact your insurance company. I'm assuming you have renter's insurance."

Olivia nodded.

"And until you get the lock fixed, you should find someplace else to stay... a hotel, a friend's."

I felt Olivia's shuddering breath against me. "Okay. We'll figure something out."

The woman offered a small smile and handed Olivia a card. "Don't hesitate to call if you need to, if either of you think of anything else or find anything."

Olivia let go of me to check out the card. "Thank you. Thanks for all your help."

"No problem. That's what we're here for."

And with that, they were off, the building's security guard coming over. "I'll get maintenance to work on your door immediately. You should be able to stay there tonight."

The silence that followed that statement spoke volumes. It was obvious to anyone paying attention that Emily and Olivia didn't want to stay there anytime soon.

I didn't know the particulars yet, but I did know enough, and I needed to take some action. "All right, Joe. Thank you."

With a serious nod, he went back to his post by the front door, making me wonder exactly how Evan had gotten into our building in the first place. But now was not the time to appease my curiosity.

Putting my arm back around Olivia, I turned her toward the elevator. "Come on. You're both coming upstairs with me and you can stay at my place. Okay?"

There was no argument from either of them. None. Zero. Two strong-willed girls who'd been knocked sideways by today's events.

A sudden burst of anger surged through me. Evan deserved a swift punch in the fucking face. Or more.

But again, I needed to keep calm for Olivia. For both of them. By extension, I cared for Emily now too. It was a strange feeling. Never in my life had I cared about the family of a "girlfriend." Now, however, Emily had crept under my skin, and I had this urge to make sure she was okay as well.

Our elevator ride was quiet, and somehow the sisters grew even more withdrawn as we walked down the hallway, a sense of dread permeating the still air. I found myself drawn to their door, my curiosity growing to a feverish level.

What exactly had Evan done? How much had he destroyed? And had he taken anything?

When we reached our apartments, part of me was disappointed to see that their door was shut. Mostly anyway. It didn't look like it was latched, and certainly, it wasn't locked.

As I keyed into my place, I said, "Don't worry.

If anyone else comes by, we'll hear them. But I'm sure it'll only be the maintenance guy."

Once we were inside with the door shut and locked, it was like a dam had been set free. They both made themselves comfortable in my living room and proceeded to talk and talk and talk, the words tumbling out, speaking over each other, only causing them to get louder. Apparently, the shock was over and now they were pissed.

And through it all, I got the gist of what had happened. Apparently, the police had scoured the security cameras and found that shortly after Emily and Olivia had left, Joe had left his post to visit the bathroom, and another resident in our building had held the door open for Evan, who was wearing dark clothes and a hoodie pulled up over his hair. Why that tenant hadn't thought that suspicious was beyond me.

Fortunately, nothing really valuable was missing, except for about fifty dollars that Olivia always kept on hand in her kitchen drawer, plus her old engagement ring that her ex had insisted she keep. She said she didn't care about it in the least and was grateful that her grandparents had always given her more sentimental, homemade gifts rather than any expensive heirlooms.

Olivia whipped out her phone to show me the pictures of the damage, not a cushion or book left alone, her bedroom violated also. What this one guy had accomplished in such a short time was unbelievable. All for fifty bucks and a stupid diamond. Absolutely disgusting.

The guy must have been desperate. And now, he had not only the Las Vegas thugs after him but also the police.

But he'd made his bed, and I was pissed as hell that he'd dragged my girl into *his* damn mess. He'd better hope that I'd never run into him.

Shoving my anger aside, I realized I needed to take charge of the situation and do what I could to help. And the most obvious problem was that Olivia and Emily didn't feel safe.

"You guys are welcome to stay here right up until you go to Italy... and when you get back too," I added. "And then we'll figure it all out."

Looks of relief spread on their faces. Sure, I'd do anything to help, but I had to admit, it'd be amazing to have Olivia right here. Yeah, across the hall wasn't that far away. But to have her in my own space, every day and all night? That'd be fucking awesome.

I insisted on ordering some Italian in for dinner, Emily and Olivia thanking me profusely. And soon after the food arrived, while we were sitting in the living room with our plates, there was a loud noise from the hallway, making Emily jump.

Hopping up, I crossed to the door, opening it swiftly, maybe not the wisest move. But it was only maintenance getting to work on Olivia's locks.

When they were done, the three of us decided

it was time to go over there and get a few things for their stay with me.

Shards of glass crunched under our shoes, and I couldn't believe the mess that'd been made. Everything was out of place, like a tornado had gone through, and anything that was fragile was broken on the floor. What kind of person did that? Evan needed to be caught.

Emily and Olivia moved quickly, clearly wanting to get the hell out of the apartment as soon as possible. The rest of the night, I did my best to take care of them, getting out the ice cream and making sure their wine glasses were always full while we watched mindless TV.

After some back and forth while trying to figure out where everyone would sleep, in the end it didn't even matter because Emily fell right asleep on my couch like she owned it. Olivia shot me a smile, slowly lifting her sister's feet to the side so she could move away from the couch. I watched as she grabbed a blanket and covered Emily.

She was so damn caring, it made my chest squeeze. Olivia always gave so much of herself, and something protective in me bloomed, wanting her to get back as much as she gave in this world. She didn't deserve any of this, and I found myself wanting to do anything possible to make her feel better.

When she turned and her eyes found mine, I held out a hand. "Come here," I whispered.

Her face spoke of vulnerability, doing nothing to ease the ache in my chest. Seeing her like this killed me.

Instead of waiting for her, I closed the distance between us, grabbing her hand and leading her to my bedroom. For a brief moment, I thought about trying to distract her by showing her *exactly* how much I cared about her. But in the end, I decided to follow her lead.

Once inside my room, I quietly closed the door behind us, my eyes on Olivia to see what she would do. She didn't even check out my belongings, her usual curiosity diminished. With a heavy sigh, she sunk down on the side of my bed. And that was my cue.

I sat down as well, behind her though, leaning against the headboard and pillows. When she looked back at me, I patted the empty space next to me and smiled. "Come on."

She didn't hesitate and my instincts told me Olivia could use some comforting. And I was right because she instantly snuggled up into my side, my arm coming around her as I kissed the top of her head, inhaling the delicious scent that was this beautiful girl in my bed.

"You doing all right?" I asked.

"Yeah, I guess." Her shoulders moved up and down as she sighed. "It's just so weird. You know?"

"Honestly, I don't know. I've never had anyone break into my place. Not even my car. So I can only imagine how awful it must feel."

"It *is* awful. It's such a terrible feeling. I know there are worse things that can happen in life. But it feels like such a violation. Someone was in my *home*, going through all my stuff, touching it, destroying it."

A shudder went through her body, and I pulled her in closer, wishing I could help somehow, do something. But what the hell could I do?

It's not like I could go after Evan. This wasn't some Hollywood movie where Olivia, Emily, and I could vigilante up and take down both Evan and the big bad criminals who were after him. God damn it, I hated this helpless feeling.

Olivia tilted her head up to look at me. "Are *you* okay?" she asked.

"Yeah, yeah. I just hate this whole thing, hate that it happened to you. I wish I could *do* something. I wish I could take it all away and make you feel better."

"You are though. Just you being here helps. You letting us stay with you makes me feel a million times better."

It didn't seem like much, but it was a start. "It's the least I can do."

With a small smile, she rested her head back against me, stretching her legs out next to mine, the ultimate distraction. "You know what? I don't think you need any more boyfriend lessons... if you ever needed them in the first place."

"So I've graduated?" I teased, happy to see this lighter side of her.

Her giggle set something free in my chest. "Yes. With flying colors."

"So summa cum laude?"

She nudged my foot with hers. "No. Magna cum laude."

"Ouch."

Again, her laugh warmed me as we played a little footsie on the bed, making my mind wander to that night on the harbor cruise. We'd been so fucking close. I'd thought about that moment countless times. Almost every single minute of the day, I replayed that nearly rapturous feeling of her sinking down on me, her long, loud exhale as I filled her.

And then the blue-ball agony of not being able to move, of being caught, of being forced to stop. In a flash, I'd gone from the upper echelons of heaven to the torturous depths of hell. Being the horny ass I was, I desperately wanted a repeat... but this time with no chance of interruption. Obviously.

"You know I'm joking, right?" Olivia broke into my thoughts. "I think I misjudged you from the start. You're not the asshole player I thought you were. You're truly an amazing man."

That struck me right in the center of my chest. "You think so?"

Her hand grasped mine, and she studied the way our fingers fit together. "Definitely." For a moment, she hesitated, and I sensed she had more on her mind that she wasn't telling me. So I squeezed her hand, hoping to prompt her. "I just think..." she finally said. "I just think you were with the wrong girls."

I couldn't help the grin on my face at her words, implying she was the right girl.

She kept her eyes on our joined hands. "I mean, not that there was anything wrong with *them*. And not that I'm—I'm—you know, the *right* one. That's not what I mean at all. Not that we're, um, you know, an item or anything, or like I'm your girlfriend or something," she quickly finished, uncharacteristically stumbling over her words.

Hold up. That was complete and utter bull. I didn't fuck around with just anyone. "You are absolutely my girlfriend."

She pulled away to glance up at me with wide eyes. "I am?"

"Hell, yeah. Unless, of course, you're still hung up on that Jim guy."

"Oh, my gosh," she scoffed, poking me in the ribs. "*Jared* and I are friends. And friends only. Plus, he hardly ever comes into the library anymore. He says he's too busy to read lately."

"Good." Thank fuck. "I know this started out as you doing your neighborly duty, but don't you agree that this has turned into something else entirely?"

"It kind of has."

"*Kind of?*" I repeated, my tone louder than

intended as I bumped her delicious thigh with mine. "Come on. What's a guy have to do to become your boyfriend? I've helped you and your sister countless times, brought over food, even cleaned your kitchen. *And* I took you on a dinner cruise which I came up with all by myself. Thank you very much. I've never even thought about doing something like that before."

"So acts of service plus a dinner cruise equals becoming my boyfriend?"

I laughed. "Yep. One-hundred percent."

"Okay. I'll have to write that down in my notes."

"What notes?"

"For the book I'm writing about this experience, of course," she said in a serious tone.

An awkward silence stretched out between us as her words whirled around in my head. A book about this? About *me*?

She busted out laughing, then clamped a hand over her mouth, looking toward the door. "You have to know I'm joking," she whispered.

The urge to tickle her until she screamed came over me, but I somehow resisted. God, I couldn't wait to be completely alone with her. Determined not to be overcome by my lust for Olivia again, I took a deep breath. Words. That's what I needed to focus on. Not her gorgeous legs touching mine. Not her warm bare skin. Not the side of her breast pushing into me.

Fuck.

"So," I said. *Come on, asshole. Think of something. Anything.* "So, uh, now that I'm your official boyfriend, why don't you tell me what *you* like, not what books and relationship experts say you should want. Tell me what you, Olivia Lindquist, want."

My girl didn't miss a beat. "Besides short fingernails and un-chapped lips?"

With a stuttering heart, I took a quick look at my nails. Thank God they were nice and short. And my lips were in good shape too.

She giggled. "Don't worry. You're summa cum laude on both."

"Well, good. I'm glad I passed that test." My heart calmed a bit. "And what else?"

That seemed to stump her for a long moment. "You know something that Henry used to do that drove me crazy? Whenever I was talking about a problem I was having, he'd always interrupt me and tell me what I should do to fix it."

"That bastard." But to be honest, I didn't see what the issue was there. Except for the interrupting part of course.

She squeezed my thigh and laughed. "Obviously, you don't see the big deal. But when I'm upset, you know what I want?"

"What do you want?"

"I want someone to *listen* to me. That's it. Just listen. Just empathize. I can usually come up with solutions on my own. But first, I need to talk it out. And Henry didn't ever give me the chance to do that."

"Did you tell him that?"

"I did. And it would just lead to an argument because he didn't understand why I didn't want his help."

What a tool. "Sounds like he was making it all about himself," I said.

"Exactly!"

"You two weren't meant to be."

"Nope. We sure weren't."

Not like us, I almost blurted out. But I stopped myself. We'd made more progress tonight than I'd ever dreamed of, and I didn't want to push it too much.

The air conditioning kicked in, and Olivia covered her legs with the edge of the comforter then settled back into my side, resting her head against me once more, the gesture so trusting, like she sought my touch as much as I did hers.

In silence, we cuddled up together, something I'd never really been into in past relationships. But I could hold Olivia all night. It felt right. It felt *good*.

A loud car drove by, the beat making its way into my room. Another car honked, reminding me of the life going on outside my window. I'd forgotten about everything else. Everything. It was always like that with Olivia. When I was with her, I thought about nothing but her. And when we were apart, she completely occupied my mind.

Once the sounds had passed, Olivia yawned, sliding farther down into the cushy pillows. "There's only one thing left on my boyfriend lessons list..." she mumbled. "But we don't have to do it if you don't want to."

"What is it?"

"I'd love to meet your family soon."

My heart sunk in a flash. The last thing I wanted to do was subject her to that. She'd probably hate me after meeting my mom and dad, and that would destroy me.

But as much as I loathed and dreaded the idea, some strange part of me also wanted Olivia to meet them. She needed to know me fully, know more about me, if this thing between us had any traction for a future.

Besides, maybe my parents would be all right. Maybe they'd changed over the years since I was a kid, and they'd be different somehow. I'd never brought any woman I'd dated to the house before, so I shouldn't be so sure it'd be a disaster.

It would also be a good distraction for Olivia, and maybe I could get Aiden and Trevor to come over again if Emily didn't want to be alone.

Olivia drifted off in my arms while I stewed about it all. I already had plans to meet with my dad this Saturday, right before this big Italy trip. Maybe I could see about turning it into a family dinner, get this thing over with, and move past this big relationship hurdle.

Yeah, that was what I'd do. Everything would

work out just fine. I was sure of it.

TWENTY-NINE

Olivia

I reached over to place a hand on Luke's knee. He was tense. More than tense. And that did nothing to ease my own nerves. Instead, it intensified everything. My anxiety swirled around in my empty stomach like the ocean churning before a storm.

Oh, this was all a huge mistake. Why had I said anything? Why had I insisted on meeting Luke's parents? I could have waited to open my big mouth until after Italy. But no. I'd wanted to get this over with before my trip, somehow thinking this would cement Luke and I together as a couple, something I could feel good about, something I could tell my family.

The only thing I could blame it on was the break-in. I hadn't been the same this past week since it'd happened. It was like my true self was sitting on the edge of my life watching this new Olivia who was a bumbling, nervous person, unsure of herself suddenly. A girl who didn't always think before she spoke, who didn't think things through.

Or maybe it was because I was so damn tired. I couldn't sleep lately. Emily either. My sleep was lighter than usual, the slightest noise waking me. So most nights, I ended up out in Luke's living room, sitting in his chair, my eyes darting back and forth between Luke's doorway and Emily tossing and turning on the couch, trying my best not to wake either of them.

We'd worked so hard to clean up the disaster across the hall, putting it all back together slowly, all the while hoping to hear something about Evan. But there was nothing. It was like he'd disappeared off the face of the earth, which wasn't exactly reassuring.

The Lindquist sisters were a mess right now. And it didn't help that Luke, my rock through this rough period, was now a tense shadow of himself at the moment.

Inhaling a long breath, I squeezed his leg, making the decision to not dwell in my head tonight. Whatever his relationship with his family, I would be there for him, like he'd been there for me.

It wasn't that I owed him that. I had quickly learned this relationship was different from my previous one. There was no 'you scratch my back, I'll scratch yours.' Anything I did for Luke was because I genuinely wanted to, and somehow I knew the same was true for him.

Luke drove through some side streets in the Clairemont neighborhood and pulled up to a well-kept two-story home. All I knew about his parents was that they were both in the tech industry and Luke was an only child.

When I'd asked questions about them and his childhood, he'd closed himself off a bit in a way I hadn't seen from him before. The only thing I could get out of him was that his mom and dad didn't get along most of the time, that they fought a lot. I knew there was a lot more to the story than that, and I was half-eager, half-dreading finding out.

Once he shut off the engine, Luke turned toward me, slightly pale with sweat beading on his brow. "You ready?"

Now, I was truly concerned. Where was my normal, cheerful Luke? "I guess?"

The smile he gave me didn't reach his eyes. "I think it'll be fine."

I didn't miss his lack of confidence. "You think?"

He rubbed his hands against his knees, facing forward. "I've never brought anyone home to meet my parents. Not since..."

"Not since?" I prompted when he paused.

Shaking his head, he turned to me once more. "You know what? That was a long time ago. And my parents are super excited to meet you. This is going to be great. Really."

My mind buzzed with worry over whatever it was he didn't want to tell me. *Had* he brought someone else to meet his mom and dad before? The words he'd said made no sense. I didn't have time to prod him further because he was already out of the car, crossing over to my side to help me out.

Clutching the bouquet of flowers in one hand, I grabbed onto his free hand with the other, ignoring the unusual feel of our sweaty palms rubbing together. Why did it have to be so hot today on top of everything else?

Together, we walked up the pathway, beautiful blooms on both sides greeting us. Someone was clearly into gardening and had a green thumb.

His parents met us at the door, both of them wearing bright smiles. They looked so nice. What on earth did Luke have to worry about?

As his mom graciously ushered us in, exclaiming over the flowers, I urged myself to relax. And even more so when we all sat down in the elegantly decorated living room, where a tray of hors d'oeuvres rested on a coffee table.

All eyes focused on me, and a new flutter of nerves settled in the pit of my stomach, but I knew I was decent at this stuff. Parents had always liked me. I was used to speaking at work a lot, so I could put on that customer service shield and make small talk with the best of them. After that mental pep talk, the questions began.

"So," Mrs. Waller said, "Luke's never brought home a girlfriend before."

I glanced at the man beside me, whose arm flexed against mine, but quickly returned my attention back to Mrs. Waller. For some reason, whenever I looked at Luke, his obvious tension seeped into me, making me more than anxious.

Putting on my best smile, I squeezed Luke's knee and answered, "Well, I feel very honored. Thanks so much for having me."

Luke's dad positively beamed as did his mom. "So Luke mentioned that you're a librarian," Mr. Waller said.

Here we go. And off I went, gushing about my job, omitting some of the things that occurred in a downtown library like the occasional needles found in the bathrooms or the people who used our sinks to wash themselves. Oh, and also, I didn't mention my judgy boss Nikki or my love of romance books. It was best to stick with the positives, I decided.

And once we moved to the table for dinner, I took the opportunity to ask them questions—about their jobs as well, their family, how long they'd been married, and anything else I could think of to keep the conversation flowing.

Luke was oddly quiet, and I grew more and more worried about him with every passing second. I was somehow carrying this entire dinner party on my back with absolutely nothing from him except a weird blank look on his face, completely out of character for him. He barely interacted with his parents at all.

He shoved around the food on his plate with his fork, hardly eating, drinking entirely too much wine. It was almost like he had shut himself down, or he'd escaped to a safe place inside his head, making me nauseous with concern as I wondered exactly why.

It was also exhausting to be the sole focus and to keep the conversation from stalling, and I grasped at anything I could think of to discuss, including gardening, hobbies, and the latest books that were popular, but I was swiftly running out of topics.

The chicken I'd just eaten gurgled around in my stomach. Oh, God, this was moving into downright painful territory, making me regret this entire idea even more.

As the minutes dragged on and we finally started our dessert, I couldn't wait to be alone with Luke again to talk to him, to drag everything out of him if I had to. Once we got in the car, well, I'd—

The loud clatter of a fork falling onto a plate startled me. Glancing up, I saw Mrs. Waller exchange a glare with Mr. Waller. Looking at Luke, I tried to figure out what was happening, but he wouldn't meet my eyes.

"Could you just drop it, Rena?" Mr. Waller said under his breath which did nothing to stop every single person in the room from hearing it.

"*You* drop it," she hissed back.

In disbelief at this strange turn of events, I tried to catch Luke's attention again. But it was like I wasn't even there, sitting right next to him.

"This time I'm really done," Mr. Waller barked out.

"No. *I'm* the one who's done," she said just as loudly. "And in front of a *guest* too."

What on earth was this all about?

A loud screeching sound interrupted the tension-filled silence as Luke's dad pushed his chair away from the table. He stomped into the kitchen, his wife following with a deathly glare splashed on her face.

My heart pounding, my eyes wide, I looked to Luke once more. "What just happened?" I whispered to him even though he was staring blankly at the empty doorway, his face pale and his entire body coiled with stress.

But there was no need for me to try to keep quiet because no one could hear me over the racket that started up only a few feet away.

"You're such an asshole," Mrs. Waller shouted over the sound of pots and pans banging.

"*I'm* the asshole? How am I the asshole? You're the one who started this whole thing," Mr. Waller shot back.

"What are they arguing about?" I tried again to get Luke's attention. "What happened? Did I do something?"

But again, he was silent, completely

withdrawn from me.

In the grand totality of life and the billions that had come before me and would come after me, what occurred around this dining room table in the middle of San Diego was nothing. It was insignificant. Truly.

However, in reality, to me, it was the exact opposite. My tiny world imploded, confusion, fear, and utter anxiety taking over every cell in my body.

But one thing I did know? I needed to get out of here. We both did.

As if coming back to life, Luke suddenly moved, making the same motion his dad had seconds before, pushing his chair back and grabbing my hand. "Come on. It's time to go."

THIRTY

Luke

I couldn't even look at her as I dragged her toward the front door.

"Luke... wait," she pleaded with a tug at my arm. "Shouldn't we say goodb—"

"No. We're leaving."

Damn it all to hell. This was my life. This was who I was. Who I'd been suppressing from Olivia, from myself, from everyone really. Trying to be the good guy, someone who was worthy of her.

But I'd never be. Because this was where I came from. This was in my blood, my DNA.

What the fuck had I ever been thinking to bring her here?

Dropping her hand, I opened the passenger door for her, refusing to look at her. I knew what I'd see in those big brown eyes. Confusion. Disappointment. Condemnation.

Without a word, I moved to the other side,

opened my door and sat behind the wheel, shutting my door behind me.

The one time I'd dared to look at her face during their stupid blow-out, it'd been impossible to miss the horror written all over her expression. And in that second I knew this thing between us could never work.

I started the car and took off, totally in my head, trying to work out the details of what I should do.

"Are you okay to drive?" Olivia's quiet voice broke into my thoughts.

"Yeah, I'm fine."

Of course, I knew I should say more to Olivia... be a man and try to reassure her. Suck it up. Man up. Not feel any pain. Not think about my childhood. Shove it down. Never express emotion. And God forbid, never cry.

But I couldn't just yet.

I didn't know what pissed me off more—my parents not being able to control themselves for one fucking night or the fact that I'd epically screwed up by pulling Olivia into this ugly mess.

Leaving the quiet neighborhood streets behind, I pulled onto Clairemont Drive, gripping the steering wheel hard, forcing myself not to take off down the road like a raging maniac.

That self-destructive streak inside me that I thought I'd beaten came back with a roar. I wanted to ruin everything in my vicinity. Life sucked. Love sucked. And I didn't want to be here anymore.

"So are we going to talk about what just happened?" Olivia suddenly said.

I clamped my lips shut, at least self-aware enough to know that nothing good could come out of my mouth right now.

"Please..."

Glancing at her, I could see her eyes welling up with tears.

Shit.

Feeling like the lowest of scum, I spotted an empty church parking lot and made a quick right, driving to the far end that overlooked the bay in the distance, the setting sun nearly blinding me as I parked.

Despite rolling down the windows, the world seemed to close in on me, the intensity of Olivia's stare burning like a laser into the side of my face. Looking straight ahead seemed easier, anything to avoid the hurt I'd see in her eyes.

"I don't even know what to say," Olivia began.

I didn't either. Still watching the water, I wished I could be there at this moment. Anywhere but here, stuck in this awful limbo with the only woman I'd ever really cared about.

The silence dragged out between us, nothing and nobody around to break it. Except the two of us.

I had to do it, just get it over with and face the truth about us before we got any deeper. "I'm so sorry that happened, so damn sorry. It makes it painfully obvious that you deserve better than this, better than me."

"What? What are you talking about?"

The experience whirled around relentlessly in my head, stirring up a tornado of feelings I thought I'd moved past. "I suck as a boyfriend. And no lessons are ever going to change that."

Dead silence. "You absolutely do *not* suck as a boyfriend. You have got to be joking right now."

At the frustration in her voice, I took off my seatbelt and finally turned to face her, a whole heap of emotions evident in her expression, her cheeks a splotchy pink. Just the sight of her made my chest hurt.

"I wish I was joking," I said.

"Oh, no, no, no." Olivia stared me down through determined eyes. "I'm not going to listen to any of this you-deserve-better-than-me crap."

She somehow perfectly mimicked my voice when she said it too. The absurdity of it all nearly made me laugh, but the painful lump in my throat stopped me. And the tear making a slow trail down Olivia's cheek squelched it also.

"It's true though," I argued. "You didn't deserve to see that. *This is who I am*. And you're... you're better than that. I mean, look at you." I heaved out a sigh. She'd never get it. Really. Her family was perfect. She'd been raised in a cotton candy, Disneyland world. "You don't understand."

She shook her head. "Explain it then. We need to talk about it, get it all out in the open."

As torturous as it was, she was right and I owed her that at least. "Well, now that you've met my family, you can see that your perfect parents are up here—" I raised one hand then lowered the other. "—and my terrible parents are down here."

Her face fell, and for some reason, I felt the need to continue, to really dig into the differences between us.

"You have too much lightness in you. And I have too much darkness. I can't let you see the awful parts of me because..." I struggled to find the right words. "...because you'll hate me and grow to resent me. I'll drag you down, and you'll regret it someday. You'll look back and wonder why you wasted months, maybe years, with me."

She twisted her body in her seat to fully face me. "You think I have no darkness in me? We all have darkness. We're all crazy in some way. I've never met a single *normal* person. I thought Henry was totally, completely normal. Well, guess what? He wasn't in the end. He was a coward who couldn't communicate that he was unhappy."

"Exactly." Her words only reinforced my point. "And now, don't you regret spending all those years with him?"

"That's not what I meant at all." With a ragged sigh, she rubbed her forehead. "And you think you suck at being a boyfriend, well, maybe I suck at being a girlfriend. I mean, what do I know about anything? I'm terrible at relationships. I couldn't even keep the interest of my fiancé. He—he called me boring. And he wasn't wrong."

"That's not true. You are *not* boring. You're incredible, Livs." I shook my head, destroyed that I was bringing her down too, the exact opposite of what I'd ever want. "You are absolutely incredible. That's indisputable. And it's not what this is about even."

"Then what *is* it about?"

Releasing a heavy sigh, I looked back at the bay. "I don't even know anymore. I just feel like the shittiest human being to ever walk the earth."

"Because of your parents? Or because of me?"

"Not because of you. Never because of you." A pang of regret settled deep in my chest. "Nothing to do with you at all. It's all me. One-hundred percent."

There was a long silence, the only sound some seagulls in the distance and the sounds of our breathing. Any remnants of anger left my body, now leaving me defeated, Olivia's downcast expression matching the way I felt.

"Have they always been like that? Your parents?" Olivia asked. "I mean, what even happened? I'm still so confused."

"I have no idea. It was probably a continuation of something they were arguing about before. That's what it usually is—one very long, never-ending argument. They have the most toxic relationship I've ever seen."

"And they were like that when you were a kid?"

"Yep. Always fighting," I admitted, unsure of how much to say. "Every damn day. Every damn minute."

"Oh, my God. That's awful."

The expression in her eyes was heartbreaking, like she truly cared about what I'd gone through as a child. With her empathy, a dam broke in me, and I suddenly felt the need to confide everything to her, something I hadn't done since I'd met with a therapist in my twenties.

"I couldn't have any friends over. I made that mistake once with Aiden. And I never did it again. We were maybe eight, sitting around the dinner table, and like what just happened, they had a major fight, and they ended up in the kitchen, plates being thrown. Aiden and I hid out in my room the rest of the night, and afterwards, Aiden was so freaked out he wouldn't even talk to me at school for a while."

She sniffled and wiped her nose with the back of her hand. "That's so sad."

"I hated it. I hated them. I hated home." I swallowed hard against that stupid lump. "I still do."

"Then why did we even go? Why didn't you just tell me all of this?"

"Because they always apologize to me and promise me they'll be better. So I thought maybe they could do it. I thought things would be different. With you." I'd been a goddamn idiot to think that they would ever change. "And I didn't want to tell you the extent of it because I wanted you to like me."

"I would never think less of you because of your parents' issues. Never." Her eyes were pleading with me. "And please let me see the real you that you're hiding. Let *me* decide if I can handle it. That's *my* decision. Not yours."

"You sure about that?"

"Yes, I'm sure. If we can't be real with each other, then... then... I don't know." Her hands fluttered in her lap. "Just tell me. Be honest. Be real. *Please*."

Something inside me compelled me to speak, maybe it was her words, maybe it was how at ease I usually felt around her. "Well, the truth is sometimes I can get really, really depressed and hate life... hate myself... hate everyone."

Her stare didn't waver. "Okay. So can I."

I scoffed. "*You* hate everyone? I don't believe it."

"Yes, absolutely, I can. People suck. Try working in customer service for one day, and you'll feel that."

"I don't need to work in customer service to feel that."

A small smile formed on her face. "I suppose you're right." Her smile disappeared as she fiddled with her bracelet. "And you know what? It really upsets me that you think I have no darkness. It's like... it's like you've put me on some pedestal where I'm perfect and think I'm better than you. And that's just not true."

I was the absolute worst. "I'm sorry about that. Just this whole thing is..." I shook my head. "It's brought up a lot of things I thought I'd worked through. I'm not myself right now. I'm not even sure what I'm saying or what I'm *trying* to say."

She paused for a moment, pursing her lips. "Maybe it's because you're hurting."

"You're right. You're absolutely right. See? Tell me how you're not perfect in every way."

"I am so not perfect. I can name a hundred things that are wrong with me."

"Like what?" I challenged.

"Well, for one, I'm a people pleaser to the point of completely losing myself." Her eyes turned to the water as she frowned. "I'm scared of my boss. I let Henry walk all over me. And I'm terrified to even enter my own home now."

Seeing her vulnerable like this struck a chord deep inside me. "Of course you're terrified to be in your apartment. That's totally and completely normal after what happened. And as far as the rest of it, maybe you used to be like that with Henry, but you haven't been like that with me at all. Look at you just a minute ago, demanding that we talk."

Her lips curved into a smile again. "That's true."

"And with Nikki, she *is* scary. So it's not just you."

"How do you know? You've never met her."

I scowled at the idea. "And I don't *want* to meet her. But from what you've said and the fact that Nadia feels the same way, I think it's a pretty safe bet to say the woman is intimidating to just about everyone."

She thought for a long moment, not saying anything, and something she'd said before dawned on me.

"Oh, shit," I muttered. "Did I do the Henry thing of trying to fix it and not let you vent?"

"No. No, that was different. You're just reassuring me that I'm not a total waste of space."

"Hey, don't talk about yourself like that." I really was dragging her down, just like I'd been afraid of. "This night was so fucked up. I'm so sorry."

"It's okay. It really is." Her phone made a noise, but she ignored it, instead biting her lip, deep in thought. "What I don't get is why your parents are even together anymore."

Good fucking question, something I'd been asking myself since I learned what the word divorce meant. "God only knows. It makes no sense. But I think in some warped, toxic, codependent way they must need each other. And it's not that either one of them is worse than the other. They're both awful. Believe me, I've heard enough of their fights to know they both give and get equally."

"No wonder you've never had a girlfriend over before."

"Yeah, after that one time with Aiden, I never had anyone over. Not a single friend."

"That's so unbelievably rotten. I can't even imagine having to worry about that as a kid. And all your life really." She tilted her head, her eyes studying my face. "Have you ever talked to them about it, you know, confronted them?"

I sighed heavily. "Yeah. Several times as an adult. It's all so messed up. Individually, they're fine. And in recent years, that's the only way I'll hang out with them is one at a time. And that's what I should have done with you. Just introduced you to each one separately."

"Hindsight's always twenty-twenty, though." She took a second to adjust her glasses, her mouth opening and closing a few times like she had something she wanted to ask. "Have you ever thought about cutting them out of your life completely?"

Ah, the biggest question of all, something I'd contemplated myself many times. "I have. Definitely. All through my twenties, I hardly ever saw them, but then my dad had a health scare a few years ago. It ended up being nothing major, but it made me realize I couldn't do that. So that's when I came up with the idea of seeing them each alone. Still not very often. But at least it's on a level I can live with, a balance where I'm not traumatizing myself and I'm not cutting them off. You know?"

For the first time since this disastrous night had begun, Olivia truly smiled. That beautiful smile I increasingly found myself living for. "That's pretty amazing. You do realize that, don't you?"

"Realize what?"

"That you figured that out... a way you could make it work for you."

That smile was downright contagious. "That's a very positive way to look at it. I'm just trying my best to survive a dysfunctional family situation."

"You are. You really are." Her hand landed on my knee and she squeezed before returning it to her own lap. "And for what it's worth, I think every family is dysfunctional in some way."

I arched a brow at her. "I highly doubt yours is."

"Oh, yes, we are."

"How?" I challenged.

"My mom knows everything. I mean, *everything*. And my dad just kind of goes along. Actually, all of us do."

I had no idea what to say to that. It didn't seem that bad to me.

"I know that sounds pretty mild compared to your family and what lots of other people go through," she said as if reading the expression on my face. "And it *is* mild. But it still weighs on me sometimes. And it shaped me into who I am today. I really think it's part of why I am the way I am. And Emily too."

"I get what you're saying." I truly did. "And I'm sorry to hear that."

"Thanks." She shuffled a bit in her seat before continuing. "I think everyone has *something* that they're dealing with. Life has a way of knocking us all down along the way."

She had a point, but I hated the thought that I'd been part of anything that had "knocked" her down.

Leaning forward, I grabbed her hand. "Livs, I'm so sorry about tonight. So sorry I didn't think it through more beforehand and that I brought you into this situation to begin with."

She thought for a moment. "It's all right," she said. "I get it. I understand."

A relieved breath escaped me.

Olivia's phone rang, and she rolled her eyes as she glanced at the screen. "Speaking of my mom." Her eyes darted to my face. "I should probably get it. I'm sure it's something about the trip."

"Yeah, yeah. Of course."

Staring at the water as she answered, I had no idea how to feel. Sure, Olivia seemed okay with everything and even said she understood. But the thing we needed most was time... more time together to put this behind us and move past the first hurdle in our relationship. And with Olivia leaving tomorrow for three whole weeks, we wouldn't get that much-needed time.

As I realized this conversation with her mom could last a while, I decided to start the car and drive us back home where I was sure Emily would be up and waiting for us, all excited about this trip.

Depressed as hell about how this night had turned out, the only thing I could do was vow to make some changes in my life and count down the days until Olivia returned back home.

THIRTY-ONE

Olivia

Italy was beautiful. Of course, it was beautiful. And Tuscany? It was surreal, like a stunning painting come to life. But the rolling hills dotted with vineyards, the picturesque medieval towns, and the ridiculously delicious food were totally lost on me.

Luke had stolen my brain. All I could think about was him. That last night I'd been with him swirled around endlessly in my head, leaving a sour taste in my mouth. The fact that we'd left things sort of unfinished and unresolved between us truly weighed me down. And the idea of Luke hurting and stewing about his parents? Absolutely heart-breaking.

I tried my best to hide my worries and concerns, because this trip was about my family, about the amazing life my grandparents had built and their fifty-five years together. I couldn't let my personal stuff get in the way and overshadow such a monumental celebration. So I kept quiet about it, and Emily did the same.

When Luke and I had returned home from that awful dinner, Emily and I had stayed up late into the night, packing and discussing all the craziness of our lives while Luke had left us alone, disappearing into his bedroom to give us privacy. And my sister and I had decided to continue keeping almost everything to ourselves, choosing not to discuss Evan, the break-in, or any of our drama during this vacation.

Our parents would freak most likely, and the last thing we both wanted was to upset them or the rest of our extended family. This was an event long in the making that was supposed to be a joyous occasion, and we wanted to do our best to keep it that way.

Looking at my mom laughing and talking to her parents, the Chianti flowing during yet another perfect dinner at the villa my grandparents had rented, I couldn't help but feel a burst of love for her. I'd complained about her a little to Luke, and I felt terrible about it now.

Of course, she could be a little overbearing at times. But that was part of who she was. She was also warm, kind, caring, and thoughtful, always wanting the absolute best for every single person surrounding her.

We all had our flaws. I certainly had mine. Emily had hers. I supposed even my sweet little grandma had hers. The thought made me smile. I was pretty sure my grandpa had a permanent bruise on his upper arm where she always poked him with her surprisingly strong finger whenever she got excited or worked up about something.

I drank my share of wine under the lights that brightened up our outdoor dining area, but it did nothing to numb the relentless thoughts in my mind. Instead, it only fueled the feelings, making them stronger. During the last several days, I'd snuck away a few times to call Luke, but he hadn't answered.

The nine-hour time difference didn't help. Late at night for me was the middle of the day for him. It should have worked. But most nights here were absolutely magical, and I didn't want to skip out too much on my family gathering in the rustic courtyard, my cousin strumming the guitar, everyone laughing and talking under the starlight while my dad made sure no glass went empty.

I knew these were once-in-a-lifetime memories that would never be experienced again. None of us were getting any younger, certainly not my adorable grandparents. I'd already lost my grandma on my other side and knew how much that hurt.

Staring off in the distance at some sparkling

lights, a small village filled with medieval towers and red tile roofs that we'd visited a few days ago, I jumped when someone poked me in the shoulder.

"So who's the boy?" my grandma said beside me while pulling up a chair. I tried to help her but she waved me off.

"What boy?" I asked weakly as I sat back down.

She gave me a sharp look, making us both giggle. After all, I could trace my love of reading back to my grandma, in particular her huge stash of romance novels with broken spines and worn pages that she'd read over and over. It was hard to hide anything to do with love from her.

"Okay," I admitted. "There is a boy. A man. He's in his thirties actually."

"That's still a boy." She shot my grandpa a faux glare. "I'm not sure men ever catch up to women in maturity."

Our laughter attracted Emily, who pulled up her own chair. "What's so funny?" she asked.

"We're talking about boys," my grandma said.

Emily gave me a worried look. "Oh, about Luke, right?"

"Luke." My grandma pounced on the name. "I like it. Nice name. Is he handsome?"

"Exceedingly handsome," Emily answered for me.

"And what about in the sack? Is he any good?"

I covered my giggles with my hand, meeting Emily's eyes. We both stole a glance at our mom, who was busy talking to her brother. Thank goodness. As far as our parents knew, we were both virgins. Well, they had to know otherwise. But in our family, we had a "don't ask, don't tell" agreement. Not that we'd ever talked about it. It was just the way it was because it was beyond awkward.

"Well?" my grandma prodded.

I sighed. "He's like a dream. The absolute best." At least what I'd experienced so far, but I didn't really want to go into the details.

My grandmother nodded. "And is he nice to you? Does he treat you well?"

"He does."

"He gave her a lamp," Emily interjected. "For her living room because he was worried about her reading in the dim light."

Thank goodness the lamp had remained unscathed during the break-in.

"Oh, he sure sounds like a keeper," my grandma said. "So what's the problem then?"

After a moment of hesitation, I decided to tell her all about that awful dinner with his parents, something I hadn't even fully told Emily.

Did I absolutely despise talking about it? Yes, of course. Did I hate to bring up toxic people to my sweet grandma? One-hundred percent yes. But I also knew she wouldn't stop asking until I told her. So I did, the entire sordid tale, including the terrible argument we'd witnessed and every detail of our discussion in the car afterwards.

When I finished, I had no clue what her response would be, and it took her a moment of thinking before she finally spoke. Her hand went around my forearm as I looked into her blue eyes, bright as ever, wrinkles crinkling the edges.

"You know what I think?" she asked.

"What?" Emily and I said in unison.

"I think he's a keeper. He communicated with you. I know it took a bit of pushing from you at first. But he told you all of it and confided in you. And that's very, very important, a foundation that every successful relationship must have."

I hadn't thought about it like that, appreciating how fully he'd opened up to me.

"Do you know how we made it for so long?" My grandma nodded her head toward my grandpa. "By talking all the time. And despite what you think, it hasn't just been me talking. Believe it or not, when your grandpa and I are alone, he's quite chatty. And even though we've each changed a million times since we first met, we grew together because we talked about absolutely everything."

While she paused to take a drink, I watched my grandpa, who sat quietly listening to the conversations around him, and tried to imagine him being chatty.

"It was tough," my grandma continued, "especially when your mom and uncles were little. We were both so exhausted all the time with barely a minute for each other. But late at night, when the house was quiet, we'd talk in bed, discuss anything we had on our minds."

I envisioned the two of them in their small bed that they'd shared forever, whispering in the darkness.

She cleared her throat. "If you have time for a date night, that's great, or a roll in the hay too. But even more important, in my opinion, is communication. That's the number one thing. *Respectful* communication," she added. "Don't ever let any man, any person, call you names or talk down to you."

Emily and I both nodded obediently at the fierce expression on her face.

"If he does, kick him in the nuts and get out of their fast."

And now, we both giggled because my grandma acted out the motions along with her words. Poor soul who ever dared to mess with her.

"You hear me, girls? I mean it."

I stifled my laughter to answer, "Yes, yes, definitely."

She nodded emphatically. "Now what else is bothering you?"

Glancing around at my extended family—aunts, uncles and cousins, plus a few of their little kids—I realized the other big thing. Luke's mom and dad. "I'm worried about his parents, like how that would affect any future we might have."

"Honey, every family has its issues... even ours. We're not perfect despite this beautiful image right here." She waved her hand at the picturesque tableau in front of us, lights strung above us highlighting the glowing faces set against the rustic old building. "Some have it worse than others, though. I'll grant you that."

In my mind, I pictured Luke's parents shouting at each other.

"Poor kid that he had to grow up with that." She shook her head. "Some people think it's better to stay together for the kids, but it's really not. And who knows what their deal is because they're still together even though Luke's been out of the house for a long time."

"I have no idea."

She stared into the distance thoughtfully. "The important thing is how he handles it. I think he was caught off guard, being optimistic that they'd be different in front of you, and then, when all hell broke loose, all those childhood feelings came rushing back."

My grandma hadn't studied psychology like her daughter, my mom, but she'd certainly been an astute observer of life around her.

"And again," she continued, "it's all about communication. He needs to be willing to keep discussing it with you until, together, you come up with a solution that works for both of you because when you marry, you marry each other's family too. And if you have kids, that just complicates everything."

"Oh, boy." I sighed as she gave me a sympathetic look while patting my hand.

"I doubt you remember your grandpa's mom. She died when you were a toddler. But that woman..." My grandma rolled her eyes. "She was a handful, so critical of me, like I wasn't good enough for her precious oldest son."

"Really?" This was certainly family gossip that I'd never heard about.

"Oh, yes. She criticized everything at first—the way I made my meatloaf, any little speck of dust in our living room, the way I dressed. But you know what? Your grandpa over there," she stared at him a long moment, "he stepped in to stop her. He actually said, 'She is my *wife* and I won't let you treat her this way.'"

Pride blossomed in my chest. My grandpa was the man.

"See? We all have our drama," she went on. "And after that, she clamped her mouth shut. Oh, I could tell she wanted to say stuff, and we were never close, but we made it work somehow. And that's what I think you need to do with Luke... if you have a future with this young man. And something tells me you do."

With her words, hope filled me. So we'd had a bump in the road, our first bump, a pretty significant one. But with some time together, some more time talking it out, I suddenly felt confident we could create a bright future for ourselves.

THIRTY-TWO

Luke

"Damn it," I muttered after hitting my thumb with the hammer. Again.

So I wasn't the most handy guy. But I wanted to renovate this place with my own hands, complete with my own blood, sweat, and tears. Or whatever that phrase was.

But once again, thoughts of Olivia distracted me. She consumed me. That last night with her rang around in my mind like a song on an infinite loop, the awful memories it'd brought up, the terrible thoughts in my head, like I'd returned to that godawful place called childhood.

I knew I couldn't rely on anyone else for my own happiness, and I'd done the hard work of trying to crawl out of the miserable hole that had contained my terrible roots. It'd taken me years... years of therapy and introspection.

But for once in my life, another person made

life not just bearable but actually fun. I hadn't known that was possible until that fateful night when Olivia had asked me to walk her home and offered to share her ice cream with me.

Everything I wanted in life was so close to me yet frustratingly just out of reach. I had been on the cusp of something I'd never dared even dream about—love, real actual love. And it killed me that because of that night, everything felt so uncertain right now.

"Dude, why the big sigh?" Aiden suddenly said from beside me. "I know you're having issues, but this right here?" He pointed toward the kitchen. "This is huge. *Huge*. Like life-changing huge."

Shaking my head, I tried to clear away the negativity swirling around in the old brain. "You're right, man. This *is* huge."

Aiden stared at me. "Nice enthusiasm there, bro."

The truth was as excited as I was about this whole endeavor, it meant nothing without *her*. But Aiden, who only did casual hook-ups, wouldn't understand that. "Sorry."

He turned back to his current job of staining the reclaimed wood for the bar. "Have you talked to her lately?"

I let out a breath. "A little. Not as much as I'd like."

"Why not?"

I shrugged. "I don't want to interrupt her family time with my bullshit. Like she wants to be in Italy, having the time of her life, and think about *my* fucking parents."

Aiden dipped his brush in the stain, quickly removing the excess. "Yeah, that makes sense. I get it. But she won't be gone forever, and then you can deal with this thing."

He had a point. After putting the hammer down, I looked around, trying to decide what to do next. Lay down painter's tape or sand one of the barstools. Deciding against both, I took a seat at the bar.

Aiden turned to me, a smirk on his face. "Lazy ass."

"Hey, I'm taking a break. I got started way earlier than you, just like every day."

He rolled his eyes. "Well, I stay later every day."

I couldn't help laughing before taking a swig of my water. Aiden was even more of a night owl than I was. While he returned to focusing on his task, a long silence stretched out between us, the only sound the brush moving back and forth plus the occasional car driving past outside the open front door.

Something else was on my mind, and I wasn't sure exactly how to bring it up to Aiden. We'd obviously been friends forever and discussed just about every topic under the sun... except one.

That awful night he'd spent at my house as a kid.

Maybe he hadn't thought about it in a long

time. I certainly hadn't. It'd been something forgotten in the many years since. But with recent events, it was once again at the forefront of my mind, like it had just happened yesterday. And something inside me felt horrible that Aiden had experienced that as a young child too. All because of me.

I exhaled deeply, determined to bring it up somehow in the hopes of putting the past behind me and moving into a new future... with Olivia, with my friends, with my life path.

"So, hey, man, I wanted to apologize for something," I finally managed to get out.

That certainly caught his attention, and he paused to glance at me, brows together. "What's that?"

I looked away, his eyes too intense. "I want to tell you I'm sorry for what happened when we were kids... you know, that time when you came over to my house."

A beat of silence passed, and I could practically hear the wheels turning in Aiden's brain. "Oh, right. That time when your parents went nuts in the kitchen?"

The casualness of his tone drew my curiosity enough to face him. "Yeah, that time. That was the only time."

Aiden sighed, rubbing the scruff of his short beard with his free hand. "Nah, you know what? I'm the one who should apologize about that."

"You?" I scoffed. "What do you have to

apologize for?"

"I don't know." He thought for a moment before continuing. "I guess, as a kid, I didn't know what to think about that whole experience, but it freaked me out. So I just avoided you until my mom talked to me about it and told me to stop being a butthead to you... that it wasn't your fault."

I knew I wasn't imagining things about him staying away from me, but I could hardly blame him for his reaction. It was totally and completely unfair to put a kid through that.

"I mean, honestly," Aiden went on, "neither of us is to blame. The only people at fault are your goddamn parents."

He definitely had a point. "Yeah, you're right. Absolutely right. Now that I'm an adult, somewhat, I can see that. But then..."

"Well, it's not your fault. It never was. You were just a kid, and you did nothing to deserve all that shit."

Something about hearing that from Aiden, the only person in the world to see firsthand what my childhood had been like, unleashed some deep-seated pain. A sudden lump formed in my throat. "Thanks for that," I muttered.

"Don't fucking thank me," he said in a joking tone. "You shouldn't feel so bad about it all, man. Not just with me, but I'm talking about Olivia. So she saw what your parents are really like. Big deal. Their bullshit is no reflection on *you*—she's smart enough to know that—and then you were triggered by something you thought you were over. It's gonna happen sometimes."

Jesus. The guy was killing me. "Yeah, I appreciate that. And I appreciate what you said about Olivia too."

"I don't know what you're talking about exactly, but no woman is worth the trouble," a new voice said, making us both turn around to see Trevor walking in, apparently catching the tail end of our conversation.

That was it. I had to get away.

Stepping outside into the back alley, I gulped in some air, emotions overwhelming me—the past, the present, the whole fucking thing feeling like a hot poker in my gut. The tears welled up, unfamiliar and foreign to me, burning my eyes with their intensity.

I had to let go, to let it out, something I'd never in my life done before.

Doubling over, I finally cried, silent, quiet, the tears spilling over, hot against my skin. I cried for the kid I'd been, the kid who'd had to listen to endless arguments between the two people who supposedly loved him the most, the kid who couldn't have any friends over, the kid who dreaded the dinner table, who felt sick every single fucking night.

Years of grief poured out of me, unwanted and painful.

Life could be so unfair. How could two people,

two parents, be so goddamn selfish? How could they ruin my childhood like that? And even worse, how was I still letting them affect me and my future with Olivia, by far the best thing that had ever happened to me?

For a long while, I let myself feel it, feel it all, every emotion it'd caused—the anxiety, the fear and worry, the intense sadness and depression. I hadn't known how to express it as a kid, and in many ways, therapy had helped. But in truth, I never had anyone outside of that to share it all with... until now.

The tears finally spent, I stood upright, the cold bricks at my back. Strangely, I felt a lot better, lighter and unburdened.

Years ago, my therapist had wondered why I'd never cried, and I had no answer. I had no fucking clue. But I wished I'd been able to. Because the anger and despair only moments before had suddenly been replaced by a calm determination.

I might not be perfect, but I was *not* my parents. And right now, I needed to get my shit together, wrestle these demons once more, and settle this all with my girl.

THIRTY-THREE

Olivia

I shoved my phone back in my purse. Where was he? He hadn't answered my texts, my calls or even my knock on his door.

I'd wanted to surprise Luke, so I hadn't told him I was coming home two days early. My mom, grandma, and Emily had talked me into it. Honestly, I didn't have much of a choice really, not with those forces of nature urging me to stand by for an earlier flight.

And now, hours had passed since I'd landed in San Diego—tired, exhausted, but also wired and full of anticipation. I'd been aimlessly wandering the Gaslamp, occasionally grabbing a bite or peeking in a shop, trying to distract myself from the gnawing of nerves in my stomach.

Being in the warm glow of my family had fed my soul, and seeing the happiness of my grandparents and their enduring marriage made me want that so desperately for myself.

But not with just anyone. I wanted Luke and only Luke. More than ever, I was convinced he was *the one*. I just needed to find him, talk to him, see how he was, to see if that spark, if that intangible *something*, still stood between us, or if it'd been lost in the wake of that awful night before I'd left.

Seeing that I was near a popular coffee shop that my co-workers and I all enjoyed, I veered right, telling myself that I needed to pay more attention to my surroundings. The last thing I wanted to do was run into Nikki during my time off.

"Olivia! Wait," a voice shouted from behind me.

I turned to see my boss' boss, Rachel, a stylish woman in her fifties that we rarely saw in our library because she was so busy traveling all over the city.

In an instant, I tried to hide my angst about Luke and put on a proper business demeanor. Or so I hoped. "Hi, Rachel. How are you?"

"Doing great." Her head tilted as her eyes narrowed. "I thought you were in Italy."

"Oh, I came back a few days early." I had no clue what to say if she pressed me about why, but thankfully, her expression relaxed.

"Well, I'm really glad I bumped into you." She flashed me a quick smile. "I just met with Nikki and spent the morning at your library."

I didn't know much about Rachel since she was rather new, but she gave me good vibes. "I hope everything went well."

"It definitely did. I really like what you've been doing, and I can see all the hard work you're putting in."

I knew she was good people. "Oh, thank you so much."

She gave me a sideways look that sent my heart pumping. "And I heard about your new idea..."

Oh, no, no, no. What on earth did Nikki say? So much for getting in the good graces of the library bigwigs. "Um," I hedged, my mind whirling with possible responses.

A loud truck whizzed past us as we stood there awkwardly, waiting, my little heart beating away.

"And," she finally continued, "I love it."

Forgetting about professionalism, I gasped, my eyes widening. "You do?"

She smiled. "Absolutely, I do."

"That's great." It suddenly dawned on me that she might not be talking about what I thought she was talking about, and I debated how to phrase my question just in case. Unfortunately, the jet lag made it even more difficult to think clearly.

"Nadia actually told me about your romance book club idea and said that Nikki wasn't a fan," Rachel said.

What? Nadia had been the tattler? "Um, right, right." That hesitant feeling persisted.

"Romance is the number one genre and dominates the market," Rachel went on. "And the fact that you want to capitalize on that in a way that celebrates romance readers instead of shaming them, well, that shows some very forward thinking on your part."

Pride filled me, as well as relief. So maybe those weren't exactly my reasons for wanting to start the romance book club, but I was still beyond thrilled. "Well, thank you. I really appreciate that."

"No. Thank *you* for coming up with such a great idea. I'm sorry Nikki gave you a hard time about it, and that's something we'll be discussing in the future... her management style and how that trickles top down."

The immature brat that resided in my mind wanted to shout, "Take that, bitch!" But of course, I only nodded and said, "Okay," hopefully the best course of action with such a strange, touchy subject.

"Well, anyway, that's really between Nikki and me, but since you're also in charge, you need to be aware that there will be some changes going forward."

"Okay. I'll do my best to, um, to do my part as well," I added.

"You're a bright light at the library, and I want you to know that we appreciate you." Her phone buzzed, and she gave it a quick glance. "I need to get going, but I'm so glad we could have this chat."

"Me too. Me too," I managed to say. "So nice to see you."

"You too. And I'll be around more often, so I'll see you next week."

Still in shock, I stood there until she was out of sight, and then the adrenaline shot through my body all at once, making me want to squeal with happiness right in the middle of the sidewalk on a busy weekday morning with people everywhere. But I somehow refrained, instead holding it all inside, afraid I might explode, needing to walk it off.

How had this happened? I could hardly believe my good fortune.

I couldn't wait to talk to Nadia about it all and see what exactly had occurred at the library today. And even more so, I was bursting to tell Luke who would probably be even more excited than I was.

Where, oh, where was he right now?

The need to see him overwhelmed me. I had to share this great news with him. It wasn't the same without him. Nothing was the same without him.

Not only did I crave his physical touch, an absolute first in my life, but I also craved his mind, his words, his thoughts, his constant encouragement. That back and forth that I saw with my grandparents, with my own mom and dad, the comfort, the knowing, that person who was always there for you... I wanted that so badly with Luke.

Steering myself away from the familiar path to the library, I meandered down some streets that weren't on my usual routes to work or stores I frequented. It was quieter here, a bunch of restaurants that hadn't opened yet for the day dominating the area.

I passed a nice Italian place, a waiter coming out to ready the outside seating area for the upcoming lunch rush. He smiled at me, and I couldn't help thinking of Luke and his dreams. Before I left, he'd been looking at places, but I hadn't heard anything since. So I assumed nothing had worked out yet. Hopefully, he wouldn't let that derail his plan.

Exhaustion stealing through my tired body, I felt the sudden urge to sit down. I spotted a chair outside a different restaurant and took a seat. The sun flashed through some buildings to warm up my bare legs.

For some reason, I'd decided to wear a skirt, dressing nicely for what I didn't know. Oh, who was I kidding? I'd hoped to run into Luke. But that was ridiculous. I decided to sit a few more minutes then go back to my own apartment and take a nap, even though that was probably the worst way to deal with this jetlag.

A noise across the street caught my attention.

It was another restaurant of course, but one that clearly needed some work. And judging by the stack of lumber by the front door, someone was doing just that.

But the outside was gorgeous, all faded brick and beautiful iron work, with such potential that would be absolutely perfect for Luke. My heart sunk as I realized that someone had beaten him to it. What a shame.

With a defeated sigh, I stood up, ready to go back home and wallow in self-pity. Before I did, I figured I might as well peek inside the open door of that restaurant and see what was sure to be a beautiful interior.

Crossing the street, I wondered why I felt the need to depress myself further at this ruined possibility for Luke. But here I was, admiring what looked to be an apartment or office above the restaurant with empty, paint-chipped window boxes just calling for cascading flowers.

No noise came from the interior as I approached the wide open door and peered inside. It took a moment for my eyes to adjust to the darkness compared to the sun-lit day outside.

But once they did, I barely had time to comprehend what was in front of me. Because staring right back at me was a mirage. Surely, it had to be my crazy imagination. Or some kind of walking jetlag dream.

"Oh, my God, Olivia," Luke said. His voice

seemed deeper than I remembered.

He pushed back from the bar, stood up to his full height, and strode over. Before I could think or understand that it was truly him, his lips landed on mine in a passionate, soul-scorching kiss that stole the breath from my lungs.

I clung to him, desperate, needy, my heart beating wildly as his arms wrapped around me, squeezing my body to his. Our lips melded together, our mouths explored, my mind reeling at the wonder of this moment.

He pulled back to look at me, his eyes boring into my soul. "You're home," he whispered. "You're finally home."

THIRTY-FOUR

Luke

"I'm home," she repeated with a soft smile.

God, I couldn't believe how beautiful she looked. And how the hell had she walked into this place? Of all the gin joints in all the towns... "How did you find me?" I asked.

Her eyes widened. "Did—did you not want to be found?"

Still with my arms around her, I gave her a little shake. "What the fuck are you talking about? Of course, I wanted to be found. By you," I added. I nodded my head behind me. "I wanted to surprise you with this place, so I'm kind of in shock that you surprised *me* instead."

Her smile returned. Thank God. "It was purely coincidental."

"There's no such thing as a coincidence," I said.

A noise sounded behind us, something like a scoff, and I remembered we had an audience

—Aiden, who wasn't exactly into relationships, and Trevor, who seemed to think women were now the enemy.

Olivia glanced over my shoulder. "Um, hey, guys."

I hated to do it, but I let her go. Fuck this. We needed to be alone. Without bothering to even acknowledge those two, I grabbed her hand and led her through the kitchen, straight out the back door to the empty alley. I'd show her around later. Right now, we needed to talk.

As soon as we were outside, I pulled her to me again. "I hate the way we left things. And I despised being apart from you like that."

She looked up at me, her eyes big and vulnerable. "Me too."

"I'm so sorry. So damn sorry to put you through all that, not just the dinner, but me spiraling in the car afterwards." It still utterly killed me that I'd put her through that whole ordeal.

"It's okay," she said.

"No. It's not okay. I should have communicated better, told you all about them before, absolutely everything, so we could have been prepared... or avoided it completely. But we could have decided what to do. Together. And I royally screwed it all up."

Her eyes watering, she reached up to caress my cheek. "Don't be so hard on yourself. It was just a mistake. And we're learning... still learning how to be, you know, a couple, in a relationship."

"So we're still a couple?"

"Absolutely, of course we are. Why wouldn't we be? Because of your mom and dad?"

Glancing down, that old shame from my childhood swept through me. I took a breath, remembering to let myself acknowledge that terrible feeling and let it pass through me. It wasn't me. Not anymore. I'd left that awful past behind me.

"I don't know. I just still feel like you deserve better than that," I admitted. "Because the truth is... when you marry somebody, you marry their family too. And now you know how awful my parents are."

"Marry?" Her mouth hung open.

Oh, shit. I'd gotten ahead of myself and hadn't even thought about it before *that* word had slipped out. "I—I didn't mean right now. But yeah, someday, Livs. I already know you're the one for me. I can't even imagine being with anyone else after the things we've shared. Being without you these last couple of weeks has been pure misery."

Her eyes welled up, but she didn't say anything. And I knew I needed to say more, to truly open up and tell this amazing woman how I felt about her.

I cupped her face between my hands. "You're my soulmate. I love you. I love you so damn much."

The words reverberated between us in the silence that followed as I watched the tears roll down her cheeks. "I love you too," she finally whispered.

Those words... my God... they swirled around in my chest until I thought my heart might explode with happiness. I'd had a few girls say that to me before. But I'd never said it back. Never. Because I hadn't felt it. And in reality, they probably hadn't either.

But now? Truer words had never been spoken. I meant it with all my heart and soul. And the fact that she'd said it back?

I lifted her in my arms and twirled her around, laughing, grinning, our smiles mirroring each other's. "I fucking adore you," I said. "You are the most incredible person I've ever met."

It looked like the smile and tears were battling on her face, but in the end, something else won out. "Kiss me," she demanded.

Well, okay, then. "Anything you say, my sexy little librarian."

She giggled as I let her slide down my chest, her breasts rubbing against me the whole way down. Fuck me.

At that moment, I realized what she had on because her skirt had slid up, revealing a black thong. "Oh, God," I groaned. "How did you—" I couldn't complete my thought because her lips suddenly were on me, practically devouring me.

Weeks had passed, magnifying my attraction

for this woman in my arms, and I showed her exactly how much I loved her with every caress of my lips, every sweep of my tongue into that delicious mouth of hers.

I backed her up against the old brick wall of our restaurant, the need for her rising up in me like an inferno. Flames licked my veins as she moaned into my mouth, our breaths intermingling, our bodies melting into each other.

She fit so perfectly against me, every inch of her soft curves, her plush body, touching mine. Her hands wound around my neck, her fingers in my hair, drawing me closer with such force for someone so much smaller than me.

"I want you so much," she whispered. "Let's finish what we started on the boat."

With those words, Olivia had no idea what she'd unleashed in me. Should I have called a time-out and insisted we go home? Probably. But instead, I couldn't stand the thought of waiting even a few minutes longer, and I was going to take her right here against this goddamn wall.

I ground my hips against her stomach, desperate for some action, some relief from the insane amount of tension building inside me. And her body answered me right back.

"I can't wait to finally fuck you." I sucked her lower lip into my mouth, then released it. "But first, I'm going to taste that sweet pussy of yours."

Her whimper urged me on even more, and for a second, I wondered if I could stand to wait much longer to be inside her again. But at the same time, I was determined to get this right.

So I tried to pace myself, kissing her bare arms, my grip on her strong how she liked it. Slowly, I worked my way down her gorgeous body, taking my time with her luscious breasts, palming her through the thin material of her dress, her nipples pebbling beneath my touch.

"You're so damn gorgeous," I said, sinking to my knees before her.

I lifted her skirt even more, revealing the soft skin of her thighs and stomach, my hands large on her body. She shifted her hips forward, the small triangle of her thong covering the promised land that I was dying to sink into, the tightening in my pants growing nearly unbearable.

Nudging the wet circle on her panties with my nose, I inhaled the scent of her arousal. God, she smelled incredible, and it was all for me, that fact only making me harder. I thought about just moving her underwear to the side, but I didn't want anything getting in my way, so I pulled them down the length of her legs, taking them off completely and stuffing them into my pocket.

Wondering what she thought, I glanced upwards, our eyes connecting in a moment of sexual tension, a short pause before I totally devoured her. When she gave me a small smile, something melted inside my chest. Still with that insane eye contact, I reached for one of her legs and placed it over my shoulder, spreading her open for me.

And now I was ready to feast.

Grabbing her ass cheeks, I pulled her forward, kissing her upper thighs first, working my way inwards, wanting to make her practically beg for it. I groped all that delicious flesh of her bottom as she wiggled her hips, impatient.

Fighting my smile, I kept up the relentless kisses against her thighs until she grabbed the top of my head, her fingers digging into my hair.

"Say it, babe," I demanded. "Say what you want."

"I need your mouth on me... now."

Chuckling, I could barely contain my happiness. That was all I wanted to hear. And then I gave her what she wanted, burying my face in her pussy, her moan of pleasure hitting me right in the soul.

I went right for it, sucking her swollen clit into my mouth, pulling her even tighter against my face. The leg over my shoulder dragged me closer as a loud moan echoed above me.

But I wouldn't give her relief yet, so I explored every inch of her wet heat with my mouth before I'd attempt to push her over the edge. My hands alternated between her ass and spreading her apart even more.

Pushing my tongue inside her as deeply as I

could, Olivia bucked against me, and I figured it was time. So I returned my attention to her clit, sucking then flicking her with my tongue, all the while letting my hands explore everywhere I could reach, the lower half of her body completely bared to me.

She felt so incredible, every single part of her. If I died right now between her thighs, I would at least go a very happy man. But hopefully, we'd have an entire lifetime ahead of us, of exploring each other's bodies, as life changed us, as we grew older together. And I knew I'd never get tired of this girl because my heart was hers completely.

When she started to move her hips in a rhythmic pattern, I knew she was close.

"That's it," I urged her. "Fuck my mouth."

Her whimpers intensified, and so did my movements. And when I pushed two fingers inside her, connecting with her g-spot, she cried out, her body tensing for one long moment before she shattered against my lips.

Watching her fall apart was the sexiest thing on earth, and I knew the memory would forever be imprinted on my brain for as long as I lived.

When she finally stilled, I raised myself up to my full height, taking in her flushed face and blown-out pupils, not to mention her heaving chest. She was ripe for the taking, and I couldn't wait to be inside her.

"Want to see how good you taste?" I asked.

Still breathing heavily, she nodded, and I pressed my lips to hers in a slow, intimate kiss before breaking away to rest my forehead against hers to stare into her eyes.

"Why are you so quiet?" I wondered aloud, suddenly nervous at her uncharacteristic silence. "Having second thoughts?"

"No. Of course not," she answered. "If I'm quiet, it's because I have one thing on my mind."

I pulled back, beyond curious. But I had my answer when she reached for my shorts, swiftly unbuttoning them, making me chuckle. "Ahh, I see. So you're obsessed with the big guy?"

She giggled like crazy, all the while not stopping the movement of her hands, quickly unzipping me and yanking down my shorts, leaving me in only my boxers. "Positively obsessed with the big guy."

Oh, God. The big guy pulsed right then, hot, throbbing, and straining to be inside her again.

Olivia reached for me, and I thought she was going for it, but instead her hands found the edges of my shirt, creeping underneath to caress my overheated skin, her nails raking downward to send chills cascading down my sides.

"You like that, right?" she asked, smiling smugly.

"You know I do," I breathed out.

Standing up on her tiptoes, I met her halfway, our lips colliding in a passionate kiss as our hands were all over each other in a frenzy of anticipation for this long-awaited moment. God, I couldn't wait anymore.

Neither could Olivia, apparently, because she began to stroke my impossibly hard dick through my boxers. And then, her nails dug into my hips as she finally pulled my boxers down, my cock springing free at full attention for Olivia.

The cool air hit me but did nothing for the boiling blood rushing through my veins. And the pressure only built when Olivia grabbed me then pumped her hand up and down, lingering at my tip, her thumb circling a bead of pre-cum.

Oh, good God. I might die from this experience.

Olivia stopped touching me then, her hands moving to my shoulders, and I knew instantly what she wanted. I reached for her ass, and lifted her up to straddle me, pushing her back against the wall.

The head of my swollen cock was right there, right at her wet entrance. Fucking hell. I stared down at her. She stared back. And with one forceful pump of my hips, I plunged into her.

"*Fuck.*"

I didn't move for a long minute, absolutely stunned by the amazing sensation of actually being inside Olivia again, the love of my life, the most incredible feeling in the world.

Her eyes held mine, the air around us saturated with the smell of sex and desire.

"I love you so much," I whispered.

"I love *you* so much," she whispered back, her arms circling around my neck.

God, my heart couldn't take this. And I wondered about my dick too, especially when Olivia began to move impatiently.

"You're so hard," she said.

"Too hard?"

"Just right, baby. Now fuck me. Fuck me senseless."

Drool might have escaped me at her words. Wow. And I proceeded to do just as I'd been instructed by this sexy woman. I pounded into her. Over and over. Again and again. My arms straining with the effort, my heart beating like crazy, I let myself get lost in the moment, giving her everything I had in me.

Her hands moved to either side of my face, and she captured my mouth in a sexy kiss, all tongue, all lust, only adding to the intense passion of the moment. And when she let up, she removed her hands from my cheeks to unbutton the top of her dress so her beautiful cleavage was on display. She yanked her bra down and started massaging her breasts.

Good lord. Olivia was proving once again to be my dream girl—enthusiastic, uninhibited, just as into it as I was. The passion we had for each other was unreal.

The sound of heavy breathing, moans, and groans filled the space between our mouths, against the background of skin slapping skin.

With each thrust, I pinned her against the wall, deep inside her, grinding against her, hoping to give her some friction.

I watched in awe as she kept her hands on her gorgeous tits then plucked her hard nipples.

Needing to touch her myself, I let one of her legs drop, which only made her squeeze tighter around my cock. Oh, my God. So fucking tight. "I'm not going to last much longer."

Reaching down, I found her clit, her loud moan telling me I was on the right track as I rubbed her back and forth, rocking my hips against her.

"Luke," she whispered breathily. "You feel *so* good."

Pride, lust, love filled my chest. Never in my life would I have dreamed of feeling this way. This wasn't just sex, wasn't just getting each other off. This was something different, something deeper than life itself, this connection of two hearts.

Everything in me began to tense, my balls tightened, and I knew I couldn't hold back any longer. *Please, please let us come together.* I wanted that desperately.

Olivia cried out, the sound like candy to my ears, as I watched her, her eyes closing in ecstasy while her pussy pulsed around me like a vise, the feeling beyond words.

"You're incredible," she moaned. "Come inside me, baby."

I buried my head in her shoulder, a primal grunt escaping me. With one final thrust, I plunged deep inside her and let go, finally getting relief for my swollen cock, exploding in hot spurts in an absolutely epic orgasm.

Lifting my head, I watched her, her walls still clenching around me, both of us riding it out for maximum pleasure, never wanting this moment to end.

She collapsed against me, boneless, and I held her tight to my chest. Surprisingly, I heard a strange noise, like a sniffle, and I pulled away in shock to see Olivia's eyes bright and watery. Quickly, she wiped the moisture away.

"I'm sorry. I don't know why I'm crying," she mumbled. "But these are good tears. That was... that was beautiful."

"I couldn't agree more."

Nothing in the English language could capture what had just happened.... maybe celestial, cosmic, soulmates came close.

Letting her other leg go, still inside her, I squeezed my arms around her, drawing her in, wanting to consume her, completely intoxicated by all things Olivia. I knew how she felt, a lump in my throat too at the swell of emotions.

Stroking her hair, I wondered at the mind-blowing physical connection we had, something that went deeper to make it even more magical, tying the mental and emotional together with our bodies. I'd never had anything close to this, someone who loved me so wholly.

"I'm never going to let you go," I whispered against her hair.

Her arms around my waist grabbed me harder. "You better not. Because I won't let you."

There she was, my feisty neighbor. Well, neighbor was the wrong word now, not if I had anything to say about it.

After kissing the top of her head, I let her go, pulling away to catch her eyes. "Come on, little miss insatiable, I have something to show you before you attack me again."

Giggling, she shook her head. "You're the worst."

"Am I now?" I arched a brow. "That's not what you said when you came on my cock."

She laughed even harder, and I took a moment to admire the beautiful light in her eyes.

"What do you have to show me?" she finally asked.

Slowly, I slid out of her. "Let's go clean up, and then you'll see."

After fixing our clothing, I wrapped my arm around her shoulder, leading her back inside, a swell of excitement building in my chest. "Welcome home."

"Home?" she asked. "What do you mean?"

"What I mean is I hope you're ready for an adventure."

"With you?" She nudged me with her hip. "Always."

God, I loved her so much, and I could hardly wait to start our new life together. I would be forever grateful for this woman and how much she changed everything I thought I knew about love. Olivia's boyfriend lessons were the best thing that ever happened to me.

But I might wait a while to tell her so.

EPILOGUE

Olivia

Six weeks later...

Bypassing the restaurant, I rushed up the steps to our apartment, hoping Luke would be there and not downstairs. The door was wide open, loud music from his record player pouring out, so it was safe to assume it was him and not Evan or some crazy Las Vegas gangster.

But still, I edged up to the doorway and peeked in first. And sure enough, there he was, his back to me, itching his cute butt as he studied the lamp he'd given me.

What on earth was he doing?

I decided to keep quiet and watch for a moment. After a while, he moved the lamp to the other side of the couch, then stood there looking at it again.

"Oh, no, no, no," I blurted out.

Luke whirled around, a big grin on his face. "Oh, no, no, no, *what*?"

"It looked way better on the other side."

His brows lowered. "You think?"

"I *know*."

He shot me a sideways look. "We can figure it out later. For now, my lovely librarian..." Walking toward me, he held out a hand. "...have a seat, and I want to hear all about your day."

Giddy happiness rising up like champagne bubbles in my chest, I took his hand and let him lead me to the couch where he promptly sat me down, removed my shoes, then raised my feet up and put the foot massager under them.

"Aw, babe, that's sweet of you."

"Well, it's a special day." He plopped down beside me. "So tell me how it went. How was the first official meeting of the smut club?"

I burst out in laughter. "Oh, my God," I finally said. "How long have you been waiting to say that?"

He chuckled. "A very long time. Not bad, huh?"

Rolling my eyes, I squeezed his leg. "Not bad. But Nikki would die, just die, if she heard you call it that. She practically had a stroke when the talk turned steamy and had to excuse herself to refill the beverages."

"She was there?" he asked.

"Only for a few minutes... the best minutes."

"Maybe it'll give her a few ideas."

I giggled when he waggled his eyebrows. "Maybe."

"But it was mostly you and Nadia running the show?"

"Yep, and it seriously couldn't have gone any better. So many people came that Nikki had to run out and grab more chairs."

"Well, that showed her, didn't it?"

"Sure did. When it was all over, she came up to me—I swear her face was green—and told me what a great asset I was to the library."

"Whoa. I would have liked to have seen that." Luke shot up from his spot next to me. "I'll be right back. We need to celebrate."

I watched him as he bypassed a bunch of boxes stacked up against the wall that we hadn't gotten to yet. The last few weeks had been insane. Between all the remodeling and planning downstairs, my work, and moving to this adorable place above the restaurant, we'd barely had time to breathe.

But it had all been a dream come true, every last bit of it, and we'd both been annoyingly happy. So annoying that Emily couldn't stand to be around us. She'd decided to give up her old apartment for good, hoping to find someplace new for her peace of mind since Evan still hadn't been found.

So she'd taken Aiden up on his offer to crash at his place and take one of the empty spare rooms. Even though Trevor, her new arch enemy, lived with Aiden also right now, Emily said it was worth it to get away from the obnoxious couple that Luke and I had become.

How were we that obnoxious?

But really, I didn't mind. Because Luke and I were in that can't-keep-our-hands-to-ourselves, happy honeymoon phase and needed lots of time alone to christen every corner of our new place.

From the kitchen, I heard the sound of a cork popping. While he was busy, I took a second to fix a serious wrong. Turning off the foot massager, I stood up and moved the lamp back to its original spot.

"Hey, hey, what are you doing?" Luke suddenly asked.

Hands on my hips, I turned to face him. "I'm thinking we need to have a very serious boyfriend lesson right about now."

"Oh, no, I'm scared." With an exaggerated sigh, he rubbed the stubble on his chin. "What on earth is it?"

"The lesson is that you—" I poked him in the chest. "—must acquiesce to your significant other when it comes to decorating. I get the final say, and I say the lamp stays where I originally put it."

"Oh, is that right?" He bit back a grin, instead grabbing onto my pointer finger. He lifted it to his mouth and slowly sucked my finger between his lips.

My knees went a little weak, I had to admit,

even though I'd seen this tactic from him before. "I refuse to succumb to this kind of... of..." He moved closer, his eyes going all sultry, and I lost my train of thought.

Before I could recover, he swooped down and grabbed me, throwing me over his shoulder caveman style, my ass sticking up in the air.

"What are you doing?" I shrieked.

"You want to know a little girlfriend lesson?"

"No!" I gave him a good spanking, and he gave me one right back.

He carried me to the bedroom, laughing the whole way, before he threw me on the bed. Suppressing my giggles, I stared up at him, beyond turned on.

"Well, I'm going to tell you anyway. On smut club night, a good significant other comes home and reads the best parts out loud to her partner."

I about died from laughter before I could answer. "How about we take turns?"

"Deal."

He tossed his big body down beside me, and it was at that moment, I finally spotted what was on the wall behind where he'd been standing.

"*What the hell is that?*"

His eyes followed my line of vision to the awful painting of a man's chest complete with weird nipples that I'd created on my birthday and thrown away while packing.

"Oh, that?" he said. "I hung it while you were at work. Thought it might be hot in the bedroom."

"But... but..." I sputtered, suddenly remembering that I'd asked Emily to take it down to the trash. That little traitor. "I'm gonna get her back someday. I swear."

Turning to Luke, I saw that he was trying his best to hold back his laughter. But instead, he drew me to him, wrapping me in his arms, kissing me thoroughly, our bodies coming together in an instant.

I couldn't believe how many times we'd already had sex since we'd moved in a week ago. One week ago today actually. Which reminded me...

"Hey," I whispered, "I want to ask you something."

"Right now?" he practically growled.

"Yes. Right now. You know how important communication is to me."

"Mm-hmm," he said while unbuttoning my shirt. "What is it?"

"So today marks our one-week anniversary of living together, and I'm wondering if you have any regrets? There are so many big life events happening right now—a huge career change, opening a restaurant, not just moving but moving in with your girlfriend, arguing about the thermostat..."

He laughed in my face before getting serious again, his eyes lit up. "Absolutely zero regrets. I have never been happier in my life. And it's all because of you." He peppered my face with kisses. "What about you? Any regrets?"

"None."

"Good. Now stop talking unless you have something dirty to say or you're going to compliment the size of my..." He rubbed his giant erection against my leg.

"Oh, God," I said, somehow groaning and giggling at the same time.

He continued his kissing assault, punctuating each caress of his lips with an "I love you," words I'd never tire of hearing from him, words I didn't hesitate to say right back.

I'd let him pretend he'd won the little painting battle for now and take care of it later, as well as some other questionable decorating choices he'd made while I was gone.

Girlfriend lessons. Who needed those anyway?

Thank you so much for reading The Boyfriend Lessons! I really hope you enjoyed it.

For an exclusive bonus scene of Luke and Olivia one year later, please subscribe to my newsletter!

(If you're already a subscriber, you can enter your information again to get the password.)

The next book in the trilogy, The Roommate Trouble, features Aiden and a down-on-her-luck "princess" who rocks his world.

And the third book features Trevor and Emily who definitely have a lot to overcome on their journey to happily ever after.

Lastly, to stay up to date, please follow me on Amazon and/or subscribe to my newsletter!

Thanks again for reading,
Jenna xoxo

ABOUT THE AUTHOR

Jenna has always had her head in the clouds, making up stories and creating characters. After years of working as a freelancer, she finally decided to put pen to paper and give this whole fiction thing a chance.

When she's not busy at her computer, she loves spending time with her husband, daughter, and insanely energetic dog who's always looking for trouble.

She lives in the Pacific Northwest where she's constantly raking up pine needles in her back yard and dodging wild turkeys in her front yard.

Catch up with Jenna on her website, jennafiore.com, and stay up to date on future projects!

MORE BOOKS BY JENNA FIORE

Love Lessons Trilogy:

The Boyfriend Lessons
Two neighbors, one drunken night... boyfriend lessons that will forever change their lives.

On paper, Luke's life looks like a dream come true. He's extremely attractive, highly successful, and women flock to him.

But beneath the surface, Luke is deeply unhappy with his job and an even more tumultuous dating life.

When the gorgeous librarian across the hall offers to give him boyfriend lessons one boozy night, Luke can't resist.

As Olivia helps him through the lessons, she quickly realizes that Luke isn't in need of her help

—he's just in need of love. And Luke?

He falls hard for the girl next door.

The Roommate Trouble

When a sexy chef meets a down-on-her-luck "princess," is it destiny or a recipe for disaster?

Aiden's lifelong ambition to become a head chef is finally within reach when he and his friends open their dream restaurant. Passionate and driven, Aiden throws himself into the job, determined to make it a success.

But fate has other plans when Charlotte walks in on day one, looking for a job. Despite the fact that Aiden's her boss and she's obviously hiding something, he's drawn to her and can't stop thinking about her.

When Charlotte falls on hard times and ends up living out of her car, Aiden steps in to help. And that's when the roommate trouble begins.

The Partner Disaster

A grumpy jilted groom, a sunshine partner, and an adolescent rooster... what could possibly go wrong?

Trevor's been with one girl his whole life, and she broke his heart, dumping him at the altar.

He's done with love forever. Trying to pick up the pieces and start over, he's closed himself off to the world and he intends to keep it that way.

But then a little firecracker named Emily comes crashing into his life, a woman in need of her own fresh start after getting tangled up with the wrong man. She's smart, gorgeous, and full of energy.

The only problem? They absolutely despise each other.

Summer of Rain

A steamy, emotional romance featuring a sexy movie star and the sweet heroine who steals his heart...

Rain had everything he'd ever dreamed about—a successful acting career, fame, fortune, and any woman he wanted. So why the hell wasn't he happy?

Addy had nothing she'd ever dreamed about with a life that lay in ruins.

On the busy streets of Los Angeles, these two souls collide, literally, and their lives will be forever changed.

Twenty Years Later
What happens when the good girl hooks up with the high school bad boy twenty years later?

Widowed mom Jayda and single dad Alex are two lonely souls who reconnect at their class reunion. A passionate one-night stand turns into a two-night stand that neither of them ever expected.

But Alex has settled in Miami while Jayda is tied down in Maine, making their would-be romance more than challenging. With complications of family and distance, can one steamy weekend turn into anything else?

The Crush Next Door
An engaged woman, her hot new neighbor, a whole heap of trouble.

Jessica Santoro is living the life in the big city. Well, maybe things aren't exactly perfect with her not-so-dream job, obnoxious neighbor, and long-distance fiancé. But at least she has an ocean view. Kind of.

When Jess starts watching Dodgers games with the annoying guy next door and thinking less about her fiancé, this curveball might just lead to a home run... or a strikeout with the bases loaded.

The Pinkie Pact

When a bold girl meets an inexperienced law student, sparks fly in this enemies-to-friends-to-lovers college romance.

Desperate for a fresh start, Sky makes a pact with her new roommate Kara to change their lives for the better. When she meets Kara's hot brother, however, her new life gets a whole lot more complicated.

But this is it for Sky... her last chance at the college experience. And this time, she's determined to get it right. Well, hopefully.

The Dream Pact

When an aspiring musician makes a pact with a pre-med student, they never dream they'll fall in love.

Brie would give anything for a normal life. After years of torment in high school, she hoped college would be a fresh start. But it's been the complete opposite with her bully following her to school.

Hiding out in her dorm room, she's closed herself off from the world. However, everything changes when she meets Bear and they make a pact to follow their dreams.

But breaking free of the past is never easy, and Brie will have to confront her deepest fears if she wants to find true happiness. And in the meantime, she just might stumble upon a life-changing love.

Return to Me Always

A hot Scot and an American lass pair up when the past comes back to haunt them.

Kat Ryder sets off for London, ready for the adventure of a lifetime before starting college. The very first day, she meets the gorgeous guy she's been dreaming about forever—literally the man of her dreams—and he's nothing like she'd imagined.

When Kat and her dream man are falsely accused of a crime, they're forced to go on the run together. And that's when the real adventure begins in a race for their lives as dreams and destiny collide.

Printed in Great Britain
by Amazon